Body on
Baker Street

Sherlock Holmes Bookshop Mystery
Elementary, She Read

Year Round Christmas Mysteries
We Wish You a Murderous Christmas
Rest Ye Murdered Gentlemen

Lighthouse Library Mysteries (writing as Eva Gates)
Reading Up a Storm
Booked for Trouble
By Book or By Crook

Constable Molly Smith Mysteries
Unreasonable Doubt
Under Cold Stone
A Cold White Sun
Among the Departed
Negative Image
Winter of Secrets
Valley of the Lost
In the Shadow of the Glacier

Klondike Gold Rush Mysteries
Gold Web
Gold Mountain
Gold Fever
Gold Digger

Also Available by Vicki Delany
More Than Sorrow
Burden of Memory
Scare the Light Away

Body on Baker Street

A SHERLOCK HOLMES
BOOKSHOP MYSTERY

Vicki Delany

CROOKED
LANE

NEW YORK

Copyright © 2017 by Vicki Delany

Published in the United States by Crooked Lane Books, an imprint of The Quick Brown Fox & Company LLC.

Crooked Lane Books and its logo are trademarks of The Quick Brown Fox & Company LLC.

Library of Congress Catalog-in-Publication data available upon request.

ISBN (hardcover): 978-1-68331-299-4
ISBN (ePub): 978-1-68331-300-7
ISBN (ePDF): 978-1-68331-302-1

Cover illustration by Joe Burleson
Book design by Jennifer Canzone

Printed in the United States.

www.crookedlanebooks.com

Crooked Lane Books
34 West 27th St., 10th Floor
New York, NY 10001

First Edition: September 2017

10 9 8 7 6 5

For the happy couple: Julia and
Coleman, September 2, 2017

Chapter 1

"Sherlock Holmes Bookshop and Emporium, Gemma speaking."

"Hi. I . . . I . . . uh . . . May I speak to the person in charge of author events? Please?"

"I'd be happy to help you." I put down my pen and opened the store calendar on the computer. Most of the best dates over the summer and into the fall were already booked. "Can you tell me something about yourself and your book?" As the name of my shop suggests, we focus on Sherlock Holmes and Sir Arthur Conan Doyle, but I try to support local writers whenever I can, regardless of what they've written.

"Oh, sorry," she replied. "Didn't I say?"

"No, you didn't."

"It's not me. I mean, I'm not going to be speaking or signing. I'm calling for my boss."

"Let's start with the title of your boss's book, shall we?" While my attention was distracted, Moriarty the shop cat settled himself in the center of the publisher's catalog I'd been browsing. I wiggled the edges of the paper. He hissed at me. I poked his side with a pencil. He hissed louder.

Desperate measures were called for. I feigned as if turning back to the computer and then swept in, picked him up, and put him on the floor. He managed to give my arm a light scratch.

Moriarty lived on the premises. Small and thin and pure black, he was a great shop cat. Everyone loved him. He could be counted on to be charming and friendly to shoppers and to treat their children according to their age. He seemed to be able to tell which people didn't care for cats, and in those cases, he respectfully kept his distance.

Everyone loves Moriarty. Except me.

That is because Moriarty loves everyone. Except me.

This time he hadn't drawn blood. I consider that a victory. He held his tail high and stalked across the room and out the door without as much as a backward glance of apology.

I returned my attention to my caller. "I'm sure we can arrange something. How about mid- to late August or early September? The Labor Day weekend is booked, I'm afraid, but . . ."

She cleared her throat. "I know it's short notice, but she's changed her mind, and, well . . . I was hoping"—she had a high-pitched voice and spoke as though she were not quite sure she was allowed to—"for Saturday."

"Saturday? You mean the day after tomorrow? That won't be possible."

"I checked your events listing before calling, and I don't see anything advertised."

"We don't have anything planned for that day, that's true, but I have to order the books, advertise the event. You do want me to advertise it, don't you? People need advance notice to put it on their calendars."

"She only decided to go to Cape Cod last night and reluctantly agreed to do one signing this weekend. She won't be pleased."

"Sorry," I said. I've found most writers to be extremely pleasant, lovely people, more than happy to do whatever they can to accommodate my bookshop and schedule. The odd one, however, seemed to think he or she was doing me an enormous favor by bothering to stop in and grace us with their presence.

"I understand. I do. This must be highly inconvenient for you. It's possible you have some books in stock already. It's called *Hudson House*."

"*Hudson House*?" I stared, first at the phone in my hand, and then at the boxes of books piled on the floor of my office. I have a storage room, but overflow tends to find its way in here. "You don't mean . . ."

"The author's name is Renalta Van Markoff. That's R-E-N—"

"I know. Thanks. What's your name?"

"Oh, didn't I say?"

"No, you didn't. I'm Gemma Doyle. I'm the owner and manager of the store." I am also the chief duster, the head bookkeeper, the buyer, the returner of unsold stock, the human resource manager (of the single employee), the cat feeder and litter box cleaner, and the head sales clerk. I didn't bother to tell my caller all of that. The poor woman sounded

like a bundle of nerves. I wondered if she was always so nervous or if her boss was standing over her, impatiently tapping
a ruler into the palm of her hand.

"Linda Marke. Miss Van Markoff's personal assistant."

The boxes surrounding me were full of copies of *Hudson
House*, the latest in the pastiche series by Renalta Van Markoff. The book had been released only two days ago and was
already on its way to hitting number one on the *New York
Times* bestseller list. It was also currently the bestseller in my
shop. "Are you saying that Renalta Van Markoff wants to do
a signing here, in West London?"

"Yes."

"The day after tomorrow?"

"Yes."

I took a deep breath. Wow. Two years ago, when the
first book in the Hudson and Holmes series, *An Elementary
Affair*, began to generate notice (and huge sales), I tried to
invite Renalta Van Markoff to the bookshop. I never managed to get past personal assistants, publicists, and other
interfering busybodies. I'd been led to believe that my tiny
shop wasn't big enough, *important enough*, to host Miss
Van Markoff.

Maybe none of her staff had bothered to ask the author
what she thought of that.

I would do whatever I had to do to get her here on Saturday. "I have plenty of books in stock, and I should be able to
get more in time. How about half one?"

"Half of what?"

"Sorry. I mean one thirty. Readers can have lunch, maybe
enjoy some time at the beach, and then come to the store."

"Thank you," Linda said. The relief in her voice was obvious. "That would be wonderful."

"Great. I'll see you then. Do you have any special requirements? I'll provide water for Ms. Van Markoff. Tea or coffee if she'd prefer. A signing table, pens. Anything else?"

"I'll be there this afternoon. We can talk then."

"You're coming here? Today?"

"I need to see the layout of the store. Decide where Miss Van Markoff will stand to speak and where she will sit to sign. She's very . . . particular. You do have a podium, of course."

"Of course," I said. Meaning no, but I could try to find one.

"How does one o'clock sound?"

"I'll be here."

"Thank you very much. This means a lot to me . . . I mean to Miss Van Markoff."

She hung up.

I stared at the phone for about two seconds. Then I leapt to my feet. I bolted out of the office and dashed down the stairs. I made it about halfway before turning around and running back up to open one of the boxes and grab a handful of books. They were weighty tomes. I hadn't even glanced inside one yet, but I estimated it to have 736 pages.

Back downstairs with my arms loaded with books. Moriarty tried to trip me on the bottom step, but I was ready for him, and I deftly dodged his outstretched paw.

"What's got you in such a tizz?" Ashleigh, my new assistant clerk, asked.

I dropped the books on the counter. "I want a big display of these. Along with the earlier ones in the series." Like most mystery novels, when a new book was released, the sales of the earlier in the series went up substantially.

"We already have a big display of those." Ashleigh gestured to the center table, piled high with hardcover copies of *Hudson House*. The cover showed a street of three-story white row houses with black doors, pillared entranceways, and second-floor balconies with black iron railings. A woman, dressed in a brown-and-gold silk gown with a spray of feathers in her dark hair, was coming out of a house with "221" prominently displayed on one of the pillars. The street might have been one that I'd lived on in London, but if so, it was of another time. A hansom cab could be seen disappearing into the mist. It was night, and thick fog swirled around gas lamps.

"We need more," I said.

"Why?" Ashleigh asked. She'd only been working here for a short time, and she was proving to be hardworking and reliable. She had a tendency to question everything I did. This can be good in an employee—keeps me on my toes. It can also be bad—I am the boss, after all.

"Someone from the publisher is dropping by this afternoon. I want it to look like we're promoting this book hard."

"Which we are," Ashleigh said.

"Even harder, then," I said.

At that moment, Ellen, one of my regular customers, dropped a copy of *Hudson House* on the counter. "I've been so looking forward to this one. I wish Renalta Van Markoff would write faster."

"You'll have plenty of time to get into it," I said. "Now that your husband's moved out of the house."

She stared at me. "How do you know that?"

"Didn't you mention it, Ellen?"

"I most certainly did not. Not to you or to anyone."

"Just a guess." I busied myself arranging the volumes. The covers of Renalta's three books all showed the same street. A woman coming out of (or going into) number 221. Only the time of day, the weather, and the woman's attire differed.

"That was quite the guess," Ashleigh asked once Ellen, giving me more suspicious glances, had left.

"I never guess. Ellen comes in here once a month or so. She's very fond of gaslight mysteries and buys her favorites in hardcover as soon as they come out. An excellent customer. She's always dressed well and groomed to the nines. I once overheard her complaining to a friend that her husband was drinking more than she liked. Today, I noticed that her engagement ring is dirty, meaning she's been fingering it a great deal lately and not taking the time to clean it. She's wearing sandals, but the paint on her toenails is chipped, indicating a lack of interest in her appearance. As does the unraveling hem in her blouse and the stain on the front."

"Maybe she got the stain at breakfast and hasn't been home to change."

"It was at least two days old."

"I hope you're not able to tell my innermost secrets by the way I dress or if I washed my shirt since last time I wore it."

"You," I said, "are an enigma."

"And proud of it," she replied.

I'd not yet seen Ashleigh in the same outfit twice. Not just outfit but style. She came to the interview in proper business attire—hair scraped back in a stiff bun, gray skirt to the knees, neat gray jacket, ironed white shirt buttoned to the top, flat pumps. The first day of work she resembled a California girl heading for the beach with a surfboard on top of her Volkswagen Beetle, in a swinging ponytail, short red-and-white skirt, pink T-shirt, and flip-flops. I didn't mind, as long as the skirt wasn't too short or the shirt too tight. We were a summer vacation town, after all. The following day, she appeared in a safari jacket, multipocketed khaki pants, hiking boots, and even a pith helmet. Today's outfit was "ladies who lunch at the yacht club."

The bells over the door tinkled, and Ashleigh called out, "Welcome! Let me know if you need anything."

"Ooh, you have it," the new arrivals squealed. They both scooped up copies of *Hudson House.* "I knew you would."

"If you like that series, you might also like . . ." Ashleigh discreetly led the women to the gaslight fiction shelf.

I picked up a copy of the book and checked the last page. 720. Rats, I'd been off by sixteen pages.

Along with my great uncle Arthur, I own the Sherlock Holmes Bookshop and Emporium, located at 222 Baker Street, West London, Massachusetts. As can be assumed by the name, we stock Sherlock Holmes–related books and merchandise. Not only second and later editions (and the occasional first) of the original Sir Arthur Conan Doyle books or the magazines in which the stories appeared, but modern pastiche novels, short story collections, and anthologies. As many of those as there are (and more every day), it's not enough to keep a bookshop fully stocked, so we also sell nonfiction relating to the life and times of Doyle and his contemporaries and historical fiction we call gaslight—books set in the mid- to late Victorian or Edwardian periods. The "Emporium" part of the shop's name refers to all the coloring books, games, puzzles, mugs, teacups, posters, DVDs, making-of books, and so on related to Holmes and Watson. I never fail to be astonished at what some fans will consider to be treasures.

I glanced around the shop. Ashleigh was busy with the two women, their arms now laden with books. "Personally," she said, "I far prefer Laurie R. King's Mary Russell to the Van Markoff books. But it's a matter of individual taste."

"I'll give one of those a try then," the shopper said, and *The Beekeeper's Apprentice* was added to the pile.

A family browsed the children's section, and a group of vacationing hipsters was studying the Sherlock paraphernalia, exclaiming everything to be "cool" and "ironic." I feared that we'd soon be due for a fresh interpretation of the Great Detective with unkempt beard and man-bun.

"I'm popping into the tea room," I called to Ashleigh.

She lifted one hand in reply.

My shop is attached to the building next door, number 220. A year ago, we'd knocked down part of the wall, put in a sliding glass door, and opened Mrs. Hudson's Tea Room. Uncle Arthur and I own half of that business. Jayne Wilson owns the other half and manages the tea room and serves as the head cook and baker. As well as my business partner, she's also my best friend.

"Jayne in the back?" I called to Fiona, who was ringing up a takeout coffee and bran muffin.

"Where else would she be?" Fiona asked.

"Good point." I went into the kitchen. It was eleven thirty and the kitchen was a flurry of activity as Jayne and her helper, Jocelyn, did lunch and tea prep. Mrs. Hudson's wasn't only a tea room; Jayne serves takeout coffee and baked goods all day, lunch from eleven until two, and afternoon tea from one until closing at four.

When we first began planning the tea room, I told her that one o'clock was ridiculously early for afternoon tea. She'd replied that the Orangery at Kensington Palace starts serving afternoon tea at noon. *So there.* I gave in, realizing that in the face of the modern tourist industry, some standards have to give.

"Busy?" I asked. The question was redundant, seeing as giant pots of soup simmered on the stove; Jocelyn was up to her elbows in sliced tomatoes, onions, and peppers for lunch sandwiches; a tray of raspberry muffins waited to be taken out front; Jayne's face was dotted with flour, her white apron had streaks of chocolate, and she was rolling out massive sheets of dough. But after my faux pas earlier regarding the state of Ellen's marriage, I was attempting to act more "normal" when engaging in social discourse. Whatever that means.

"What do you want, Gemma?" Jayne asked.

Definitely busy. She didn't usually snap at me. I try hard to stay out of her realm, which isn't difficult. A kitchen, of any sort, is not my natural environment.

"Something came up that I thought you might be interested in. How's the book going? *Hudson House.* Have you had time to read it?"

"Gosh, Gemma. It's so good, I've scarcely gotten any sleep for days." The store had received an advance review copy some months ago from the publisher. I'd begun the first in the series but had never finished it. Too overwrought and overwritten for my taste. I thought it read more like a historical romance than a Holmes pastiche. To my surprise, the moment Jayne spotted the copy of *Hudson House* on my desk, she pounced. She declared herself to be a *huge* fan of the series.

"My mom's number one hundred and twenty-seven on the waiting list at the library," Jocelyn said. "She's close to breaking down and buying herself a copy."

"They have a waiting list of one hundred and twenty-seven people?" I asked.

"It's fabulous," Jayne breathed. "Even better than *Doctor Watson's Mistake.*"

"Tell your mom to come to the Emporium on Saturday," I said to Jocelyn. "Around one."

"Why?"

"That's what I've come to tell you," I said. "Renalta Van Markoff herself will be here to do a signing at one thirty."

Jayne actually screamed. "Oh, my gosh. Are you kidding me?"

"Nope. I've just had a call from her PA. Saturday it is."

"That's not much notice," Jocelyn said.

"We can manage," I said. "Her PA's coming to the store this afternoon at one to check things out."

"Do you think she'll want us to do a tea?" Jayne asked. "We can put on a tea party. That would be so exciting. I can use my special Sherlock Holmes tea set."

"We'll have trouble accommodating the expected crowds as it is. No way can we fit everyone into the tea room."

Jayne pouted prettily. Jayne did everything prettily. She was tiny and blonde with sparkling blue eyes and a heart-shaped face.

11

"We'll talk more at our regular partners' meeting later," I said. "But I thought you'd want to know."

"She's going to give a talk, I hope."

"I expect so."

"I'll come in early on Saturday to get most of tea prep done ahead of time so I can come."

"I'll tell my mom," Jocelyn said. "And she'll tell about a hundred of her closest friends."

Chapter 2

I left Mrs. Hudson's through the door to the street so I could check the window display. The tea room didn't normally feature merchandise from the Emporium, but space had been made among the teacups, cake plates, and three-tiered trays for a couple of the Van Markoff books. After all, the name of her series was a good match to the name of our tea room.

Next door, the windows of the Emporium were all about summer reads. We'd arranged a pile of sand, a child's bucket and pail, a short-legged beach chair, and a stack of colorful fluffy towels. Books, *Hudson House* prominent among them, were arranged on the chair and towels. At the moment, Moriarty was basking in the sunny window. I decided to dismantle the beach-reads theme and make the window all about Renalta Van Markoff. There wasn't time to get any advertising into the *West London Star*; my store windows would have to be our advertisement.

I checked my watch. Quarter to twelve. Linda said she'd be here at one.

I went into the shop and climbed into the window. Moriarty hissed at me and stalked off to find another place for his nap. I studied the display and decided not to completely clear the beach scene but to add more Van Markoff books to it.

I was thinking about placement when I realized three small children were standing in the street, licking ice cream cones and watching me. I struck a pose and stood very still.

They giggled. I held the pose.

Their father came up to them and said something. I moved, and he jumped in surprise. The children roared with laughter, and he gave me a grin.

"Hand me some of those books, will you?" I said to Ashleigh.

She did, and I arranged them. "The author's coming on Saturday for a signing. Short notice, but that's what she wanted."

"Okay," Ashleigh said.

"You're not a fan?"

She shrugged.

"Spread the word to people you think might be interested. Tell those who buy the book today or tomorrow that if they bring it back on Saturday, the author will sign it. Encourage them to get it today, though, and not wait. We might not have enough."

Window done to my satisfaction, I went upstairs to my office and put in a rush order for more copies of the entire series. My distributer told me they'd try to get it to me by Saturday morning. I then made up posters to put in the windows advertising the signing. The box nearest my desk was still half full. I leaned over, plucked a book out, and flipped it over. The author photo filled the back cover. It showed an olive-skinned woman in her early forties, makeup applied with a trowel (although a very expensive trowel) with deep-red lips, green eyes, and a mass of black hair of a color not found in nature piled on top of her head. She held her chin in one hand, and the giant ruby on her finger glowed as though a fire burned within. I checked the author's web page and found the same picture. I downloaded it to print on the posters alongside the book cover image and giant black letters advertising the time and date of the author's appearance.

When I got back downstairs, I was surprised to see that more than a handful of excited women had gathered on the sidewalk, armed with cameras, notebooks, and copies of Renalta Van Markoff's novels, some well-thumbed and others new and pristine.

"Where did all those people come from?" I asked Ashleigh.

"You told me to spread the word about Saturday. I did that, and I also mentioned that she's coming here today to check out the store."

"The author herself isn't coming," I said. "Just her PA."

"Doesn't matter. They'll be looking forward to Saturday even more if she doesn't show up today."

I spotted Jocelyn's mum in the crowd. Jocelyn had also helped spread the word apparently.

The fans were not to be disappointed. I'd just finished taping the posters to the doors of the Emporium and Mrs. Hudson's Tea Room when a glistening black Cadillac Escalade pulled up out front and parked in the loading zone. As one, the crowd surged forward.

A woman, short and thin, jumped out of the front passenger seat the moment the car came to a stop. She wore a knee-length brown skirt, a white shirt buttoned to her throat, and sensible shoes and carried a large brown leather bag slung over her shoulder and across her chest.

The driver, a good-looking young man, ran around the car and opened the back door to allow an older woman to step out. The onlookers let out a collective gasp. People darted across the street or hurried down the sidewalk to see what was going on, and shopkeepers poked their heads out of their stores. Passing traffic screeched to a halt.

The older woman paused for a moment, one perfectly manicured hand resting on the car door. She stood there smiling while cameras and smartphones clicked. It was a hot summer afternoon, but she was draped in a black ankle-length cape with a scarlet satin lining that shimmered as she moved. Her ruby-red shoes had four-inch heels. Her black hair was gathered behind her head in a tumbled mass, and ruby earrings gathered the light of the sun and threw it at us. The driver took her arm, and they walked slowly through the gaping crowd into the Sherlock Holmes Bookshop and Emporium. The younger woman scurried along in their footsteps.

"Bit over the top," Ashleigh said in my ear.

I ignored her and plastered on a smile. "Welcome. You must be Renalta Van Markoff. You look exactly like your author photo." Although the photo had been taken at least twenty years ago.

She extended her hand toward me, and I was enveloped in a cloud of Chanel No. 5. Expensive and classic. For a moment, I wondered if I was expected to kiss the ruby ring. Instead I took the offered hand in mine. "I'm Gemma Doyle. Owner and manager."

"An Englishwoman. How perfectly delightful. And so suitable." Her eyes were an unusual shade of emerald green. Colored contact lenses, I suspected.

The younger woman stepped forward. "Hi. I'm Linda. We talked on the phone."

"Pleased to meet you in person," I said. Linda was in her late twenties, I guessed, with brown eyes, short dark hair, and heavy black eyebrows. She wore no makeup, had done nothing with her hair, and dressed so plainly as to be almost dowdy, but her bone structure was excellent, her skin almost luminescent, and although she kept her head dipped down most of the time, her eyes brimmed with intelligence.

"Kevin Reynolds," the driver said. "I'm Miss Van Markoff's publicist." He was older than Linda but a good deal younger than Renalta. He was tall and lean and strikingly handsome, and the spark in his eyes when he studied my face told me he knew it. He handed me a small rectangle of stiff white paper. "My card." I stuffed it into my pocket.

"Your store is much smaller than I expected," Renalta said.

The Emporium isn't very big, that's true. The office, storage room, and staff washroom are accessed by a steep staircase at the back, and the main floor is just one large room. The sections—Conan Doyle, pastiche, gaslight, nonfiction, children and young adult, merchandise—are separated into individual areas by a careful arrangement of shelving and tables. A cozy reading nook with a comfortable, well-worn leather chair, side table, and lamp is set into a corner of the large bay window overlooking the street. I myself like nothing better than to curl up in that chair with a good book, a cup of tea, and a scone slathered in strawberry jam and topped with clotted cream on winter days when traffic in the shop is slow.

"The shelves are on wheels," I told Renalta. "They can be moved against the wall to clear the center space. We'll set out rows of chairs and can extend next door if necessary." I pointed toward the tea room where people were gathered at the entrance, watching us. Jayne stood at the front, her eyes aglow.

Renalta sniffed. "I certainly hope you'll be able to manage an event of the numbers I attract. This is not a visit by some self-published author with a memoir about teaching in a one-room schoolhouse, who can be counted on to have her daughter's bridge club turn up and no one else."

"I can manage," I said.

"I suppose it will do," Renalta said.

"I think it's charming," Linda said.

"You would," Renalta said without looking at her. "On Saturday, I'll require two bottles of water, Riviera brand preferably, on the podium and another two bottles at the signing table. All of them with the seal broken ahead of time but the cap left on. It can be difficult sometimes to get those seals off."

"Miss Van Markoff will speak for precisely twenty minutes," Kevin said. "And then she'll move to the signing table. I'll escort her over, and Linda will be waiting there to open the books to the proper page."

"I was hoping for twenty-one minutes," Ashleigh mumbled. I refrained from laughing.

"I assume a sufficient quantity of my backlist will be on hand?" Renalta asked.

"I'm doing my best," I said. "You didn't give me a lot of notice, you know."

She waved that triviality away.

Moriarty had climbed to the top of the gaslight shelf. He sat there, his tail twitching, amber eyes glowing, watching everything. The muscles in his back legs tensed. I read the signals and leapt to intercept him, but I was a fraction of a second too late. He launched himself directly at Renalta Van Markoff and landed squarely in the center of her chest. Only her heavy black cloak protected her from being badly scratched. She screeched. Her arms flew up, and she batted at the cat. Moriarty clung on.

Some women screamed. A handful laughed.

Linda calmly stepped forward and plucked him off. "Aren't you a naughty cat?" she cooed, giving his black nose a light tap.

"Are you all right, Renalta?" Kevin brushed invisible hairs off the front of her cloak.

"I . . . I . . ."

"I am so sorry," I said, totally mortified. "He's usually extremely well behaved. I have no idea what got into him."

"Perhaps Miss Van Markoff should sit down for a moment," Ashleigh said.

Kevin guided his boss to the chair in the reading nook.

Jayne hurried over with a glass of water. She handed it to Kevin, and he gave it to the shaking author who gulped it down. "Goodness," she said. "That was unexpected."

"He was only being friendly," Linda said. "Weren't you, you lovely thing?"

Moriarty rubbed the side of his head into Linda's chest, and she stroked his back. One malicious amber eye looked at me. I glared in return. He'd never before attacked a customer. What a choice for his first victim.

"Perhaps the cat can be kept out of the main room on Saturday," Kevin said to me.

An excellent idea.

A woman's voice rang throughout the shop. "I've told you and told you, Gemma Doyle, that animal is a menace. Someday he'll go too far. And then you'll be sorry." If ever I was inclined to get rid of Moriarty, the one thing that would stop me would be the "told you so" I'd get from Maureen of Beach Fine Arts, located across the street at 221 Baker Street.

"I'm surprised to see you here, Maureen," I said. "I didn't know you could read."

"Of course I can read," she snapped. "I just don't care for the sort of silly rubbish you sell. And your prices are far too high. But now that I'm here . . . and the author's here . . . I might, just this once, make a purchase." Maureen snapped up a copy of *Hudson House* and hurried over to the reading nook.

Renalta was still sipping her water while being fussed over by Kevin. Maureen held out her book.

"I'm sorry," Kevin said. "Miss Van Markoff isn't signing today. I hope you can come back on Saturday."

"Don't be silly, Kevin. I'd be delighted to sign her book." Renalta gave a light, tinkling laugh. "Who shall I make it out to?"

I refrained from rolling my eyes. That scene had been a total setup. The stern publicist; the author willing to do anything for her fans.

I turned quickly and caught Linda's secret smile. She flushed and put Moriarty onto the floor.

Jayne snatched a book off the top of the stack and fell into place behind Maureen. Jocelyn's mother and the other onlookers rushed to follow, and the buying frenzy was on. Ashleigh staffed the cash register while I tried to direct satisfied customers to more of our stock. People were standing at the windows, peering in, wondering what all the excitement was. When they shifted, I caught a glimpse of the parking enforcement officer stopping at the Escalade and pulling out her ticket book.

I snatched a stack of books out of a carton behind the counter and brought them into the reading nook. "Just a signature and date for store stock, please." I shoved the books at Kevin. Might as well take advantage of her while she was here.

He gave me a poisonous look but took the books and placed them on the table.

Kevin didn't let the signing go on for too long. After about twenty people had had a chance to meet the Great Author, he lifted a hand. "I'm sorry, everyone, but we have to be on our way. Miss Van Markoff has a prior engagement. Let her take a few minutes to sign books for Ms. . . . uh . . . for the store." Some publicist. He'd forgotten my name already. Linda opened my books to the title page and handed them, one by one, to Renalta, who signed them in red ink with an enormous, elaborate flourish.

"Don't forget, everyone," I said, "Renalta will be here on Saturday at one thirty for a longer visit."

The crowd murmured in appreciation.

"Excuse me, excuse me. Make way for the press." Irene Talbot, crack reporter (also the only full-time reporter) of the

West London Star pushed her way through. "Can I have a picture for the paper?"

"I'm dreadfully tired," Renalta said as she leaned back in the chair and struck a pose. Head to the side, cape tossed over her shoulder, hand to her throat. Kevin quickly rearranged some books so the spines were facing Irene and then stepped out of the way. Irene snapped a few pictures while cameras and smartphones clicked behind her, and then she asked, "What brings you to our town, Miss Van Markoff? *Hudson House* came out two days ago. I would have expected you to be busy touring with the new book."

"I should be, *my darling*, I should be. A book tour can be so *dreadfully* exhausting. Before I plunge back into the fray, I need a few restorative days on the Cape. My absolute *favorite* place on earth." The onlookers murmured their approval. Renalta did a good imitation of offspring of an old-money East Coast family, but she didn't quite have the rougher edges smoothed out. The Bronx, I thought. Maybe Queens. I haven't been in America long enough to get the finer details of regional accents sorted out.

"No matter how exhausted she is," Kevin said, "I can never convince Miss Van Markoff to miss an opportunity to meet her fans."

She threw him a smile, and then she wiggled her fingers at the crowd. Kevin took her arm and helped her stand. The throng opened before them, and they walked slowly to the door.

I followed. "Thanks for coming," I said when we were all standing at the entrance.

"Get that horrid animal out of here before I come back." Her voice dropped to a whisper, and every trace of charm and old-money manners disappeared in a flash. "You don't have nearly enough books."

"More are upstairs."

"Upstairs doesn't do me any good, does it? Linda, this bookstore wasn't a good idea. It's simply too small."

"It will be fine, Miss Van Markoff. I'm sure Gemma's hosted many author events before."

"Unlikely of my caliber," the Great Author sniffed. "Very well. If it's a disaster, let it be on your head." She sailed out of the shop. Kevin opened the door of the car for her. She turned and threw a huge smile to the onlookers and then, with a whirl of her cape, clambered inside. Kevin went around to the driver's door.

A piece of paper had been slipped under the windshield wiper. Linda pulled the parking ticket free and stuffed it into her bag. She got into the car, and they drove away.

I went back into the shop.

"Isn't she marvelous?" Jayne said. "So sophisticated. So gracious and charming." Clutching her new book to her chest, she drifted back to the mysterious depths of her kitchen.

"Did she meet the same person we did?" Ashleigh asked.

"Ah, fame," I replied. I glanced around the shop. Most of the Van Markoff fans had left with their precious signed books, but a few still browsed. "Twenty-seven hardcover copies of *Hudson House*. Twelve paperbacks and two hardcovers of *An Elementary Affair* and seven paperbacks of *Doctor Watson's Mistake*. Not bad for a half hour's work."

"I haven't had time to run the tally yet," Ashleigh said. "How do you know?"

I refrained from saying, "Don't you?" Jayne had told me not to do that. That, she said, tends to make people feel inadequate. "Just a guess." I, as I have said, rarely guess. I simply observe. And today I observed that twenty-seven hardcover copies of *Hudson House*, twelve paperbacks and two hardcovers of *An Elementary Affair*, and seven paperbacks of *Doctor Watson's Mistake* had been taken off the main display table and the new books rack.

"Are we going to have enough on Saturday?" Ashleigh asked. "I don't want to be the one to tell her we've run out."

"There are more upstairs, and I've put in a rush order. We should be okay. I'm worried about the space though. We really are going to have to pack them in. I'll order extra chairs from the rental company."

A customer put a copy of *Echoes of Sherlock Holmes* on the counter, and Ashleigh rang it up. She popped the book into an Emporium shopping bag and bid the woman a good day. I took the copies Renalta had signed off the reading nook table and put them into their box. I'd hold some of them back for those of my regular customers who weren't able to get to the shop for the author's visit.

"Twenty-eight," Ashleigh said as I was tidying the center table.

"Twenty-eight what?"

"According to the computer, we sold twenty-eight copies of the book. Not twenty-seven."

"The computer's wrong."

"It's not wrong, Gemma. If it reported less than you thought, I'd think someone stole one. But it says twenty-eight hardcovers of *Hudson House*."

I counted the copies that remained. Thirteen. We'd started with forty. We had therefore sold twenty-seven. I looked around the shop. Moriarty sat by the cash register, allowing Ashleigh to rub the top of his head. They gave me identical smirks.

I ran to the window. "Aha!" One of the display copies had been removed. "I neglected to check over here."

I turned around quickly. Ashleigh might have been in the act of rolling her eyes, but I couldn't be entirely sure.

The door chimes rang.

"Donald," I said, "nice to see you."

"I cannot believe you allowed that woman to step foot in your store, Gemma."

I didn't have to ask what woman Donald Morris was referring to. He was a frequent visitor to the shop, prominent Sherlockian, member of the Baker Street Irregulars, noted Conan Doyle collector (if he could afford what was being offered for sale), and Holmes scholar. In the winter he wore a deerstalker hat and a houndstooth-check Inverness cape. In the heat of summer, he was more likely to wear some sort of Holmes-related T-shirt. Today it read, "You Know My Methods."

"I assume you mean Renalta Van Markoff, Donald. Of course I allowed her into my shop. I was hardly going to throw her into the street and bar the door. I sold a lot of her books."

"Twenty-eight of the newest one," Ashleigh called.

Donald sputtered. About once a year, he tried to start a chapter of the Irregulars in West London, but it never lasted long. Donald's insistence on strict adherence to the canon and on doing everything his way ensured that the less committed (or the equally stubborn) soon dropped out. "Those books are an outrage! An insult to Holmes's memory." Donald pointed to the bookshelves. His index finger quivered in indignation.

"Donald, you're wearing a T-shirt with one of his sayings on it. If Holmes was a real person, which I will once again remind you he was not, he'd be offended at that."

"Sherlock Holmes would have adapted to the changing times, Gemma."

"I'm not standing here arguing with you, Donald. You'll chase my customers away."

He approached the center table and picked up a book. His lip curled.

"Step away from the books, slowly and calmly," Ashleigh said, "and no one gets hurt."

"You are not helping," I said.

"I thought better of you, Gemma." Donald shook his head mournfully.

"Sorry. Now what was I doing? Oh, yes, running a business, selling people what they want."

He put down the book and picked up the stand displaying the poster I'd done for Saturday's event.

"She's coming here *again*?"

"Yes, Donald. You may not like her books. I don't even like them all that much, although I don't object on principle the way you do. But lots of people love them. I'm happy to serve my customers."

"You're right."

"I'm what?"

"You are right, Gemma. It's your role to give the public what they want. Or what they think they want. None of my business at all. I can be satisfied to remain apart from the mindless rabble." He plucked a book off the table and carried it to the sales counter with a look that indicated a mouse might have expired between the pages. "I suppose I should see what the fuss is about. Purely in a research capacity, of course. Much like an economist might read *Das Capital* without being a Marxist."

"The comparison is hardly apt, Donald," I said.

"You look very striking today, my dear," he said to Ashleigh.

"Thanks." Ashleigh rang up the purchase and handed him the book. "Striking" was a good word. She wore blindingly white capris, a navy-blue jacket with gold buttons over a blue-and-white T-shirt, and espadrilles. Her light-brown hair had been heavily sprayed into a shoulder-length flip.

"I'll have a bag, please. It will do my reputation no good to be seen carrying this work of so-called popular fiction around with me."

She dropped the book into a store bag.

Donald accepted it. "Good day, ladies." He left the shop.

"What's got his long woolen underwear in a knot?" Ashleigh asked.

"Van Markoff's books have some of the more traditional Sherlockians upset. Mrs. Hudson—you know who that is, right?"

This time Ashleigh did roll her eyes. "Everyone knows who Mrs. Hudson is, Gemma. Sherlock Holmes's landlady. She's always objecting to his clients and to the poor street urchins he calls the Baker Street Irregulars."

"That's right. In this series, Mrs. Hudson is Holmes's lover."

Ashleigh laughed. "The wily old dog."

"Right. In the original books, Mrs. Hudson has no first name, no past, not even a present outside of 221 Baker Street. She does nothing other than scold Sherlock, serve kippers to Dr. Watson, and show visitors in."

"What are kippers?"

"A fish. Traditionally served for breakfast."

"You people eat fish for breakfast? I thought you had fried eggs and sausages and fried tomatoes and such. With toast. Lots of toast. And marmalade."

"And kippers. Not to be confused with kedgeree, which is a dish made with smoked haddock, rice, and eggs. But that is somewhat beside the point. The premise of these books is that Mrs. Hudson, whose first name is Desdemona—"

"Desdemona?"

"Yup. Desdemona Hudson and Sherlock Holmes live together, in the modern sense of that phrase. They love each other desperately but cannot marry because Mr. Hudson, one Randolph, who happens to be a minion of Professor Moriarty . . ."

My cat's ears picked up.

". . . won't give her a divorce."

"What about Dr. Watson?"

"Watson lives with them, *not* in the modern sense of that phrase, but to provide them with a cover of respectability."

"It was more respectable for two single men to share an apartment than a man and a woman?"

"Actually, it was. Anyway, the premise of the Van Markoff books is that in his stories about Sherlock, John Watson is only pretending that Mrs. Unknown-First-Name Hudson is just the landlady. Meanwhile, Desdemona is not only Holmes's lover but his smarter partner. And, of course, she is the estranged daughter of an earl, extremely beautiful, an expert at disguise, fluent in many languages, and trained in exotic Asian arts of unarmed combat."

Ashleigh laughed. "As earls' daughters usually are, I'm sure. I wasn't going to read those, but you're making them sound good."

"Aside from the premise, guaranteed to offend any serious Sherlockian, the books tend toward the bodice-ripping side of the aisle. Lots of heaving alabaster bosoms in low-cut gowns. Desdemona is faithful to Sherlock, and he to her, but everyone else spends most of the books bed hopping. I think the second book had a subplot about women being forced to work in high-end brothels. Mrs. Hudson objected to that."

"I'd hope so. I guess I can see why Donald wouldn't like it, but he doesn't have to read the books, does he? I'm glad he decided to let it go," Ashleigh said.

"Let it go? Oh, no. He'll be here on Saturday. Guaranteed."

Chapter 3

It's Jayne and my custom to meet in the tea room every day at twenty to four for our business partners' meeting. We have a cup of tea and enjoy the day's leftover baking and tea sandwiches, if there are any.

"I'm expecting a record-breaking crowd on Saturday," I said. We'd taken my favorite table, the one tucked into the window alcove, and I faced the street. Traffic was heavy as the first weekend of the summer approached. Pots of flowers overflowed outside the shops, and the branches of the ancient trees lining the street, lush with soft new leaves, swayed in a light wind. "I'm worried I'm not going to be able to fit everyone in."

Jocelyn placed a two-serving teapot in the center of the table. She wore the tea room uniform of knee-length black dress, black stockings, and white apron with the Mrs. Hudson's Tea Room logo of a steaming teacup next to a pipe. I poured my own tea, and fragrant steam rose into the air.

"We can use the tea room," Jayne suggested. "If we arrange a couple of rows of chairs in the doorway."

"I was hoping you'd say that. It will interfere with your business, though, and Saturday's your busiest day."

"Might help to draw additional customers in. By the way, I've hired Lorraine Dobbs to work here part time over the summer. The way this season's starting, I'll need the extra help."

"Good." I sipped my Darjeeling. Delicious, as always. "She's always reliable, and she knows enough about retail that she can help in the Emporium in a pinch."

"No poaching my employees, Gemma," Jayne warned.

I smiled at her over the rim of my teacup. "I meant when she isn't working here."

"Back to this Saturday. If we have chairs arranged in the tea room, we can't be serving also. We'll close food and drink service at one and reopen when Renalta finishes speaking. Some of her fans are sure to stay for tea after her talk. I can't believe I got to meet her in person. Wasn't she amazing?"

"Absolutely charming," I said dryly.

"And now I have my own signed copy. I'm so pleased. I told Robbie I can't see him tonight because I want to finish the book."

"I'm sure that went down well."

"He understands."

I doubted that very much. Robbie was Jayne's boyfriend. I didn't much care for him, and the feeling was mutual. I thought he was a no-account layabout. He thought I was an interfering friend.

On a recent occasion, Jayne and Robbie's timely arrival saved me from a knife-wielding maniac. I could have handled the situation myself, thank you very much, but Robbie figured he'd single-handedly saved my life. Nevertheless, I had thanked him. More than once. I was getting weary of him constantly reminding me about the supposed Chinese belief that if you saved someone's life, you were responsible for it from then on.

"My mom's planning to come back on Saturday for the talk." Jocelyn put a plate of lemon tarts and smoked salmon sandwiches on the table. "She's sure excited about it. She's thrilled to have her own signed book."

"Thus reducing the library waiting list by one. Tell her to come early." I helped myself to a sandwich. "I'm expecting a big crowd."

"What are you going to do about chairs?" Jayne asked. "You don't have anywhere near enough."

"I've arranged with the wedding rental place to drop them off Saturday morning. I've ordered one hundred."

Jayne whistled. "You are going to pack them in."

"I might have to get Maureen called out of town on a sudden emergency."

"Maureen? What's she got to do with anything?"

"My greatest fear is that the fire department is going to close us down for exceeding capacity. Trust Maureen to keep a steely eye on the number of patrons passing through our doors."

"I'll pop over to her store with some baking in the morning. Tell her it's our thanks for all she does for the street. That might mollify her."

"It might. I'd better get back to work. We're pretty busy today. News about Renalta is spreading."

"How's Ashleigh working out?" Jayne asked.

"Good so far." Ashleigh had always wanted, she told me at her interview, to live by the sea. But rather than go exploring, she'd married her high school sweetheart as soon as they graduated and settled down to a life of domestic bliss in Lincoln, Nebraska. Domestic bliss had been in short supply, and the couple divorced after a few difficult years, whereupon Ashleigh, at twenty-three, finally left the cornfields and flatland behind and headed east seeking the ocean with a suitcase crammed full of an odd assortment of clothing. She was delighted to be in West London, and I was delighted to have her working in my shop. She was a good and conscious employee. That made a change from what I was used to.

"I might even allow her to close up so I can get off home at a decent time some nights. Although I do wish she'd do something about her dress sense."

"What's wrong with her dress sense?" Jayne asked. "She always looks presentable."

"Presentable yes. More than presentable. 'Eclectic' might be the word. I don't want to have to worry about what she's going to show up in next."

"Bikini babe or Catholic nun? Who do I feel like being today?"

"I can't begin to imagine what the size of her closet must be."

Jayne laughed. "I'm looking forward to seeing what she wears next. It adds a bit of excitement to the drudgery of my day."

"One thing we don't need any more of around here is excitement. As you've already told Robbie you're busy tonight, why don't you meet me for dinner? I'll go home at six, walk and feed Violet, and then come back to the store around eight. That should give you time to finish the book. Ashleigh can close up at nine."

eight. That should give you time to finish the book. Ashleigh can close up at nine."

"Sure. Where shall we go?"

"How about the Blue Water Café?"

"We'll never get a reservation with such late notice, not on a Thursday in summer," Jayne said.

"You make the call," I said. "Speak to Andy. He'll find us a table."

"You think?"

"Guaranteed." Our friend Andy is the chef and owner of the Blue Water Café. It's my goal in life to see Jayne ditch Robbie and get together with hardworking, respectable, smart, kind Andy. He adores her, but she just can't see it. He'd make sure Jayne got a table tonight if he had to turn the president away.

The door to the street opened, and Grant Thompson's head popped in. "Is this a private meeting or can anyone join?"

"Come on in," I said. "We're closing in a few minutes, but we can always find something under the counter. And the coffeepot hasn't been emptied yet."

"Coffee'd be nice, thanks. Any muffins left?"

Jayne called to Fiona, who was stacking chairs on the tables prior to sweeping the floor.

"Tell you the truth," Grant said, "I'm here for more than coffee and treats. I want to talk to you, Gemma."

"Why?"

"I heard Renalta Van Markoff was in the Emporium earlier."

"Yes!" Jayne squealed. "She was talking to people and signing books. She's so friendly and gracious. I got a book signed."

"I also see," Grant said, "by the sign in the window that she'll be back on Saturday."

"For a formal talk followed by a signing," I said.

"I'm hoping you can reserve a couple for me," he said.

"I can, but I wonder why you want them." Grant was a rare book dealer. He specialized in late nineteenth- and early twentieth-century detective fiction. I couldn't see that the works of Renalta Van Markoff would be of any interest to him.

"I concentrate on one area," he said, "but it doesn't do to be too limited. Signed books are worth holding on to. Some-day, I might find a buyer."

Fiona put a cup of coffee and a muffin on the table in front of him. "Are books worth more if the author has signed them?"

"Usually," Grant said.

"Don't they have to be old to be valuable?" she asked.

"Age helps. Rarity helps even more. Renalta Van Markoff's books aren't exactly rare, far from it, but they might be of some value someday. I've heard it rumored that she has arthritis in her right wrist so she doesn't sign an excessive amount of books." That, I thought, might explain why she wanted her water bottles to be unsealed. Good thing I'd asked her to sign some store stock for me before she tired.

"I'm a book dealer," Grant continued. "I buy and sell. Sometimes I can sell right away, but sometimes I have to hold onto what I buy for a while. That's the nature of the business. I'll plan on coming on Saturday. What's your reserve limit?"

"Three." Visiting authors usually sign books that have been preordered, in most cases for those who couldn't make the personal appearance. If I didn't have a limit on the number a single buyer could take, it would be an unfair monopolization of the author's time.

"Three's good. Signature and date." He finished his coffee. He smiled at Jayne. Jayne smiled back. Grant cleared his throat and looked at me. "Do you happen to be free for dinner tonight, Gemma?" The green flecks in his deep-brown eyes sparkled in the afternoon light, and his thick brown hair curled around his ears in the moist sea air.

Before I could invite him to join Jayne and me, she leapt in. "No. Gemma has to work until late, and then she and I are meeting for dinner. We have important business to discuss, and that's the only time we can get together."

He glanced around the tea room. Four elderly ladies, Mrs. Hudson regulars, were shaking the last drops from their pot. Two women, shopping bags piled around their chairs, were handing Jocelyn their credit cards. "Another time, maybe," he said.

"What got into you?" I said once the door had closed behind Grant. "That was rude. We aren't having any business meeting tonight. We're just going out for dinner. Why shouldn't a handsome single man come with us?"

"He didn't want to have dinner with *us*, Gemma. He wanted to have dinner with *you*."

"So?"

"So. He's not the man for you."

"What are you talking about?"

"How's West London's hottest detective?"

"I assume you mean Ryan Ashburton, and I have no idea. Having not seen him since the conclusion of the Longton case."

"Which, Gemma, is precisely my point. You should be having dinner with Ryan. Not Grant. The man's mad for you, and I have to say, it seems to me as though the feelings are returned."

I stood up. "I've told you, Jayne, Ryan and I are finished. We had something once, but it didn't work out. I'll thank you not to interfere in my love life. I'll meet you at the Blue Water Café just after eight. Things should be quieting down in the kitchen by then. Why don't you get there early and ask Andy to join us for a drink?"

* * *

At five minutes after eight, I texted Jayne to say I was running late but would be at the restaurant soon. I thought that would give her and Andy time to have a nice quiet chat before I arrived.

When I did arrive at the café, it was eight twenty-five, and Jayne was sitting alone at a table for two. The advance reading copy of *Hudson House* was open in front of her, next to two menus and a lurid pink concoction approaching the bottom of a martini glass.

"Sorry I'm late." I dropped into a chair. "Last-minute rush of customers." Okay, that was a lie. "Where's Andy?"

"Night off."

"What?"

"It's his night off. He's entitled to one now and again, you know. I sometimes think I'd enjoy a day off. I wonder what that's like."

"You can have a day off in January."

"If I live that long." She sipped her drink.

"I'll take the day too. We can go to the beach. It won't be crowded."

Jayne laughed.

"Evening, Gemma." The waiter gave me a smile. "Can I get you something?"

"Sauvignon Blanc, please."

"Ready for another, Jayne?"

"Not quite yet, thanks," she said.

I glanced at Jayne's book. The bookmark, a white cocktail napkin from the tea room, was about twenty pages in. "I thought you were almost finished with that."

"I have finished it. I'm reading it again."

"Really?"

"I want to get some of the nuances I missed the first time."

"Nuances? She hammers you over the head with every clue."

"Well pardon me for liking it."

"Sorry," I mumbled.

The Blue Water Café occupies a prime space on the edge of the small harbor next to the boardwalk. The outdoor dining area, packed as always at this time of year, is suspended over the water. To the east, looking over the Atlantic Ocean, the sky was a deep purple. To the south and west, across town toward Nantucket Sound, the clouds were streaked pink and gray. Boats bobbed gently at their moorings, and charter fishing and pleasure craft returned to port, leaving no wake as they passed. Harbor seals played in the water around the pier while tourists leaned over the railing to take pictures. The hum of conversation and gentle laugher drifted around the deck. Candlelight glowed from inside hurricane lanterns, wineglasses sparkled, and marvelous smells filled the air.

My drink arrived, and the waiter recited the daily specials. I handed him the menu without opening it. I always have the same thing when I come to the café. I know what I like. Why try something else and risk being disappointed? "Clam chowder and the stuffed sole, please."

Jayne asked for a green salad followed by the lobster pasta, and the waiter departed.

"When's Arthur due back?" Jayne asked.

I shrugged. "You know him. He'll be back when he gets back." Great Uncle Arthur Doyle is the one who first came to West London. He bought the building at 222 Baker Street on a whim and, being a lifelong Holmes lover, took advantage of the address and opened the Sherlock Holmes Bookshop. His whim didn't last long, nor did his desire to settle in one place, and when he tried to sell the business, it was the worst possible time for independent bookstores, so he couldn't find a buyer. At the same time, I was in the process of getting a divorce from my cheating husband and extracting myself from the mystery bookstore we jointly owned, close to Trafalgar Square in London. I jumped at the chance to start fresh, came to West London, and bought half the store from Uncle Arthur, as well as a share of his 1756 salt-box house with a view of the ocean. I took over the store, and he was content to leave me to run the business. Uncle Arthur is fast approaching ninety years old, but he can still be counted on to wake up one morning and decide to go exploring in his prized 1977 Triumph Spitfire or join one of his old Royal Navy buddies on their sailboat for a cruise around the Mediterranean.

I'd refused a third glass of wine, the waiter was clearing our plates—scraped clean—when a buzz began in the hallway leading to the deck. I was seated with my back to the room, facing out to the harbor. I swiveled in my chair to see what was happening behind me.

"Oh, my gosh," Jayne said. "It's her."

Renalta Van Markoff swept into the room, followed closely by Kevin and Linda.

It was nine thirty, and the restaurant was thinning out. The hostess showed Renalta and her group to a table for four smack-dab in the center of the deck. Renalta didn't exactly wave to the watching diners, but she did lift her head and glance about the room before taking her seat. Tonight she wore an ankle-length black cotton dress under a bold-red jacket with giant black buttons and black stitching around the collar and cuffs. Her shoes were red patent leather with four-inch heels. The hostess lifted the hurricane lamp to light the candle nestled inside, and Renalta's ruby earrings flashed in the light. Kevin was dressed in dark jeans and an open-necked white shirt under a blue jacket with a white handkerchief in the breast pocket and two inches of starched white cuffs showing. His hair was flicked casually back, and stubble was dark on his chiseled jaw. I wondered if his striking looks were part of her public image.

Linda was still wearing what she'd had on earlier at the Emporium. She kept her head down and slipped into her seat without making a sound.

Waiters descended with menus and pitchers of water. Kevin made a show of an intense study of the wine list. Renalta fluffed her napkin and patted her hair while Linda buried her head in her menu.

"You're staring," I said to Jayne "That's not polite."

"She isn't trying to be incognito. Do you need any extra help on Saturday? Renalta Van Markoff does seem to attract a crowd."

"I don't think so. She'll give her talk and then sign books. Kevin said she'd speak for twenty minutes. I don't know if that's in addition to time for questions. I'll check when they arrive. I'll keep the lineup organized, and Ashleigh can run the cash register."

"I miss the days when cash registers went ca-ching ca-ching," Jayne said. "The sound of money being made."

"You're not old enough to remember ca-ching ca-ching. Neither am I."

"No, but my mom tells me all about it."

We drank our coffee and talked about mutual friends. By the time we were ready to leave, full dark had fallen over West London. I turned around to look for our waiter so I could ask for our check.

A woman walked into the dining room, trailed by a very anxious-looking waiter. The new arrival didn't appear to be here to relax and enjoy a nice meal and a glass of wine. Even in the dim glow from the row of electric lights lining the railing and the tabletop candles, I could see the fury in her eyes and the determined set of her square jaw.

"Please, madam," the hapless young waiter said.

She ignored him. Spotting her quarry, she set her shoulders and marched across the deck with firm steps.

Renalta Van Markoff and her companions had been served their first courses. Kevin lifted a glass full of deep-red liquid to his lips. He was the first to spot the new arrival, and his face paled. He almost dropped his glass as he jumped to his feet in an attempt to intercept her. He was too late.

"There you are," the woman yelled. "I'd say you're enjoying the fruits of your labors, but you've never worked at anything in your life."

Renalta didn't so much as bat a fake eyelash. She was seated and the intruder stood over her, but the author managed to look down her long nose at the newcomer. "You again," she said. "And just when I was enjoying some peace and quiet. How dreadfully tedious this is."

"Get out of here, Paige," Kevin said.

She glared at him. "Or what? Are you going to have me thrown out? You'd like that, wouldn't you? Wouldn't you love to see me humiliated once again?"

"Yes." Kevin jerked his head toward the waiter. A small crowd of staff had gathered, attracted by the woman's raised voice. The hostess slipped away. All conversation stopped as everyone watched the altercation. Linda dove under the table and came up clutching her cavernous bag. She pulled out her phone and snapped a picture of the furious intruder.

"You're nothing but a pretty lapdog," Paige said to Kevin, almost spitting out the words. "In a fair world, you'd be working for me, not trying to get me tossed into the street." She swung back toward Renalta. "I saw your car in the parking lot. That hideous, ostentatious, gas-guzzling vehicle. You have to advertise everywhere you go, don't you? I'm surprised you don't have your picture posted all over it. You're nothing but a joke."

"Clearly," Renalta drawled, her fake old-money accent firmly in place and her voice pitched high enough that everyone in the room could hear, "you are not laughing." She lifted her glass to take a sip of wine. The woman, Paige, knocked it halfway across the room.

The watchers let out a collective gasp. In the distance, getting closer, came the sound of a siren.

Paige turned to face the other diners. "You all think she's some great talented writer. But I'm telling you she owes everything to me. Everything! She stole my book! I thought I was helping her, and she stabbed me in the back. Without me, her best line would be, 'Do you want fries with that?'"

A few people tittered, more in embarrassment than amusement. Kevin placed himself firmly in front of Paige. He was careful, I noticed, not to touch her. Clearly this wasn't the first time this had happened. She, however, wasn't quite so circumspect. She shoved at his chest. He took a step backward and held up his hands. She was in her early sixties, tall, and very thin. Her slate-gray hair was cropped short, and the bangs were ragged as though she'd cut them herself with nail scissors. The skin on her haggard face and neck hung in loose folds, and her eyes blazed with rage. She had, I thought, remembering my Shakespeare, "a lean and hungry look."

Linda was on her feet now, snapping more pictures. In case they needed them in court, probably. Renalta reached across the table and grabbed Kevin's glass. She swiveled in her chair so she faced into the outdoor room. She held the wineglass up as if in a toast and took a drink.

The police arrived, led into the dining room by the hostess.

I recognized Officer Johnson from the WLPD. She headed immediately for the center table. "What's happening here?"

"This *lady*," Kevin said, "has interrupted our dinner and refuses to leave."

"She owes me for a glass of wine," Renalta said. "A very expensive glass too. Thank heavens she didn't throw the bottle." She sipped. Her eyes sparkled. She was enjoying this.

"You've been asked to leave." Johnson put her hand on Paige's arm. "I'm sure you don't want any trouble here. Come with me, please."

Paige made no move to shake Officer Johnson off. "I'll leave," she bellowed, also playing to the audience. "Not because of *her*, but because this nice young officer has asked me to. You all know the truth now. I won't rest! I'll never give up! Not until I get my rightful recognition. You haven't heard the last of me, Ruth!"

"No," Renalta said languidly, "I'm sure I haven't."

"Let's go." Johnson began to lead Paige out of the room.

"Oh, Officer," Renalta called, holding her glass high, "please do come back as soon as you've disposed of the trash. An officer of the law is always welcome at my table. Waiter, we'll have another bottle."

The diners laughed.

"And," Renalta exclaimed, "because I am so *dreadfully* sorry to have been the inspiration for that hideous interruption to your lovely, peaceful evening, a round of after-dinner liquors for these nice people, please."

The diners applauded.

Johnson led Paige away, and Kevin followed them. A bus-boy hurried forward with broom and dust pan to sweep up the shattered remnants of Renalta's glass.

"Wasn't that awkward," Jayne said to me. "Do you think there's any truth in what she said? That Renalta stole her book?"

"Probably not. I've heard of this sort of thing happening before. Some people can't accept failure. They haven't achieved their dreams in life, so have to believe someone else stole it from them."

"Poor Renalta. How absolutely awful for her. She handled it with her usual grace and charm though."

I wasn't so sure. Renalta had adored the attention. She practically lapped it up. Perhaps I'm cynical, but I wouldn't be surprised if she paid people to follow her around and pretend to be stalkers.

"The woman called her Ruth," Jayne said. "Do you suppose that's her real name?"

"Renalta Van Markoff does sound excessively dramatic, don't you think?"

A few women, who'd been too polite to approach the author earlier, had gathered around her table now, expressing their sympathies. Renalta sipped her wine and waved her hand in the air. "The price of fame, *darlings*. It is such a dreadful burden sometimes. The poor deluded dear simply pursues me everywhere. I feel so terribly sorry for her. Don't worry, my darling Kevin will sort everything out. He'll see that she's not treated too harshly."

Cameras and mobile phones began to come out of bags, and soon bulbs were flashing and shutters clicking as the author posed with her beaming fans. Eventually the women returned to their seats. Waiters moved from table to table, taking after-dinner drink orders to be added to Renalta's bill. The hostess whispered something to Renalta, who replied that they would not wait for the gentleman.

"I won't have another drink," Jayne said. "It's long past my bedtime, and I have an early start tomorrow."

I shuddered at the very thought. Jayne got up at four AM, seven days a week in tourist season, to start the bread.

"Time for me to be off too," I said. I could only hope that Paige had learned her lesson and wouldn't pay a visit to the Emporium on Saturday.

Chapter 4

Until I came to West London, I'd never had a pet. My mother is highly allergic to dogs and cats and not overly fond of rodents or fish either. I'd always lived in London: at my parents' home, in student digs, in a miniature flat in a soulless modern high-rise, and finally in a row house with my husband. Life had simply been too busy.

I hadn't realized what I'd been missing until the day Great Uncle Arthur came home with a cocker spaniel puppy he'd named after Violet Hunter of *The Adventure of the Copper Beeches*. With the first wag of her stubby tail, Violet enriched both my life and my heart. She's supposed to be Arthur's dog, but he travels so much, most of the responsibility for her care now lies with me. It can be difficult to get away from the store in the middle of the day in the busy season to take her for a walk, but it's a task I always look forward to.

One of the best things about owning a dog, I've found, is when I arrive home at the end of a long, tiring day to be greeted with that boundless passion and sheer joy of living.

After I got in from dinner with Jayne and Violet and I had exchanged a round of enthusiastic greetings, we set out on our nightly walk. I live on Blue Water Place, a street of leafy old trees, neat gardens, white picket fences, historic homes, and friendly neighbors. The boardwalk and the harbor lie at the end of my block, and several of the houses on the street are B and Bs, so traffic in the tourist season can be a great deal heavier than in the winter. But the B and Bs are gracious and tend to the more expensive end of the scale, and we're far from the restaurants and bars in town, so once darkness falls, all is calm and peaceful once again.

Violet and I strolled through the silent streets. While she checked out the latest news from the doggy neighborhood, I thought about Renalta Van Markoff and Saturday's signing. I also thought about the woman named Paige who seemed intent on making trouble.

It was late when we got home, but after I filled Violet's water bowl and got into my pajamas, I went into the den. I switched on a single light, curled up in my favorite wingback chair in front of the cold fireplace, and made a call.

"Gemma." The deep voice said my name like a caress. "Nice to hear from you. What's up?" In the background, people laughed, music played, glasses and cutlery clinked.

I could have called the West London police station with my concern. But it was too late, I told myself, for what was not an emergency. I could have called in the morning. But, I told myself, I wanted to do it while the thought was fresh in my mind.

What I didn't tell myself, however, was that I wanted to hear his voice.

"I know it's late," I said, "but it sounds like you're still up."

Ryan Ashburton said, "I'm having a drink with some of the guys and girls."

"If this isn't a good time . . ."

The voices fell away as he moved to a quieter space. "Time for me to be heading home anyway. Jim Erickson got a promotion, so the celebration might go on for a long time yet. Do you need me to come around?"

I breathed. "No. I have a quick favor to ask."

"Go ahead."

"You might have heard that a famous author's doing a book signing at the Emporium on Saturday."

"I heard. Something Van something."

"Renalta Van Markoff. She was involved in an incident at the Blue Water Café earlier this evening. A woman accosted her. I suspect the woman is a stalker. She was certainly known to the author and her group. The police were called, and Officer Johnson ordered her to leave. Which she did, with no trouble, but things could have gotten ugly."

"You're worried she might come to the store on Saturday?"

"I am. I wanted you—the WLPD, I mean—to know. I'm hoping a uniformed officer can pop around, keep an eye on things. The program begins at one thirty. I expect people will start arriving a long time before that."

"I'll see that it gets done."

"Thank you, Ryan."

Silence poured down the phone lines. Then he said, "If that's all, Gemma, I'll say good night."

"Good night."

I pressed the red button to end the call. I sat back in my chair with a sigh and picked my book off the side table. I was starting *These Honored Dead* by Jonathan F. Putnam. The idea of the young Abraham Lincoln as a cosleuth was an intriguing one, and I was eager to see if Putnam could pull it off. But tonight my mind was on other things. I soon gave up trying to pay attention to the story, put it aside, and reached for my iPad.

It was looking as though Saturday's appearance by Renalta Van Markoff was going to be unlike any book signing I'd had before. Some hugely successful authors have been in my shop, but they didn't descend from Cadillac Escalades as though they were the Duchess of Cambridge attending a charity gala, and they weren't followed by a team of flunkies, never mind crazed stalkers. I like to know who I'm dealing with, so I searched for what I could find about Renalta Van Markoff. The bio on her web page was probably as false as her accent, but I didn't consider that to be a problem. Plenty of celebrities fudged their biographies. When Robert Galbraith's first book was published, his bio said he was a former SAS soldier. In reality he was a middle-aged woman from Scotland. A woman who had achieved some fame under her own name of J. K. Rowling. Of considerably more interest to me at the moment was the number of bookstores I found with "postponed" slapped over their events pages. Renalta had been due to attend three book signings this weekend. One tomorrow night in New York City and two in Boston on Saturday. On Monday evening she was supposed to be in Scottsdale, Arizona, for an appearance at the Poisoned Pen.

As I well know, bookstores don't take kindly to authors canceling at the last minute. Particularly when they have no reasonable excuse. Linda had told me Renalta suddenly decided she wanted to go to the Cape for the weekend. Obviously the canceled appearances didn't bother her one bit, but her publisher would be beyond furious. I suspect Kevin had to do some serious convincing to get her to even agree to come to the Emporium so as not to completely ruin the all-important first weekend of sales.

I could almost hear Renalta's voice now. *Sooooo tedious, darling.*

Chapter 5

Friday at the Sherlock Holmes Bookshop and Emporium was all Renalta Van Markoff all day. If people weren't buying her books, they were inquiring about tomorrow's talk. The phone was ringing off the hook—and isn't that an outdated expression?—with people wanting to make a reservation. I told them it was first come first serve but warned them to arrive in plenty of time. I debated asking Jayne if we could sell muffins and sandwiches and cold drinks to the early-arriving throngs of fans but discarded the idea on the grounds that we'd never manage to do that and run the tea room at the same time. Surely there were some people in West London who weren't Van Markoff fans.

Ashleigh arrived at one to begin her shift. Today she was done up like a lawyer heading for court in a severe black suit with the skirt cut precisely to the knee, gray blouse, neutral-colored nylon stockings, and black pumps with one-inch heels. All that was missing was the leather briefcase.

"Where," I asked, "do you get all those clothes?"

"All what clothes?"

"Most people have a certain style." My personal style was "as little effort as possible." "You have a different look every day. Even your hair." Today, it was pulled back into a tight bun.

"I like my attire to match my mood," she said. "We'll be getting ready for the big author signing tomorrow. In case there are any legal complications, I am in the moment."

"Okay." I suppressed the thought as to what mood she would be in around Halloween. "Just keep it professional at all times, okay?"

She held out her arms and gave me a quizzical look. "Isn't this professional?"

"It's fine. Thanks for closing up last night." I'd been pleased to arrive this morning and find everything shipshape. The floor swept, the countertops dusted, all the stock neatly in its assigned place. Even a content and well-fed Moriarty snoozing in his bed under the center table.

"Not a problem," she said.

"I've been getting queries all morning about Renalta's visit. We're not taking reservations, and if anyone calls to ask us to put aside a personalized book, take their details, but make no promises. Renalta seems the sort who might decide that she doesn't feel like signing books after all."

"Got it," she said. "I was thinking last night, if you don't mind a suggestion . . . That guy who came yesterday, Donald. He was wearing a Sherlock Holmes T-shirt. You should stock some of them."

"This isn't a clothing shop."

"But you have all that other Sherlock stuff. The mugs, the games, the puzzles, the dish towels. Why not T-shirts?"

"We're primarily a bookshop. Because our stock of books is highly specialized, we expanded into Sherlock . . . uh . . . stuff. I don't want to lose focus on books."

"Nope, but T-shirts would be a good seller."

"I don't want . . ."

"I'll look into suppliers and prices. Don't worry. I'll do it in my own time. I'll keep thinking about other ideas too. How about . . ."

I reminded myself that Ashleigh was keen, and that was a good thing. I was saved from replying when a man came into the store. He wore handmade Italian loafers, khaki trousers with seams pressed to a knife point, and a blue-and-white-checked shirt buttoned to the neck. His slate-gray hair was short and expensively cut and his hands smooth and spotlessly clean. Maybe the business look was the in thing for today after all. Who knew?

"Good mornin'," he said to us with a smile full of blindingly white teeth. "How are y'all doin' today?" His accent was so North Carolina, he could have done the voice-over for their tourism ads.

"Good morning, Mr. McNamara," I said. "Everything is in place for tomorrow. You don't have to worry."

"I . . . uh . . . do I know you, ma'am?"

"No," I said. "You're Robert McNamara of McNamara and Gibbons Press."

"How did you . . . ?"

"Never mind her," Ashleigh said. "It's her party trick. Can I grab a coffee from next door, Gemma? I didn't have time to get one."

"Sure." I smiled at the man. That he was not a casual Cape Cod vacationer was obvious by his clothes and by the closeness of his morning shave. That he was not a shopper was obvious by the way he'd studied the window display before coming in, as though ensuring it was satisfactory. That he was not interested in anything else I had for sale was obvious by the way he looked only at the center table where Renalta's books were arranged.

That he was worried was an obvious conclusion based on the research I'd done last night.

Renalta was not published by one of the big five publishing houses. McNamara and Gibbons Press was a midsized company out of Raleigh, North Carolina. They had a handful of midlist authors, both fiction and nonfiction, but Renalta Van Markoff was their only major bestseller.

Details on the website informed me that the publisher and owner were one and the same: Mr. Robert McNamara. The web page didn't have a picture of him, but I didn't need to see one to know that this was the man standing in front of me.

"Your store is small," he said.

"We'll manage fine. The shelves can be pushed aside, and I have a hundred chairs coming in tomorrow." If one more person complained about the size of my shop, I'd . . . I'd do something.

"That should be fine." He let out a long sigh. "It's good of you to do this at the last minute's notice."

"We have a mutual interest," I said. "Renalta's books consistently sell well here, but there's nothing quite like an author visit to encourage sales."

His strained smile only served to emphasize the worry lines under his eyes. "Is there anything I can do to help?"

"Everything's under control. I have plenty of books in stock, but I've ordered more. I checked with my distributor this morning, and the books are on their way. They should arrive later today. Tomorrow morning at the latest."

"Good. I'll be here for Renalta's visit. To keep an eye on things."

"I assume Renalta needs keeping an eye on."

"You don't know the half of it. The difference between authors and petulant children is that children eventually grow up. But Renalta takes it into a whole new league. After she arbitrarily canceled a weekend full of appearances at the last moment—to my horror I might add—I thought I'd better be here in person. Tomorrow afternoon's my mother's ninety-fifth birthday party. I am not happy about having to come to Cape Cod instead."

I made a sympathetic face. Moriarty yawned.

"To make things worse, my wife's away on a business trip. Not that Mama'll notice if we're not there, but my brothers and sisters certainly will." He forced out a smile. "You can call me if anything comes up." He recited his number, and I put it into my own phone.

*　*　*

At three o'clock the door flew open, and Renalta Van Markoff burst into the store. I blinked and looked again.

It wasn't Renalta, but darn close.

She wore a long scarlet cape and red stilettos; her black hair was piled into a wind-blown mass on the top of her head. Her eyelashes were false, her eyes outlined with thick black liner, and purple shadow had been excessively applied. Her red lips matched the polish on her fingers and the earrings in her ears. She swooped down on me with a dramatic swirl of the cape. "My darling, I hope I'm not too late to sign up for tomorrow."

"You mean the talk by Renalta Van Markoff? We're not taking reservations."

"In that case, I will be sure to arrive in plenty of time." Closer up, I could see that her cape had a tattered hem and was almost worn through in a couple of spots. The earrings were red glass, and her hair tilted ominously to one side. A wig.

Was this supposed to be an early Halloween costume? If so, I doubted Renalta Van Markoff would be amused. I made a mental note to ask Ashleigh not to impersonate a certain famous author tomorrow.

"You're so lucky to have her coming here. Imagine, Renalta herself, in your tiny store." She clutched her hands to her chest and fluttered her eyelashes at me. "My dream come true."

Not just a costume then, but something, dare I say, creepy.

"I'm Nancy. I'm the president of the Renalta Van Markoff Fan Club, New England Chapter, and her greatest admirer. We have so much in common." She waved her hand in what was rapidly becoming a very familiar gesture. Her ring, being a cheap piece of dull glass, chipped and tarnished, did not throw back the light. "We've met many times, of course, but I never tire of hearing her speak."

"The program begins at one thirty," I said. "You should come early if you want a good seat. I suggest buying your book ahead of time to avoid possible disappointment."

She ignored my hint. "I was planning to go to her signings in Boston tomorrow, but then the Renalta fan page on

Facebook said she was coming here instead. So much more convenient for me as I live near New Bedford." She glanced around the room, checking that no one was listening. Other than Ashleigh arranging the children's books that had been tossed by a family who'd just left (after buying nothing, I might add) and a woman flipping through a book on the making of the BBC series *Sherlock*, the Emporium was empty. Nancy leaned across the desk. "Has she been here yet?"

I saw no reason not to answer. It wasn't exactly a secret. "She came in yesterday. To meet the staff and check out our facilities."

Nancy shivered. "That is so kind of her. She's always like that, you know. So many other writers just assume everyone will jump at the idea of hosting them. Did she leave anything behind?"

"Why would she do that? We have her books in stock already."

"I mean like a signing pen, maybe. A small token of her affection. Something I could have. If you don't need it, that is."

Creepy all right.

At that moment, the phone rang, and I was saved from continuing with that conversation. "Sherlock Holmes Bookshop and Emporium, Gemma speaking."

It was yet another Van Markoff fan asking what time she should arrive tomorrow. Nancy wandered off to check out my shop. She didn't seem terribly impressed and soon gathered her cape around her. "Until tomorrow, then. Oh, one more tiny thing. You don't know where Renalta's staying, do you?"

"No, I don't."

"We're such good friends. I know she'd be thrilled if I took a room at the same hotel."

Creepy. "Why don't you call or send her an e-mail and ask?"

"I would, of course, but that silly girl who answers her phone and reads all her letters won't put me through. Personally, I think it's long past time Renalta fired her. But she's much too kind." She waved her fingers at me and left with a swirl of the cape. Her wig slipped and she grabbed at it as the door shut behind her.

"Weirdo," Ashleigh said.

"Yup," I replied.

"Your store attracts weirdoes," she said. "I mean, anyone who thinks Sherlock Holmes is a real person or who cares if he was having a secret affair with his landlady is a weirdo by definition."

Most of them, maybe. Great Uncle Arthur is a Sherlock fanatic, but no one would call him a weirdo. Not to his face, anyway. "Don't let it bother you. They're harmless."

"Bother me?" Ashleigh roared with laughter. "I think it's great!"

Chapter 6

Saturday morning people began arriving even earlier than I expected. Fortunately, I'd thought to ask Ashleigh to come in early. We pushed shelves against the walls and moved tables aside while Moriarty supervised. I set the podium, borrowed from the library, at the front of the store and dragged the chair out of the reading nook to put it against a table we'd cleared for the signing. Boxes of books arrived yesterday afternoon, and I'd stacked them behind the sales counter, with instructions to Ashleigh to fill up the center table and the shelves as needed. I'd added some copies of Laurie R. King's Mary Russell series and Carole Douglas Nelson's Irene Adler books, hoping to appeal to those interested in the women in the Great Detective's life.

I'd brought my camera to work today and placed it under the counter. "Once she arrives, I'll be kept moving," I said to Ashleigh, "so I want you to take pictures, if you don't mind. I'd like shots of Renalta when she's speaking or signing. Try to get something that shows the size of the crowd and people holding their copies of the books."

"Happy to," she said.

The rental company van pulled into the loading zone, and two men carried the chairs in and set them up in neat rows. They'd barely left when the first of the patrons arrived. Four women, heavyset, dyed hair ranging from light blonde to brassy red, and garishly dressed in the worst of summer vacation wear (including black socks in Birkenstocks), plopped themselves into the front row. They'd never been in my shop before. Once settled, they pulled sandwiches out of cavernous handbags, opened thermoses, and poured iced tea.

"You might want to buy your books ahead of time," Ashleigh said to them. "Then you can have them signed as soon as Miss Van Markoff's ready." Today my assistant looked almost normal in a colorful summer tunic worn over black leggings.

They laughed. "Don't you worry, young lady. We've got our copies right here. We preordered them on Amazon."

I gritted my teeth. Fortunately, the next bunch who came in were buyers, and I was kept busy as the flood of patrons began. Many picked up snacks or drinks at the tea room first, and book sales were brisk. Ashleigh was turning out to be a good salesclerk. She deftly guided the Renalta enthusiasts to other Holmes-pastiche books or suggested selections from the gaslight shelves. This wasn't a Holmes-loving bunch though; they mostly just liked Desdemona Hudson and the historical setting, so the Conan Doyle books and most of the associated merchandise were left untouched.

Jocelyn's mother came in and gave me a wave as she made a dash for the last available seat in the front row. She sat down and pulled out the book she'd bought on Thursday.

I was ringing up a paperback of *An Elementary Affair* for a young woman when the bottle of water in her hand caught

61

my attention. I mentally slapped my forehead. The lineup at the cash register was three deep. I glanced around the room. Ashleigh stood next to the shelves, helping a highly indecisive patron make a selection. She'd been with that patron for what seemed to be forever.

I called her over, and she made her apologies to the customer. "Thanks for the rescue," she whispered to me. "She'll never decide."

"I forgot about getting water for Renalta."

"Oh, yeah. Four bottles. The caps unsealed."

I opened the cash register and took out a ten-dollar bill. "Run to the convenience store on the corner and buy them. She wants Riviera." I added another ten. "That's the expensive stuff."

Ashleigh dashed off. She stepped aside to let Jayne and Maureen through the front door. Jayne was dressed in her working apron, and Maureen was, wonder of wonders, smiling. I was immediately suspicious.

"Goodness," she said. "You've got quite the crowd in here."

"I told Maureen you'd ensure she got a good seat." Jayne gave me a wink from behind Maureen's shoulder.

"I will?"

"It was so thoughtful of you to ask Jocelyn's mom to hold the seat for her."

"It was? Yes, it was. Very thoughtful of me."

Jayne winked again as she rubbed her thumb and index finger together. The universal gesture for a payoff.

Why hadn't I thought of that? I was getting sloppy.

Jayne led Maureen to the front row, and I continued ringing up books.

A short while later, Jocelyn's mum put a *Sherlock Mind Palace* coloring book, a DVD of the first season of the BBC *Sherlock* program, a Benedict Cumberbatch wall calendar, DVDs of the *Complete Sherlock Holmes Collection* starring Basil Rathbone, a copy of *The Associates of Sherlock Holmes*, and a thin copy of *The Red-Headed League* illustrated by P. James Macaluso Jr. on the counter. "Thanks so much, Gemma. I got a start on my Christmas shopping. My oldest granddaughter has the biggest crush on Benedict Cumberbatch—don't you just adore that name?—my son enjoys reading short stories, my father-in-law says Rathbone was the best Holmes of them all, and I'm sure Eddie—that's my grandson—will love those illustrations. Sherlock Holmes depicted in Lego. Have you ever seen anything cuter? Jayne said I had to show you what I'm taking, so you could mark it off against inventory."

"Show me? Oh, right." If this was the cost of keeping Maureen from calling the fire department on me, it was cheap.

A uniformed police officer approached the counter. "I'll be close by, Ms. Doyle, in case you need any help."

"Thank you," I said. I'd met Officer Richter for the first time a couple of weeks ago at a murder scene. He was balding and trying (and failing badly) to disguise it with a greasy combover. He weighed a good twenty-one stone—that's about three hundred pounds. The day was warm, although not excessively so, but Officer Richter pulled a handkerchief out of his pocket and wiped rivers of sweat from his brow and cheeks. When we'd first met, I estimated he was due for a heart attack in less than a month. I could only hope it wouldn't be today.

He glanced around the room. The audience was more than 90 percent women, the majority of them middle aged and up. With half an hour to go, most of the seats had been taken, and an excited buzz filled the shop. Women chatted, drank coffee and nibbled on snacks, or were engrossed in the books they'd just bought. "Doesn't look like the rioting sort to me," he said.

"You never know," I said.

"You got that right," he replied.

I watched a line of sweat drip down the side of his face. "Why don't you go into the tea room and get a glass of water. Or maybe an iced tea. Tell them I said it's on the house."

"Thanks," he said. "I could use something cold."

"Be sure and ask for an unsweetened tea," I called after him.

Ashleigh appeared bearing four bottles of Riviera-brand water. "What do you want me to do with these, Gemma?"

"Break the seals, as she asked, and put two on the shelf under the podium. I'll keep the other two here on the counter until they're needed. Then you can take over for me at the register."

I took a position by the doors to keep an eye out for the author's arrival and to direct patrons to the few chairs still unoccupied. This spot was directly underneath my office on the upper floor, and the bone-chilling howl of the Hound of the Baskervilles came through the ceiling. Or that might have been Moriarty's cries of indignation. I absent-mindedly rubbed at the bandage on my left hand. I'd cleverly lured him upstairs with a special treat of Temptations, whereupon he had, after gobbling up half the snack, equally cleverly deduced my intentions and made a break for the stairs. I'd managed to escape the office before he could, but it had been a hard-fought battle.

At quarter after one, Grant Thompson walked into the Emporium.

"Surprised to see you here," I said. "I put your books aside, as you asked." I'd had a number of other requests to have books signed, and they were stacked in a neat pile on the table awaiting the attention of the author.

"I wanted to see what all the fuss is about. And it looks to be quite a fuss indeed. Not many seats left, I see. I'll stand."

"You're a true gentleman," I said.

He gave me a grin. Grant Thompson was handsome, charming, clever, well read, well traveled, and highly educated. What more did I want in a man? *True love*? No, I'd had that once. Twice, counting my marriage. It hadn't worked out. True love belonged between the pages of a Renalta Van Markoff novel. Not in the real world.

Not in my world, anyway.

I was about to hint to Grant that I'd be looking forward to a drink and dinner this evening, if anyone felt like suggesting that, when Ryan Ashburton arrived. I didn't recognize the young girl with him.

"Wow," he said. "Looks like we should have come earlier." He gave Grant a nod.

"Detective," Grant said.

"I didn't mean for you to come yourself," I said to Ryan. "Officer Richter is here. Somewhere."

"I was planning on attending anyway. Gemma Doyle, this is my niece, Madison. Madison and her family are visiting my folks, and I figured she'd enjoy meeting Renalta Van Markoff."

"Hi," the girl mumbled. She buried her head into her chest. She was twelve or thirteen, all freckles and curly red hair, knees and elbows.

"Are you a fan of Van Markoff's books?" I asked.

"No," she said.

"Madison wants to be a writer," Ryan said. "She's really good. I thought maybe Ms. Van Markoff could give her some tips."

The girl blushed furiously.

"Not many seats left," Ryan said. "You grab one, Madison, and I'll stand over there."

She scurried away. The last rows of chairs, the ones leading into the tea room, were now almost full. People were squeezing onto the bottom of the stairs.

"She's sweet," I said.

"Smart as they come," Ryan said. "But so shy, it's painful to watch."

"She'll grow out of it." I knew of which I spoke. The teenage years were rarely kind to smart, awkward girls.

Ryan took a place with his back against the wall, and Grant went to stand against the sales counter next to Irene Talbot. She had a digital recorder in her hand and a camera slung around her neck.

By one twenty the room was packed solid.

At one twenty-one, my worst fear was realized when Donald Morris sailed into the Emporium dressed in his full Sherlock getup. Houndstooth Inverness cape, deerstalker hat, unlit pipe clenched between his teeth.

"Don't you dare cause a scene," I hissed at him.

"Me? Perish the thought, dear lady. I'm here in order to hear what words of wisdom the great Renalta Van Markoff has to expound on the nature of Mr. Sherlock Holmes."

"You are not."

"Yes, I am."

"Please, Donald, don't make trouble."

"I'll stand over there, next to Mr. Thompson and Miss Talbot. You won't even know I'm here. I will imitate Dr. Watson's words: 'Silent and furtive were his movements.'"

I groaned.

At one twenty-two, my second worst fear was realized when Paige, last night's stalker, strolled into the shop.

I decided that beating about the bush was not in order today. I walked up to her. "I am the owner of this shop. I was in the Blue Water Café Thursday night at nine thirty."

"Were you now?"

"Yes, I was. That was quite a scene you caused. The police took you away. Weren't you charged?"

"Ruthie wouldn't do that to me. That's never good publicity. I promised I'd be a good girl, and her tame monkey told the police he wouldn't press charges." She gave me a smile that put me in mind of Andrew Scott in the role of Moriarty (the human Moriarty) in *Sherlock*. "I'm only here to observe. I'm preparing my suit, and my lawyer told me to get as much ammunition as I can."

"Your suit?" Despite myself, I had to ask.

"Oh, yes. I'm suing Ruthie for all she's worth. And then some. She stole my idea and turned it pretty much verbatim into *An Elementary Affair*. Looks like all the seats are taken. Guess I should have come earlier." She sauntered across the room. Grant shifted aside to give her space to stand next to him.

I spotted Officer Richter outside doing some crowd control. Fans had gathered on the sidewalk to await Van Markoff's arrival, and another bunch was curious as to what all the excitement was about. Richter was telling everyone to keep to the sidewalk.

Robert McNamara, Renalta's publisher, was next to arrive. I was beginning to feel like the Queen at a Buckingham Palace garden party greeting my guests. "Good afternoon. Standing room only, I'm afraid."

"That's what I like to see," he said. "A full house. Renalta's a wonder."

At one thirty on the dot, the Escalade pulled up to the front of the Emporium and parked in the loading zone. Middle-aged women squealed like fangirls at a boy-band concert, and the crowd pressed forward. Many of them held up phones to take pictures and others waved books.

The passenger door opened, and the waiting women squealed once again. A great sigh of disappointment echoed down Baker Street as Linda got out. Her jaw was tight and her eyes dark with repressed anger. She made no attempt to look happy to be here, but that didn't matter. No one was interested in her anyway. Kevin leapt out of the driver's seat and walked around the back of the car to open the door for Renalta. She stepped out in a swirl of black and scarlet.

I decided that as the host, I should greet my guest. "Excuse me, excuse me. Coming through." The mob parted politely.

Renalta glared at Linda and whispered something short and sharp. That taken care of, the author broke into a radiant smile and extended her hand to me. We shook, and I felt the giant ruby dig into my palm and a wave of Chanel No. 5 wash over me. "*Darling*," she breathed, loud enough for the back of the crowd to hear, "such a wonderful greeting. So many marvelous fans. You truly are a miracle worker."

"We're very happy to have you here," I said.

"How wonderful to see you, my darlings," Renalta trilled to the onlookers. "So lovely of you to all to come."

"Please allow Miss Van Markoff through," Kevin said. "She'll be delighted to sign your books and pose for pictures after her talk."

Squealers or no, this was a group of middle-aged women after all—they stepped back politely, making a path to the door.

All of them, that is, except for Nancy, the rabid fan. She shoved the woman in front of her so hard, she would have fallen had I not grabbed her arm. "Renalta, it's me. Nancy. Yoo-hoo! Over here! I've come all this way to see you. Let's have dinner later."

A look that I can only describe as horrified came over Renalta's perfectly made-up face. She snapped her fingers, the sound so loud it cracked in the clear air. Kevin dropped her arm and stood in front of the intruder. "Get lost, Nancy."

"Renalta, tell that man to get out of my way."

Officer Richter stepped forward. "We don't want any trouble here."

"Trouble? I'm not making trouble. I'm only trying to arrange a time for Renalta and me to have dinner later. This is a public street. You tell *him* to get out of my way. Renalta, wait!"

I held the door for Renalta and she sailed into the shop, trailed by the scowling Linda. People had risen to their feet and were clapping enthusiastically. I swear more than one woman was almost in tears at the sight of her idol.

I led a smiling and waving Renalta to the front and took my place at the podium. I glanced down to check that the two bottles of water were on the shelf. I tapped the microphone.

People gradually resumed their seats, and the mutter of conversation died down.

Maureen beamed at me from the front row. Next to her the Amazon-buying group who'd been first to arrive perched on the edges of their seats. I looked across the rows of tightly packed heads to see Ryan Ashburton leaning against the wall next to the door to the tea room. Jayne stood on one side of him, and on the other was a life-sized cutout of Benedict Cumberbatch as Sherlock. I chuckled to myself, seeing them together. The fictional detective and the real one. Ryan gave me a thumbs-up, and Jayne silently capped her hands together over her chest.

Ashleigh stood behind the cash register. She lifted my camera and snapped a picture. Irene Talbot, Grant Thompson, and Donald Morris stood in front of the sales counter along with Robert, the publisher; Linda, the PA; and Paige, the stalker. Nancy slipped into the shop, glanced around for a seat, and, seeing none, joined them. She was followed by Kevin, who didn't look at all happy. I suspected he'd failed to convince Officer Richter to keep her out of the shop. Richter himself took his position beside the front door, feet apart, arms crossed, scowl firmly in place.

In the monetary hush, the Hound of the Baskervilles could be heard calling across the Great Grimpen Mire. I hoped no one would call the SPCA to report me for animal abuse.

"Thank you, everyone, for coming," I spoke into the mic. Like the podium, it was on loan from the library. "I know we're all delighted to have Renalta Van Markoff with us today." A round of enthusiastic applause. "After she talks to us about her hugely popular Hudson and Holmes series and the latest novel, *Hudson House*, Renalta will be happy to sign your copies." Someone cheered. "Mrs. Hudson's Tea Room will then be reopening to serve afternoon tea." Another cheer. "Now let's give a big Sherlock Holmes Bookshop welcome to Renalta Van Markoff."

I clapped my hands together, and the audience joined in. I stepped back to give the stage to Renalta. She hesitated, and for the briefest instant, the look on her face was of nothing but sheer unbridled panic. My heart went out to her as I realized that the poor woman was absolutely terrified of public speaking. I touched her elbow and guided her to the podium. I grabbed a bottle of water and handed it to her. She took it in shaking hands and gave me a weak smile. "When you're ready," I whispered.

She pulled the loosened cap off and took a long drink. She breathed heavily, put the bottle down, flung out her arms, and said, "Darlings! What a marvelous welcome."

I joined Ashleigh at the cash register. Once Renalta started to speak, she was fine. She talked about her writing routine—seven days a week, three hours a day. She talked about her lifelong love of Sherlock and about her new book, giving little hints at the plot and at the developing relationship between Desdemona Hudson and Sherlock Holmes. She finished the first bottle of water and reached for the second. She drank water constantly. I suspected it gave her time to organize her thoughts and helped calm her nerves.

Paige snorted when Renalta discussed her writing routine, and Donald snorted whenever Renalta mentioned the name of the Great Detective.

After about fifteen minutes, Kevin caught Renalta's eye, and she nodded. He stepped into the center aisle. "Perhaps we have time for a few questions from the audience." Hands shot up.

"I have a question," Paige bellowed without waiting to be called upon. "When are you going to acknowledge the true author of those books and . . . ?"

She didn't get a chance to finish the question. I'd pointed her out to Officer Richter as the person I wanted him to keep an eye on. He had hold of her arm and was hustling her out the door before most of the people in the room had a chance to turn and see who was speaking.

Nicely done, I thought.

I should have asked them to send two uniformed officers.

"What makes you think," Donald called, "that you have the right to interfere with one of the greatest literary characters ever created?"

"Not that question again," Renalta said.

"Sherlock Holmes is a Victorian gentleman. A man of great integrity. Honored by his sovereign and trusted by his government at the very highest of levels. Your suggestion that he would take up a sordid affair with a married woman of lax morals is impossible to comprehend."

Kevin took a step forward.

Renalta raised one hand in the universal stop gesture. "Allow me to answer the question. Sherlock Holmes, I hate to tell you, is not a real person."

The audience laughed.

"I am perfectly aware of that," Donald said.

"And as such," Renalta continued, "I am free to use my imagination as much as anyone else is."

"Preposterous. Sir Arthur Conan Doyle's greatest creation—"

"Why, take a look at you, sir. It's a long time until Halloween, so I assume you're pretending to be Sherlock yourself. Talk about using your imagination."

The audience laughed again. Some thought Renalta's dig was terribly funny. Some laughed out of embarrassment. Donald turned bright red.

"Sherlock Holmes," Renalta went on, "is so much more than a Victorian gentleman, as you call him, sir. He is all of us." Her voice rose. "He is our better nature. He is our better selves. He is what we all want to be. Not only intelligent and perceptive, but compassionate and kind."

"You tell him, Renalta," someone called from the middle row.

"He is not an adulterer," Donald shouted.

"Sherlock Holmes is not trapped in hypocritical Victorian morality," Renalta said. "But it seems to me as though you, sir, are. Am I right, ladies?"

The audience cheered.

"How dare you. Your interpretation of Mrs. Hudson is . . ." A vein began to pulse in Donald's forehead.

I slipped out from behind the counter and put my hand on his arm. "Let it go, Donald. Please. You cannot win this argument."

But Renalta wasn't finished. She was enjoying herself far too much to stop now. "And thus we come to the crux of your complaint, sir. My Mrs. Hudson is a woman of courage and conviction. Not to mention smarter than your Victorian gentleman. She is a woman of the modern world. That, sir, is what you are so afraid of."

The audience applauded enthusiastically. Renalta's speech was nicely delivered, but it had the ring of being exactly that. A speech. Written and rehearsed, tested and delivered many times.

"Renalta would be delighted to sign your books now," Kevin said. "If you could form an orderly line."

"Someone needs to put a stop to you and end this travesty," Donald yelled.

"Donald, that is quite enough," I said. "Maybe it would be better if you left."

He turned and leaned over the counter. His breath came in harsh gasps. I put my hand on his back. "It's okay. Just breathe." The two remaining bottles of water for Renalta were in front of us. I grabbed one and handed it to him. "Here. Do you want this?"

He shook his head. "No. I'm fine. I don't hate intelligent women. You know that, Gemma. I only want Holmes to be left as his creator intended."

"I know." I put the bottle back down. "If you need to sit, go into the tea room. You can rest in the kitchen."

"I'll be fine," he repeated.

I left him and headed for the signing table. People had formed an orderly line down the center of the store. Renalta sat at the table, surrounded by stacks of books. Linda stood beside her, turning the pages to the proper place for the author to sign. The PA no longer looked furious, just not entirely happy, but Renalta glowed with pleasure. Clearly signing books and talking to individual fans was not a problem for her.

I'd put slips of paper into the ones that had been pre-ordered, indicating if they were to be personalized or only needed a signature. Linda opened them to the title page, Renalta signed, and Linda then put them to one side. When she'd taken care of them all, Renalta looked at the lineup, stretching to the back of the store, and smiled. "Thank you so much for coming, my darling," she said to the woman who'd nabbed the first spot in line. "I am so sorry about that rude interruption. The poor man. Some of these people can carry their delusions to an extreme, don't you agree?"

The woman tittered in delight, and then she leaned across the table. "My friend and I have a bet as to which of the original Holmes stories influenced you the most. I think it's totally obvious, judging by what happened in *An Elementary Affair*, but she disagrees."

Renalta blinked. "My favorite story is . . ."

"I don't mean favorite, but the one you consider most influential."

"Heavens, there are so many, each one as marvelous as the others, wouldn't you agree?"

"Not really. Some are better than others. Some aren't very good at all." She stood firm, waiting for an answer. The people standing behind her shifted from one foot to another. A woman took a picture with her phone.

"I suppose," Renalta said. "If I must say . . . it's, uh . . . it's . . ."

Linda leaned over and whispered in her boss's ear.

"*The Specked Band*, of course," Renalta exclaimed. "That incredibly brave young woman was such an inspiration to Desdemona and to me."

The woman beamed and turned to her companion. "Told you so!"

I picked up the pile of signed books. "Do you need anything here?"

"Where's my water?" Renalta asked in a voice that didn't project to the line. "For heaven's sake, Linda, can't you do anything right?"

Linda flushed but said nothing.

Renalta clearly wasn't an easy person to work for. "Sorry, my fault," I said. "I'll get it."

I waded through the crowd. Several of my regulars stopped me to thank me for bringing Renalta to the shop. A couple wanted to ask when their favorite author might make an appearance. Ryan's niece had joined the end of the signing line. "I'm sorry the questions got sidetracked," I said to her. "When everyone has had their books signed, I'll introduce you to Renalta, and perhaps you can talk to her for a few minutes."

She blushed furiously and mumbled something into her chest. It might have been thank you.

The two bottles of water were on the counter where Ashleigh had put them. Donald had dropped into a vacated chair, where he sat with his head in his hands, cape spread around him, the very picture of humiliation and dejection. Ryan chatted to Jayne, and Robert and Grant discussed classic books. Nancy was telling a woman, whose expression could be used to illustrate a dictionary definition of "bored," that she was the head of the Renalta Van Markoff Fan Club (New England Chapter) and that Renalta was "soooo" grateful to her for everything she did.

I dumped my armful of books, swept up the two bottles of water, and once again fought my way through the crowd. I put the bottles on the table. "Here you go." Renalta picked one up, twisted off the loosened cap, and drank deeply. Then she beamed at the woman next in line. "How do you spell that, my darling?"

"M-A-R-Y. It's such a pleasure to meet you. *An Elementary Affair* is my favorite book of all time."

"You are too kind." Renalta's signature was as large and flamboyant as she herself.

"I didn't like *Doctor Watson's Mistake* nearly as much."

Renalta's smile cracked ever so slightly. Linda's eyes widened.

"Still, I'm sure the new one will be good. Is there any chance at all that Desdemona will eventually be free of her husband? I can't bear . . . Are you all right?"

"I . . . I . . . Linda . . . I don't feel too well."

Linda leaned over the author. "It's been a long, hard week. Miss Van Markoff, do you need to take a break?"

Renalta's eyes were so wide, she put me in mind of Silver Blaze recognizing that his handler was trying to cripple him. She gripped her throat, and her ruby ring flashed.

"We need an ambulance here. Fast," I shouted. The summer dress I wore, a nice light flowing thing, was without pockets, so I was without my phone. "You"—I pointed to the woman who'd been taking pictures—"call nine-one-one. Now."

Renalta gasped for breath. She tried to stand, but her legs gave way beneath her.

Renalta Van Markoff toppled forward onto the table, landing face first on a copy of *Hudson House*. Her right arm thrashed. And then she lay very still.

Chapter 7

Linda screamed. Everyone in the immediate vicinity began to scream. Chairs were overturned as people either scrambled out of the way or ran forward to try to help.

As she fell, Renalta knocked over her bottle of water. It rolled toward the edge of the table, spraying liquid as it went. I snatched it the moment it tumbled into the air.

Ryan Ashburton pushed his way through the crowd, followed by Grant, Kevin, Irene, and Robert. "Stand back," he yelled. "Everyone stand back. Grant, call nine-one-one. We need an ambulance here ASAP." He gave me a look, and I held up the bottle to show him I had it. He approached the still form on the table. He leaned over her and gripped her shoulders. "Can you hear me, Renalta? Can you hear me?"

She didn't move. Kevin put his arms around Linda and held her close. She sobbed into his chest.

"What happened, Gemma?" Irene asked.

"Heart attack," someone whispered. The words spread through the store as if carried on a tsunami.

"Did you know she had a bad heart, Kevin?" Irene asked.

"No," Kevin said. "She could stand to lose a few pounds, and she didn't get much exercise, but I never thought . . ."

"Exhaustion," Robert said. "Stress. The pace of touring is too much for her." He sounded as though he was trying to convince himself as much as Kevin and Linda.

"Help's on the way." Ryan touched the side of Renalta's neck and then lifted her hand. "Pulse is almost gone," he said in a very low voice.

"I'm a doctor. Let me through. I'm a doctor." I recognized one of my store regulars, Dr. Jennifer Burton. I scooped up the cap to the water bottle and grabbed the unused one. Before closing it, I lifted it to my nose and sniffed.

Bitter almonds.

I leaned toward Dr. Burton and whispered in her ear, "Poisoned. Probably cyanide."

She nodded.

I then left Ryan and the good doctor to do what they could and made my way toward the front of the store.

"Stand back, please," I said to the barrage of questions. "Help's been called. Everything is under control."

Ashleigh stood behind the cash register, her eyes wide and her hand to her mouth. "Is she going to be okay?"

"Give me a plastic bag, quickly."

"Why?"

"Don't ask. Just give it to me."

She did so, and I slipped the water bottles inside and tied the bag shut with a firm twist.

"What happened?" Ashleigh asked. "She's going to be okay, right?"

"Okay? Uh, sure. Maybe."

Jayne leaned toward us. "You sound awfully unsure of that," she whispered. "How can you know what's happened? You're not a doctor."

"I smelled bitter almonds. Cyanide."

Ashleigh gasped. Jayne said, "You're kidding, right? Sorry, I forgot who I'm talking to for a moment. You never kid. Don't be telling people that, Gemma. You'll cause a panic."

I glanced around the room. No one was paying me any attention. Most people were frozen in place, gaping, not knowing what to do. Some were leaving the shop.

Officer Richter burst through the front door. Sirens sounded in the distance, coming closer.

"Open the tea room," I said to Jayne. "Offer hot or cold drinks to anyone who wants one. No charge." I glanced at the bag in my hand. "Maybe don't offer them water."

Thank goodness we'd bought Renalta's water at the convenience store and not gotten it from the tap in Mrs. Hudson's.

"You think something might have been in the water?" Jayne said.

"I know it was." I crossed the floor and grabbed Officer Richter's arm. "You need to stop people from leaving. The detectives will want to question everyone."

"No need," he said. "She had a heart attack."

We stepped aside as the paramedics arrived with a stretcher.

Mindful of Jayne's reminder that sometimes people don't react well to total honesty, I said, "Better safe than sorry."

"Thanks, Ms. Doyle, but I think I can handle this," Richter said.

"She might have been poisoned," I said. "Detective Ashburton said so."

Ryan had said no such thing, but I figured Officer Richter wouldn't take my word for it.

"In that case." He moved to block the exit.

I ran to the back of the room. Ryan had ordered people to keep away to give Dr. Burton room to work. Most of them had complied. Linda stood watching, her pose the same as Ashleigh's: eyes wide with shock and hand to mouth. Kevin's arm remained around her shoulders. Robert McNamara shook his head silently, and Irene observed the scene dispassionately.

The paramedics loaded Renalta's unmoving form onto their stretcher.

"People are leaving," I said to Ryan. "You need to secure the scene."

"You think this was deliberate?"

I kept my voice low enough to be heard only by people in the immediate vicinity. "The water was poisoned. No doubt about it. Dr. Burton, didn't you smell anything?"

She shook her head. "If it's what you seem to be suggesting, Gemma, I might not be genetically disposed to detecting the scent. Many people aren't."

"Which might be why Renalta took such a deep drink," I said.

"I'll get this place locked down." Ryan pulled his mobile phone out of his pocket and walked away, talking rapidly.

I turned and saw Irene Talbot standing closer to us than I'd realized. Her ears were flapping. "Don't you dare repeat a word of that conversation. It's pure speculation."

"My lips are sealed," said the ambitious reporter.

"We're ready to go. Are you coming with us, Doctor?" one of the paramedics said.

"Yes," she replied.

Linda burst into another round of tears. "I need to come too. Please."

"No room," the paramedic said.

"I'll drive her," Kevin said. All the color had drained out of his handsome face. He held Linda tightly to him.

"I'm sure it's nothing," Robert McNamara said. "Stress on top of exhaustion. She's been working so hard lately."

"Of course, you're right," Kevin said over Linda's head. I could tell by the look on his face that he didn't believe it for a moment.

"I'll tell Detective Ashburton where he can find you," I said.

Kevin gave me a nod of thanks, and he hustled Linda away. Robert followed. People shouted questions at them, but Kevin merely said, "Excuse me, please," while Linda wept.

At the front of the store, Ryan had clipped his badge onto his shirt, and Officer Richter guarded the door. Cruisers screeched to a halt out front and parked half on the sidewalk, blue and red lights flashing. Outside, the curious gathered. Inside, people were either trying to get someone to tell them what was going on or continuing to shop. Ashleigh had resumed ringing up purchases.

I slid up beside her. "Where's my camera?"

"Under the counter where you left it."

"Did you take many pictures earlier?"

"Some."

I found the camera and quickly flicked through it. Ashleigh had been at the sales counter, and she'd pointed the camera at the back of the store, toward Renalta standing at the podium or moving to the signing table. Lots of shots of the back of people's heads with Renalta facing the audience. A couple of close-ups of Renalta, holding a copy of *Hudson House* to illustrate a point she was making. Not one picture was of the group lining the counter, standing near the bottle of water.

Some of these pictures would have been great for promoting the store. The packed house, the rows of attentive readers, the dramatically gesturing author holding up her book.

All now completely useless. It would be tawdry beyond belief to try to get any promotion out of Renalta Van Markoff's last signing.

No one else was saying it, but I was positive this would indeed prove to be her last signing.

I went into the tea room where Jayne and Fiona were pouring glasses of lemonade and iced tea and Jocelyn was making coffee.

"How can I help?" I asked.

"Load those glasses on a tray, take them into the bookshop, and pass them around," Jayne said.

I did so. Donald was sitting alone, where I'd seen him last. He'd found a book and was reading. I offered him a drink, but he shook his head without looking up. I circulated through the store, handing out iced tea and lemonade. Grant Thompson had sat down next to Madison, Ryan's niece, and was telling her about a rare copy of an early Agatha Christie book he'd recently bought. She actually looked interested. I gave him a smile. Maureen snatched a glass off my tray while continuing to tell a group of tourists that she wasn't at all surprised the Great Author had taken ill in the Emporium.

"Can I have your attention, please?" Ryan shouted.

Words were left unfinished as conversation died immediately. The only sound was Moriarty howling. Maureen gave her companions a "told you so" smirk.

"Until we determine exactly what happened here," Ryan said, "I have to treat this as a crime scene."

Murmurs swept through the store.

"Please give your contact information to one of the officers. We will be in touch later. If you believe you saw something significant, please let me know. If you took any pictures here this afternoon, you will be given an address where you can send them. Thank you for your cooperation."

He turned to me. "How many people would you say are still here, Gemma?"

"Including those sitting in the tea room, ninety-seven."

"I was going to say 'approximately.' I should know better by now."

"I might be off by one or two," I admitted. "People keep moving around. We had seats for one hundred people. That plus standing room only and those who sat on the stairs meant one hundred and twenty people were here at the height of Renalta's talk. I did a count when I was at the front introducing her. After Renalta collapsed, a handful slipped out under Officer Richter's watchful eye before he secured the door. Maybe twenty got away—I mean, left. I don't see Jocelyn's mother. Knowing her, she was well mannered enough to want to get out of everyone's way. Kevin and Linda went with the ambulance. Robert accompanied them."

"Who are those people?"

"Publicist, personal assistant, and publisher. All the *P*s in a writer's life." I held up my tray. "Would you like a glass of lemonade?"

"No, thanks. I'm afraid you'll have to keep the store closed for the rest of today. Maybe tomorrow."

"Understood. Ashleigh took some photographs of the event. I was hoping to use them for promotion. I doubt there's anything significant, but you should look. My camera's under the counter. Ask Ashleigh for it."

"Thanks. Here's Louise now," Ryan said. I scurried away before Detective Louise Estrada could accuse me of being the guilty party. Estrada and I had met before. We did not depart as friends.

The two detectives huddled in a corner. More than a few people casually wandered close to them, heads tilted to one side. Ryan gave them a hard stare. The effect, I thought, was spoiled somewhat by Benedict Cumberbatch peering over his shoulder.

I headed into the tea room for another load of drinks.

"I hope," a man shouted, "you're going to arrest that guy over there."

I turned to see him pointing at Donald.

"Why do you say that, sir?" Detective Estrada asked.

"He threatened Renalta. I heard him. We all heard him." Heads nodded, and people murmured their agreement.

"Threatened?" Estrada said. "What do you mean by that?"

"He said someone had to put a stop to her. You heard it too." He jabbed a finger at Ryan.

"I heard an angry exchange in public," Ryan said. "If we arrested everyone who threatened to kill someone in a moment of anger, the streets would be empty."

I glanced at Donald. His attention remained fixed on the pages of his book.

"An exchange of opinion," I said. "It happens sometimes."

"Sounded like more than just a disagreement to me. He said he'd put a stop to her writing her books. Looks like he succeeded, doesn't it?"

* * *

At last we were alone in the tea room, sitting together in the window alcove, each of us wrapped in our thoughts.

"Heck of a thing," Jayne said.

"Yup," I said.

"I want to go home," Donald said.

Everyone who'd been at the author talk had given their details to the police and had been either allowed to leave or politely but firmly shown the door.

Everyone, that is, except Donald. The police wanted to talk to Donald about his so-called threat.

Rather than customers shopping for the latest best-seller or Sherlock-themed gadget, the Emporium was full of white-suited men and women searching for evidence. Madison, Ryan's niece, had begged to be allowed to stay, and he allowed it if she promised not to get in anyone's way or to touch anything. She watched everything they did with a single-minded concentration I could only admire, although I could have told the forensics people they were wasting their time.

Every surface would be a mass of fingerprints. Hundreds, maybe thousands of people have passed through the shop. They pick up everything and put it down again. They go behind the counter, where they aren't supposed to, and even try sneaking up the stairs to see if I have special merchandise there. What sort of goods they thought I might need to keep hidden, I didn't dare ask. I dust and clean the shop regularly, but I don't polish the books or rub down the Sherlock-themed mugs and plates with disinfectant.

I thought Jayne might have a heart attack of her own when Estrada said they would also do the tea room. Fingerprint powder could be dusted off my goods, but it's not so easy to do in jars of jam or containers of flour. I'd managed to convince Ryan, if not Estrada, that they didn't need to check the tea room. Renalta had not gone in there on either of her visits, and the water in question had not come from Mrs. Hudson's.

It had fallen ominously quiet upstairs. Moriarty had either given up hope of rescue or escaped through a crack in the floorboards. I was afraid to go up and check.

At last, Ryan and Estrada came into the tea room. Ryan took a seat at the table in the far back corner, while Estrada marched up to us. "We'll talk to you now, Ms. Doyle."

"Can I get you something, Detective?" Jayne said. "We have plenty of sandwiches I'd intended to be served this afternoon, or I can make—"

"This is not a social call," Estrada said. "I'm not here to have high tea."

"We don't serve high tea," I said. "We serve afternoon tea. 'High tea,' more commonly just called 'tea,' is a working

family's early-evening meal, whereas afternoon tea is . . ."
Estrada looked as though she were about to arrest me for
excessive talking. "A common mistake," I added meekly.

I took a chair opposite Ryan. Estrada plunked herself
down between us.

"Have you heard from the hospital?" I asked.

Ryan nodded. The expression on his face was an answer
all of its own. "Ms. Van Markoff was pronounced dead on
arrival."

"How's Linda holding up?"

"You mean the PA?"

"Linda Marke. Yes. She was particularly upset when her
boss collapsed."

"I don't know. Louise and I will be going over there as
soon as we've finished here. You seemed pretty sure it was
cyanide poisoning, Gemma."

"Perhaps too sure?" Estrada said.

I ignored her. "That bitter almond scent, so beloved of
classic crime fiction, was a giveaway. That plus the speed at
which she collapsed. Couldn't have been more than three or
four minutes, if that, between taking a drink and dropping."

"Witnesses have told us that she drank from a bottle of
water you handed her," Estrada said.

"The water was purchased at the convenience store on
the corner about half an hour before it was consumed," I said.

"We've ordered all bottles of Riviera water pulled off the
shelves," Estrada said.

"No need," I said.

"And what," she said, "makes you so sure? Did you perhaps tamper with it yourself, Gemma?"

I did not dignify that accusation with a reply. "Ashleigh, my shop assistant, bought four bottles for Renalta."

"That confirms what she told us," Ryan said.

"Of course it does, because that's what happened. Renalta requested that the bottles be unsealed before given to her. It's rumored that she has arthritis in her wrist, so I assumed she finds it difficult to break the seal."

"Have the autopsy check for that," he said to Estrada. She made a note.

"Presumably she didn't want to appear to be struggling with a bottle in front of her audience," I said. "I noticed that she drank a considerable amount of water. The . . . fatal one . . . was her third bottle in half an hour. She was nervous speaking in public, so I suspect the water acted as a crutch to give her something to do and something to keep her hands busy."

"She didn't seem at all nervous to me," Ryan said.

"Thus proving the effectiveness of the crutch," I replied.

"Whatever," Estrada said. "You do go on, Gemma." She glared at Ryan as though that was his fault.

"I am not *going on*. I am explaining the pertinent details to those who might not be capable of following along."

She half-rose in her seat. "Now see here . . ."

"Enough," Ryan said. "Gemma's right. The amount of water she drank is pertinent. I assume she consumed that much water at all her talks. We'll check with her PA."

Estrada lowered herself back down.

"And," I said, "if that was her habit, our killer might well have known that and thus been able to plan ahead."

"Tell us about the water bottle. Was it left unattended for a period of time?"

"Yes, and I'm sorry to say, that was my fault."

"You're admitting it?" If Estrada's hands didn't go immediately to the handcuffs on her belt, I'm sure they wanted to.

"Don't get too excited, Detective. I'm confessing to carelessness and nothing else. We were so busy, so many people, so much going on, that I put the two bottles to be used in the signing portion of the event on the counter and left them there. After Ashleigh had broken the seals."

"You're saying that anyone in the room had access to them," Ryan said.

I leaned back in my chair. Estrada opened her mouth to say something, but Ryan gave her a look. I closed my eyes and drew up a mental picture of the Emporium as it had been when the afternoon's program began. I stood at the podium to welcome Renalta; from there I could see everyone in the shop.

People sat in their chairs, excited and expectant. The overflow had taken seats on the stairs. A few stood against the walls, Ryan and Jayne among them. A handful more stood along the windows. Aside from the swish of traffic on the street outside, the rustle of fabric as people shifted position, and the sound of Moriarty begging for freedom, all had been quiet.

I moved my mental gaze across the room to the sales counter. "Grant Thompson, Irene Talbot, Kevin Reynolds, Linda Marke, Robert McNamara, Donald Morris, and Paige and Nancy, surnames unknown, were standing at the counter, with their backs to it."

"You have a good memory," Estrada said.

"Thank you," I said. "As they were standing, they shifted about quite a bit. I'm sorry, but I can't place the exact position of the water bottle. By the time I went back for it, everyone had moved off."

"Donald Morris was there?" Estrada said.

"Yes."

"The same Donald Morris who was heard to threaten Ms. Van Markoff?"

"His so-called threat is irrelevant. He said it in a fit of anger. As Detective Ashburton here said earlier, people say things like 'I'm going to kill him' all the time. They don't mean it."

"But sometimes they do," she pointed out. "And in this case, the object of the threat was dead not more than a few minutes later. Detective Ashburton, we need to take Donald Morris into the station for a little chat."

"Preposterous," I said. "You're taking two completely unrelated events—the so-called threat and the killing—and combining them to make an unwieldy conclusion. Your thought process is like that of a child mixing mud and water and thinking they've made a cake."

Louise Estrada was a good-looking woman. Tall, lean, olive-skinned, black-haired, brown-eyed. She always made me think of a racehorse, poised to leap out of the starting gate. She sucked in a breath, and in front of my eyes, the horse turned into a panther. Her dark eyes blazed fire, and a deep line appeared between her eyebrows.

"Enough, Gemma," Ryan said. "You've gone too far."

"Goodness, it sounds tense over here." Jayne put her hand on my shoulder. "Can I get anyone a glass of water? There's some coffee still in the pot. Not to mention all the sandwiches and tarts I made for afternoon tea, which will now not be needed."

"Water for everyone would be good," Ryan said. "Thanks, Jayne."

She squeezed my shoulder and bustled off. Estrada let out a breath and sank back into her chair.

"The average person does not go around with a jar of cyanide in their pocket," I said.

"We don't know it is cyanide," Ryan said. "Let's wait for the autopsy results."

"A mere formality."

"You seem to know all about poisons," Estrada said.

"No more than the average educated person." I knew Estrada didn't like me, but she could at least hear what I had to say. "Therefore, we must conclude—"

"We must, must we?" she mumbled.

"Yes, we must. Obviously the murder was premeditated. Therefore, the fact that Donald and Renalta got into a minor tiff in public—an argument, which, I will admit in the interest of being fair, ended with him totally humiliated—is irrelevant."

"If he was angry at her," Ryan said, "it didn't come out of nowhere, Gemma. He might have come here today expecting a fight."

I didn't think this was a good time to mention that Donald had been angry on Thursday when he came into the bookshop. I twisted in my chair. He was sitting where I'd left him, reading. I wasn't surprised that he'd buried himself in a book in a time of crisis. "So might any one of a number of people. If not the fight, then the anger. We must conclude . . ."

I was saved from any more of Estrada's mumbles as Jayne put three glasses on the table. "From the tap," she said, "just so you know."

". . . not only that the killing was premeditated but also that the killer had to have some knowledge of and ability to obtain cyanide. One does not stroll into Wal-Mart and ask what shelf the deadly poisons are on. Donald's a retired lawyer, not a chemist."

Ryan's phone rang. "Ashburton." He listened for a moment and then said, "They can go back to their hotel. Someone's to stay with them until we get there." He put his phone away and took a sip of water. "That's it for now, Gemma. If our people finish here tonight, you can open the store tomorrow." He stood up.

"That's it?" Estrada said. "You're not going to take him in?"

"Not at this time."

"That's it?" I said. "What about the other suspects? There's Paige and Nancy and . . ."

"When we need your advice, we'll ask for it," Estrada said.

Ryan walked to Donald's table. Donald tore himself away from his book and blinked at the detective. "We might have further questions for you," Ryan said. "Don't leave town."

"I've no plans for a vacation," Donald said.

"Glad to hear it." Ryan turned and spoke to Estrada. "Let me check in with the forensic guys. Van Markoff's party has left the hospital. We need to talk to them. We can drop Madison at my folks' place on the way."

Ryan and Estrada went into the Emporium. Jayne busied herself rearranging the display of loose-leaf teas and china pots on the shelf.

"Time you were off home, Donald," I said.

He closed his book. *The Sign of the Four.* "I didn't kill that woman, Gemma."

"I know you didn't, Donald."

He shook his head. "They, the police, think I did it."

"It'll all be sorted out soon."

"Help me, Gemma."

"Me? What do you mean?"

"I'm not a total fool." He pointed to his book. "I wasn't getting much reading done while you and the police were talking, and the acoustics in this room are surprisingly good when it's empty. Detective Estrada wanted to arrest me on the spot. Detective Ashburton persuaded her not to. *At this time,* I believe he said."

"I don't know what I can do."

"Do what you did with the Longton case. You solved that. You didn't need the police."

"The police would have eventually come to the same conclusions I had."

"By then it might have been too late. Please, Gemma. I need you. You said it yourself, there are other suspects. I wonder if the police are even going to look at them."

Jayne had finished rearranging the shelf and joined us. "Gemma will get to the bottom of it, Donald. Don't you worry. Would you like some sandwiches to take home?"

What could I say?

Chapter 8

"You've got to stop baiting her," Jayne said once Donald had packed away *The Sign of the Four*, gathered his cape around him, put his hat back on, accepted the bag of food she pressed on him, and left. I decided not to point out that he'd taken the book off the store shelf and not paid for it.

"Baiting who?"

Jayne threw up her hands. "Detective Estrada, of course."

"I'm not baiting her or anyone else. I'm only trying to help. Some police officers seem to need my help more than others."

"That's my point, Gemma! You ridicule her. You mock her. Even Ryan thought you'd gone too far this time, talking about children and mud pies."

"Cake, not pie."

Jayne groaned.

"I know she doesn't like me . . ."

"That's the understatement of the year. She's going to complain to the chief about Ryan and you. Again."

"How do you know that?"

"Because I eavesdropped, of course. I must be learning something from you. She said he's been blinded, once again, by your interference in a police case. She said the only reason he's not interrogating Donald is because you told him not to."

"Preposterous. I didn't tell him not to. I merely pointed out that Donald is an unlikely suspect and they would be better spending their time investigating others." I let out a long sigh. "Jayne, I can't pretend not to notice the things I notice or force myself not to arrive at logical conclusions."

Jayne touched my arm. "I know. But you don't make it easy for yourself sometimes."

Which was precisely why my relationship with Ryan Ashburton had ended. We'd met when a string of arsons struck the shops on Baker Street. I had simply observed what others had not and took my observations to the police. For my pains I'd been accused by the lead detective (now thankfully retired) of starting the fires because I craved the attention. Fortunately, newly promoted Detective Ashburton convinced his bosses to listen to what I had to say. The arsonist was caught—exactly where and when and whom I had deduced.

The chief of police thanked me for doing my civic duty, and I'd fallen head over heels in love with Ryan Ashburton. Ryan (I thought) loved me in return.

But love wasn't enough. *Too clever by half,* he'd called me on more than one occasion. After I ruined his big surprise proposal by guessing (deducing) what he was up to, he told me he was leaving to take a job in Boston. He'd been away for a while but recently returned to West London when the position of head detective opened.

My sources—meaning Irene Talbot—told me Louise Estrada had thought she was guaranteed the job and had not been happy when Ryan was brought back to take the position. She didn't like me, and she didn't trust me, but it was more than that. I feared she saw me as a way of undermining Ryan.

"I'll try to be nicer to Louise next time," I said. "Maybe we can have dinner together one night or something."

"I wouldn't go that far," Jayne said. "Are you going to help Donald?" She looked at me, wide eyed and expectant.

"I'll do what I can. I find him irritating much of the time, with his die-hard devotion to the canon, but I have to admit to a certain a fondness for him. Eccentricity can be endearing, if it isn't taken too far. We English are known for our love of our eccentrics, aren't we?" I didn't point out to Jayne that she was being highly contradictory. On one hand, she was telling me not to annoy Estrada—which any involvement on my part in the case would do—and on the other hand, she wanted me to help Donald.

"I have insights the police do not, as I've had prior contact with Renalta's employees and some of her fans. We should talk to Linda and Kevin first, of course, because they're closest to Renalta. However, Ryan and Louise are on their way to do that now, and I don't think it would be wise for us to show up and ask to sit in on the interview. That will have to wait. Find out where they're staying."

"How am I going to do that?"

"I put Kevin's business card somewhere in the Emporium. Check the drawer beneath the cash register."

"Suppose he doesn't want to tell me? I'm sure they want their privacy at this time."

"You'll think of something." Jayne went off to find the card, and I drummed my fingers on the tabletop. Finding Paige and Nancy might prove to be more difficult.

I pulled out my phone and made a call.

"Gemma! Nice to hear from you," Great Uncle Arthur bellowed into his own phone. Despite the wonders of modern technology, Arthur seems to think it necessary to shout at the top of his voice to be heard in West London from wherever he might be. And having spent his career in the Royal Navy, rising to the position of captain of one of HRH's battleships, he had a mighty powerful outdoor voice. "How's Violet?"

I wasn't offended that his first question was about the dog. "She's well. Healthy and happy but missing you."

"Glad to hear it. I'm missing her too."

I strained to listen for background noise. There didn't appear to be any. "Where are you?"

"Still in the Outer Banks. I'm having a marvelous time. I met a retired Royal Navy chap the other day, and he's been taking me out fishing."

"I didn't know you liked to fish."

"I don't. I don't like him either, but I like being on his boat. His sister is a widow."

Fancy that.

"Why are you calling, Gemma?"

Straight to the point, as always.

"Your euchre partner, Mrs. Johnson, left something in the shop this morning, and I want to call her about returning it. Do you have her number?"

"Just a minute."

I waited while he checked his phone's contact list. Jayne came in waving a small square of paper. I gave her a thumbs-up. Next door, investigators were still moving things about and walking in and out to their van. Upstairs, the silence continued. "Here you go," Arthur said at last.

"Thanks. Catch a big one for me."

Jayne stood by the window to make her call. I dialed the number Arthur had given me. "Hi, Mrs. Johnson. It's Gemma Doyle here, Arthur Doyle's niece. How are you today?"

Her bunions, apparently, were acting up. Last night's dinner, liver fried with potatoes and onions, hadn't agreed with her, and . . .

"Sorry to hear that. Arthur's still in North Carolina, but he sends his love. I have something I'd like to talk to your granddaughter about."

"Which one?"

"The West London police officer. What's her name? So sorry, it's momentarily escaped me."

"Stella."

"Of course! How silly of me to forget. Such a lovely name. I seem to have misplaced Stella's phone number."

Silence.

"Do you have it? I hate to bother you, but . . . the book she ordered is here."

"A book! I'm so pleased. All Stella ever seems to read anymore is that policing stuff. Rules and procedures and true crime books about serial killers and criminal gangs. You sell such sweet books at your store. I have her number right here. I'll be just a moment."

She soon came back and rattled off the number.

I thanked her profusely and gave her Uncle Arthur's love one more time.

Small towns. *Gotta love 'em.* I would never have been able to pull that off in a city such as London. Stella Johnson had not been among the officers who answered the 9-1-1 call to the Emporium earlier. I'd seen her Thursday night in the Blue Water Café, so she was probably working nights. It was now almost five o'clock, meaning she should be up and getting ready for work. I made the call.

"It's Gemma Doyle here. Sorry to bother you, Officer Johnson."

"How did you get this number?" Another one who got straight to the point.

"You know West London," I said. "Nothing's a secret."

"True enough. What can I do for you, Gemma?"

"Have you heard about the death this afternoon at my shop?"

"Yes."

I decided that any pretense of this being a social call, and by the way did she happen to know where Paige was staying, would be a waste of time. Instead, I also got straight to the point. "You were called to the Blue Water Café Thursday evening when a woman made a scene. You escorted her out."

"I remember."

"The woman, Paige, came into the Emporium earlier today. I have something of hers I'd like to return and thought she might have told you where she's staying."

"The Ocean Side Hotel. Mr. Reynolds said they didn't want to press charges so I let Ms. Bookman go with a warning."

Mr. Reynolds was Kevin, and Bookman (*Bookman?*) must be Paige.

"Thanks." I hung up before Stella Johnson could ask me any questions in return.

"Renalta's party's at the Harbor Inn," Jayne said. "Ryan and Louise arrived while Kevin was on the phone with me."

"Excellent. Let's go."

"Where?"

"The Ocean Side first and then the Harbor Inn. It is, as you know, a capital mistake to speculate without evidence. However, I am going to do so and speculate that Paige Bookman is the most likely person to have wanted Renalta dead. I will then gather evidence to support my theory."

"The game's afoot!"

"So it is."

*   *   *

I needed to check on Moriarty before leaving. The shop was closed, but the police were busy in the Emporium, and they were unlikely to want to go about their business with a curious cat underfoot. It was possible he was pulling the old prison trick of pretending to be dead so the foolish guards would rush in and leave the door unlocked, in which case I ordered Jayne to act as backup. I took fresh water and a bowl of kibble with me.

"On the count of three, I'll open the door and run in," I said. "You close it behind me."

"You make it sound like we're SEALs attacking terrorist headquarters."

"The principle is similar. One . . . two . . . three . . ." I burst into the office. The door slammed shut behind me.

Moriarty lay on the windowsill, basking in the soft rays of the evening sun. Lazily, he opened one eye. Seeing it was only me, he shut it again.

"You don't fool me," I said. I refilled his food and water bowls. He'd indicated his indignation at being confined by kicking kitty litter all over the office floor.

I kept my eye on him as I backed up toward the door. "Coming out!" I called to Jayne. "Be ready!" I turned, threw the door open, dashed through it, and kicked it closed. I leaned up against it with a sigh, my heart pounding. "Safe?"

"You give Moriarty far too much credit, Gemma. He's a house cat, not a criminal mastermind. If Arthur had named him Midnight or Blackie, you wouldn't have this fixation."

I grumbled something noncommittal. Downstairs I told the forensics officers I was leaving through the tea room doors. I reminded them to lock up when they left, and a gray-haired woman gave me a look.

I always walk to work, and today had been no different. The Harbor Inn is in easy walking distance of the center of West London, but the Ocean Side Hotel's on the outskirts of town, so it was necessary to go home and get my car.

Jayne and I trotted quickly down Baker Street to the boardwalk that runs parallel to the small harbor, and then we turned up the hill into Blue Water Place. The day had started off hot and sunny, but as often happens close to the tempestuous sea, the weather changed quickly: dark clouds were now gathering over the ocean, and the scent of rain hung heavily in the air.

I would have liked to have collected the car and sneaked away with Violet being none the wiser, but I had to go into the house for my keys. The cocker spaniel greeted me in her usual exuberant manner before lavishing attention on Jayne. That done, I let Violet into the backyard to do her business while I tapped my foot impatiently. Once business had been taken care of (and the dog had confirmed that no itinerant squirrels had taken up residence on her property), I told Jayne to wait outside and lured Violet into the house with a bowl of fresh water and an early dinner. Then, guilt stricken, I dashed outside and shut the door behind me. Violet loves nothing more than a ride in the car, but that wasn't possible. I drive a Mazda Miata, and there's no room for the dog if I have a passenger.

The Ocean Side is a midrange hotel, located across the road from a stretch of public beach on the Atlantic side of the peninsula on which West London is located. I parked beside the lobby entrance, and we went inside.

"We're here to see Paige Bookman," I said to the receptionist. "But I've forgotten her room number. Can you call and let her know we're here, please? I'm Gemma and this is Jayne."

She said, "Sure," and pressed a couple of keys on her computer.

The last time I'd seen Paige, she was being escorted out of the Emporium by Officer Richter. I was the one who'd ordered her to be removed from my property, and I hadn't followed up, so it was unlikely she'd been arrested. It was early on a Saturday evening, and threatening rain or no, there are plenty of things to do in West London, so there was no reason for the woman to be hanging around in her room, but my luck held. The receptionist spoke into the phone, said my name, and handed it to me.

"Who are you?" asked a raspy voice.

"Gemma from the Sherlock Holmes Bookshop and Emporium. We met earlier today."

"Oh, yeah, you. The one who had me dragged into the street as though I was something the cat had brought in."

"Sorry about that. I thought perhaps we could talk."

"Why would I want to talk to you?" she said.

"Did you hear what happened after you left?"

"No, I didn't. What happened? All I know is that one minute I was standing on the street telling that fat cop to unhand me and the next his radio was squawking and cop cars were tearing down the street. He ran off and left me standing there like last night's garbage. So I came back to the hotel."

"I think you'll be interested in what I have to say. What's your room number?"

"I'll come down. I need a smoke anyway."

I handed the phone to the receptionist. "Thanks."

"No problem."

Paige came into the lobby not more than a minute later, already pulling a pack of cigarettes out of her pocket. "Let's walk."

The moment we stepped outside, she cupped her hands against the wind and lit a cigarette with a disposable lighter. She then headed across the hotel's parking lot at a rapid trot. Jayne and I scurried after. We crossed the road and met up with a small boardwalk winding through scruffy vegetation to a stretch of public beach. Waves pounded the shore, and whitecaps broke on the sandbar.

"You two were at the restaurant the other night," Paige said when we caught up to her. "I only wanted to talk to little

Ruthie, but they threw me out. They seem to make a habit of that in this town. I assume you've come to talk to me about her, so spill, what happened?"

While we'd waited for the elevator bearing Paige to make its laborious journey all the way down from the second floor, I'd told Jayne to break the news. Now she cleared her throat. "Renalta Van Markoff died."

I watched Paige closely. The news seemed to take her by surprise, but I've been wrong before. Her jaw dropped. She gaped at Jayne, and then she let out a bark of a laugh. "Son of a gun. And I missed it. Her heart finally gave out, did it? It always was two sizes too small."

"The police," I said, "are treating it as a suspicious death."

"Good thing I wasn't there then, isn't it? I assume that's why you're here. You want to ask me if I bumped off Ruthie Smith."

"Did you?" I asked.

"As I wasn't there, obviously I couldn't have."

I didn't bother to enlighten her as to the cause of death. Paige had the opportunity to put the poison into the water before being evicted from the Emporium.

"If not a heart attack then what happened?" she asked.

"The police aren't revealing details pending the results of the autopsy."

"Is that Renalta's real name?" Jayne asked. "Ruth Smith?"

"Ruthie Smith, a.k.a. Miss Renalta Van Markoff. A name as fake as her so-called talent. She stole her first book from me, you know. All I ever wanted was credit, and all I ever got was the back of her head."

I'd wondered how I'd get Paige to talk. That obviously was not going to be a problem. "How did you meet?"

"A creative writing class at a community college in Brooklyn. I wanted to fine-tune my craft. Ruth wanted someone to tell her the easy route to publication. She'd been working on a book for years about some pig farmer's daughter in Iowa but was having no luck getting an agent or a publisher. That came as no surprise to anyone when she read parts of the thing to the class. Total dreck. I felt sorry for her and befriended her. My mistake."

We reached the end of the boardwalk and stepped onto the deep sand. The wind whipped my dress around my legs. The few people still out were enjoying playing at the edges of the surf. Out to sea, dark clouds were gathering, and they were moving fast our way.

"My manuscript in progress was about a noble-born English woman in the time of Queen Victoria who falls on hard times when her no-good husband deserts her and her family abandons her. She opens a detective agency in order to survive. Sound familiar?"

"If I may say," I said, feeling bold, "I'm a bookseller. That's not a unique plot."

She turned to me, the rage in her eyes terrible to behold. I took an involuntary step back.

"It's my plot! My story! The characters are mine. The idea was mine. She stole it. She pretended to be all sweet and friendly and suggested we form a critique group with some of the other people in our class. Her writing was absolutely garbage. Dreadful. Laughable. How do you think she went from that to being so successful? Huh? You tell me that, Miss Bookseller." She jabbed her finger into my chest.

I didn't bother to say that no one claimed Renalta Van Markoff penned great works of literature. "Did you stay in the group for long?"

She took a deep drag on her cigarette. The wind tore at her hair. Fortunately, it also blew her smoke out of my face. "No. It was a total waste of my time. All the other members were at her level. Far beneath what I was writing. I dropped out. I wanted to stay friends with Ruthie. Like I said, I felt sorry for her, but she cut me off. A couple of years later, I found out why. Can you imagine my shock when I happened to see a review of this hot new book and the author photo was of her? The picture was photoshopped, of course, and made her look about twenty years younger, but I recognized her, all right. I bought the book and read it in one sitting. It should have been my name on the cover, my picture on the back. The advance in my bank account!"

"Did you get a lawyer?" Jayne asked.

"I tried, but no one would take my case. They said I had no evidence to prove she'd stolen it from me."

"Couldn't you compare the published book with your manuscript?" I asked.

Paige's intense gaze shifted away from me. "I didn't . . . uh . . . have enough. The lawyers I spoke to said ideas can't be copyrighted. But they should be!"

So that was it. Paige had a nebulous idea for a not unusual storyline, and Renalta had grabbed it. Renalta, not Paige, had added the Sherlock Holmes angle, turned a vague idea into an entire novel, and then went on to write another two books, each one more successful than the previous.

"All I want," Paige wailed, "all I ever wanted was for her to acknowledge me. And now you're telling me it's too late."

"What brought you to Cape Cod this week?" I asked.

"I keep my eye on her. She has a blog. I assume her secretary writes it because it's not half bad. It talks about where she is and what she's doing and all the wonderful adoring people she meets. She doesn't exactly keep her *public appearances* secret, does she? I buy every one of her books the day it comes out, to see if she mentions me in the acknowledgments. Never a word. Never a single thanks. On and on she goes, thanking her editors and publicists, her faithful PA, all the great fans she meets. Never a word about me. Certainly not an offer to share in the profits."

"You mean you've been pursuing her for years?" I'd thought Paige just happened to be in West London when she found out that Renalta was here and so decided to catch up on old times.

Paige threw the butt of her cigarette onto the sand and ground it out with her foot. I wondered if she was imagining Renalta Van Markoff's face.

"I lost my job a couple months ago. I was a copywriter for a small advertising company, and they got bought by a big corporation. Out the door I went, and at my age, jobs in advertising aren't easy to come by. Not that I'm old, but I'm not a simpering, brain-dead twentysomething either. I got a small payout, but it's not going to last me into my old age. What else can I do but try to get what I'm owed? I wrote to her several times, but she never replied. I hoped that if I met her, face-to-face, she'd do the right thing. Okay, so confronting her at the restaurant the other night might have been a mistake. It wasn't the right place. I was sure that this time, at your bookstore, she'd bring me up on the stage and tell everyone she wouldn't be where she is today without me. But she died. And now it's too late. I'll never get what she owes me. Never." She stared out to sea.

"I don't see how getting a thank-you in her book is going to help you find a job," Jayne said.

"I was planning to ask her to introduce me to her publishers so I can show them my new manuscript. It's the least she can do in return for everything I did for her. I know they're going to love it, and with her recommendation, it'll be an instant bestseller."

That, I thought, *was taking delusional to a whole new level.*

"What are you going to do now?" Jayne asked.

"Go back to New York. One thing about being out of a job—now I can finish my own book."

"You're trying to find a publisher for a work that's not finished?" I said.

"Perhaps it's for the best. I've had total writer's block. Now that Ruthie's out of the way, my creative muse will be free to express herself. I don't want anyone to think I'm trying to imitate her. *My* new book is about a star of the dance halls who joins forces with Wilkie Collins to solve crimes. Totally different."

"Totally."

Suddenly, she whirled on me. "You're not writing a book, are you?"

"Me? No."

"I shouldn't have told you. It's my idea. You won't steal it, will you?"

"I wouldn't dream of it," I said. "Besides, I sell books. I don't write them."

"What about you?" she snapped at Jayne.

"Too busy baking."

"Will you look at the time," I said. "We'd better be going." I dashed for the boardwalk, Jayne hot on my heels, as the first drops of rain began to fall. We left Paige trying to light a fresh cigarette in the wind.

"Loony tunes," Jayne said once we'd reached the Miata.

"I fail to get the reference, but I have no doubt as to the meaning. Delusional might be an understatement."

"She's held a grudge against Renalta all these years."

"So it would seem. Instead of simply getting on with it and attempting to write something of her own, it appears that all Paige is capable of producing is some vague unoriginal idea."

"Do you think she killed Renalta?"

"I have no trouble believing that Paige *wanted* to kill Renalta. But to actually do it? I suppose that's possible. The manner and scene of Renalta's death—at a book signing, surrounded by her adoring fans—would be the sort of thing Paige would consider fitting."

"Are you going to tell the police this?"

"Not necessary. Paige made a point of being hostile on two occasions and being escorted off the premises by the police. They'll track her down soon enough."

"Sad."

"Almost Shakespearian. At first Paige told us she was sorry Renalta's dead, because that meant she wouldn't get the acknowledgment she was after. Then she changed her mind as fast as a raindrop could fall and said Renalta's death had freed her. When her so-called muse doesn't magically appear, she'll soon be back at resentment. All Paige has is her bitterness. She's totally committed to their *danse macabre*."

"What's that?"

"The dance of death. But not in the literal sense. She wouldn't want it to end. I think it possible, but unlikely, Paige is the killer."

I turned the engine on and put the Miata into gear. "Then again, I have been wrong before."

"You have?" Jayne said. "I must have missed it."

"Most amusing. I'd very much like to talk to Nancy."

"The over-the-top fangirl?"

"I can think of no way of locating her. I don't even have a last name. Let's go to the Harbor Inn and see if the police have finished with Linda. We can offer our condolences."

"I'll call Kevin and ask if they're available now."

"No," I said. "I want to talk to her privately."

On the way up the long, curving driveway to the Harbor Inn, we passed a WLDP car coming down. Louise Estrada was driving, Ryan Ashburton in the passenger seat. It would be impossible for them not to see me, so I tooted my horn cheerfully and waved. They did not wave back. Once again, I wondered if I should get a less conspicuous car. I checked my rearview mirror as we drove into the parking lot, but flashing red and blue lights did not break through the rain.

In the nineteenth century, a wealthy and politically influential Boston family built the house that is now the Harbor Inn to be their summer home. The family ran out of money and/or interest in the mid-twentieth century, and the property was abandoned for years, slowly falling into gentle disrepair. It was saved from complete collapse by a budget hotel chain that did some quick and cheap renovations to turn it into an unremarkable two-star hotel with nothing going for it but a fantastic view out to sea. Andrea and Brian Morrison, a highly ambitious and hardworking young couple, bought the property a few years ago and restored it to its stately grandeur. It's now one of the nicest (and one of the most expensive) hotels in West London.

Andrea herself was behind the reception desk when Jayne and I came in, following a family returning from a day at the beach loaded down with umbrellas, towels, beach bags, and coolers. The adults were so pink skinned, I wasn't at all surprised to hear them chattering among themselves in strong Irish accents.

Andrea turned to me with a welcoming smile. "Good evening, Gemma. Hi, Jayne. Are you two here for dinner?"

"A tempting suggestion," I said, "but no. I'm looking for a hotel guest. Linda Marke?"

Andrea's face settled into serious lines. "Oh, yes. Renalta Van Markoff's assistant. The police have just left. I heard Renalta collapsed at your store earlier. It's so tragic."

"Did you meet Renalta?" I asked.

"I did. I know I'm supposed to treat every one of our guests the same as any other, but I have to say, I was so excited when I realized who she was. I can't believe I was talking to her only hours before she died."

"You spoke to her today?"

"Yes. I'm a huge fan." Brian Morrison had popped into the bookshop yesterday and bought *Hudson House* as a gift for Andrea. "I managed to get away from the desk when she was in the restaurant having breakfast and ran up to our apartment for my copy of her book. Here, let me show you. It's my pride and joy. Be right back." She slipped through the door behind the reception desk and was back moments later with a thick hardcover.

The hotel was quiet at the moment, and no one needed to be attended to. Andrea opened the book, flipped to the front, and showed me what was written on the title page with as much pride as a new mother showing off her baby: *To Darling Andrea. With thanks for a marvelous stay.* It was signed, in red ink and dramatic script that took up half the page, R. Van Markoff.

"How far have you gotten?" Jayne asked. "Gemma gave me an advance copy and I've finished it."

"I'm about half through. I was up far too late last night reading," Andrea said. "It's so exciting. Don't you just love Desdemona's husband, Randolph? He's so mean, it's wonderful to see the way she cleverly puts him down."

"Ahem," I said. "Can we leave the fan club meeting for another day?"

"I won't spoil the ending for you," Jayne said, "but it finishes with a zinger of a cliffhanger."

"Oh, don't tell me that. I hate cliffhangers. You have to wait a whole year to find out what happens next."

"But now we'll never find out." Jayne gave her head a sad shake. "There won't be any more books."

I was rapidly losing control of this conversation. If it didn't end now, I'd soon find myself in the private rooms having tea and biscuits and discussing who would be the best choice to play Desdemona in the movie version.

"Absolutely fascinating," I said. "Clearly a conversation for another day. Now may I remind you, Jayne, we are here to extend our condolences to the author's employees?"

"Give me a call when you've finished it," Jayne said. "We can have a little book club meeting or something."

"That would be great," Andrea said. "I know I'll have lots of questions. Do we ever find out why Sherlock . . . ?"

"Did many people want to meet Renalta?" I interrupted.

"Oh, yes," Andrea said. "Everyone was so excited that she was staying here. She was never too haughty to talk to her fans, either."

"Were you here when she left for the signing at my store? That would have been shortly after one."

"I still can't believe it." Andrea wiped her eyes. "I was behind the desk. A handful of people were waiting in the lobby with books to be signed. She was so charming and gracious. She signed them all and invited everyone to come to the bookstore for her talk. I would have loved to have been able to go, but we're so busy on summer weekends, I couldn't get away."

"Tell me about the people who were waiting. Did anyone seem particularly agitated, interested, nervous maybe?"

She shrugged. "Not that I noticed. That good-looking young man who's always with her tried to hurry them along, but she insisted she had time for her fans."

"You mean Kevin, her publicist?"

"Kevin Reynolds, yes."

"Who made the bookings here and for how many rooms? I promise you I don't have a prurient interest."

"I know you're no gossip, Gemma. Linda Marke called me on Thursday morning, very early, to ask for three rooms. She was lucky to get them. We're pretty much full with the season starting, but I'd had a cancellation of two rooms the night before. The main suite wasn't booked, so I gave her that one as well. They're all charged to Linda's credit card."

"Thanks, Andrea. Can you call Linda's room for me? Tell her I'll meet her at the bar." I thought Linda would be more comfortable chatting in a public place than in her hotel room.

Andrea placed the call. "She'll be right down," she said to me.

I was saved from further conversation about Renalta Van Markoff's latest, and last, tome by the arrival of a group wanting to check in.

A quick glance had shown me that the outdoor restaurant was almost full, but the small, comfortable lobby bar was empty. Rain continued to fall, but as it often does on the edges of the ocean, the clouds were quickly heading inland. A few people had to move to a more sheltered table, but most of the patio restaurant was covered by umbrellas or awnings, which protected diners from anything but the most driving rain.

In contrast to the flower-filled patio restaurant with views out to the ocean, the bar is more of a winter place. Leather sofas and chairs, low tables, dark wainscoting and striped wallpaper, deep-red carpets, a glass-paneled wall reflecting rows of bottles. The sort of place, I always imagined, in which Holmes and Watson would feel completely at home. Jayne and I took seats around a small table next to the large, thankfully now unlit, fireplace. "A cheese platter, please," I said to the waitress. "And some of the nuts and olives. We'll order drinks when our guest arrives."

"Why were you asking about people having their books signed by Renalta?" Jayne settled herself comfortably into a deep leather chair. "Seems natural enough, once they realized the author was staying here."

"No reason," I said.

Jayne looked as though she didn't believe me, but I was saved from further questions when Linda came into the bar. She was dressed in the same clothes, plain verging on dowdy, which she'd worn to the Emporium. Her eyes were not wet, but they were tinged with red, and traces of dried tears were written all over her face. She twisted a white cotton handkerchief in her fingers.

Jayne and I stood up as she approached our table. "Thanks for seeing us." I gestured to the tray of cheese, olives, condiments, and crackers. "I thought you might not have eaten lately."

She gave me a tight smile. "That was kind of you."

We all sat down, and the waitress bustled over. I asked for a glass of Sauvignon Blanc, and Linda said, "Same for me." Jayne nodded in agreement.

"First of all," I said, "my condolences."

"Thanks."

"Have you worked for Renalta long?" Jayne asked.

"Two years."

"Since her first book came out," I said.

Linda cut off a thin slice of blue cheese, placed it on a cracker, and added a dab of relish. She studied the food but made no move to lift it to her mouth.

"It went further than a business arrangement, didn't it?" I said. "Your relationship with her."

She placed the cracker on a cocktail napkin. She didn't look at me. "Renalta Van Markoff was my mother."

I tried not to look shocked. I'd guessed they might be distant relations. Marke. The obvious pseudonym of Van Markoff. Renalta's casual rudeness toward Linda. But mother and daughter? I had no idea.

Jayne glanced at me. When I said nothing, she said to Linda, "If I may say, you don't look much alike."

"I mostly take after my father's side of the family. My coloring's more like my mother, but she dyes . . . dyed her hair, and her contact lenses are a false color." Linda sighed. "We always had an unusual relationship. She was never much like a real mother to me. The way other girls' mothers are, taking their daughters to school, arranging playdates, going to the playground together or on shopping expeditions. She was always distant, I'd suppose you'd say. I was an only child. My parents divorced when I was in middle school, and they shared custody of me, although I spent a lot more time at Dad's."

"Where's your father now?" Jayne asked.

"He died shortly after I graduated high school."

"I'm sorry," I said.

"He was a writer also. They started out together, both struggling to get their first novels published. Neither of them got anywhere, and rather than taking comfort in each other, they got more and more bitter. It was not a nice place to be, between them."

"But your mother was a huge success," Jayne said.

"That only came much later, after my dad died. She wrote for years, has drawers and computer files crammed full of unpublished stuff. She wrote what's called literary fiction: you know the sort of thing, Gemma, multigenerational drama and angst in a small town in middle-of-nowhere, USA, surrounded by fields of wheat or rows of corn. It was only when she adopted a pen name and turned to historical mysteries that she got published. The first of those books was an instant success, and she . . . well, she needed an assistant. I'd been laid off when the independent literary agency where I worked closed, and the only work I could get was freelance editing. So we decided to work together. It wouldn't suit her persona, as she saw herself, having a relative working for her. I don't think she wanted anyone to know she was old enough to have a daughter my age."

Jayne snorted.

"She wanted me to call her Miss Van Markoff in public. And so I did. It all grew from there." Linda picked up her cracker again. She put it down again. "Sometimes I even forgot she was my mother."

"Does Kevin know?" I asked.

"Yes. I sometimes think he lives in our pockets, so it was hard for him not to know. Otherwise, it's a secret."

"What about the publishers and her agent?"

"Renalta doesn't have an agent. Not a proper one. We got our first contract with McNamara and Gibbons without one, so we never bothered. We didn't really need one. With my experience working at an agency, I can negotiate the contracts. As for M and G . . ." She shook her head. "They had no need to know about our personal relationship."

"I assume she got the name Van Markoff out of Marke. Is that your father's surname?"

She nodded. "Mom legally went back to her maiden name of Smith when they divorced. I kept Dad's name."

The waitress placed three glasses of wine on the table. Jayne and I sipped at ours while Linda stared off into the distance.

At last Linda turned back to us. "The police asked me who would want to kill my mother."

"And what did you say to that?"

"I said I have no idea. And I don't. My mother wasn't exactly easy to get along with. She could be distant, imperious, even openly rude sometimes. Her success went directly to her head, I'm sorry to say. She absolutely loved being an author. The fans, the book signings, the writers' festivals, the gushing e-mails." Linda's shook her head. "But to kill her?"

"Paige Bookman?"

Linda sighed. "Oh, yes. Paige. Poor, sad, lonely, pathetic Paige. She was exactly like my mother, but on the flip side of fame. I don't see Paige killing anyone though. Is that what the police think?"

"I don't know what the police think," I said. "I'm just mentioning it because she'd been thrown out of my bookshop earlier."

"Were there other Paiges in your mom's life?" Jayne asked. "Other people who resented her success and thought it should have been theirs?"

Linda let out a sad chuckle. "Paige is an original. Thank heavens for that."

"Did Renalta have any trouble with overly enthusiastic fans?" I said. "'Fan' is derived from the word 'fanatic,' after all."

"Renalta had her fame, but it was hardly on the Brad Pitt or Angelina Jolie level. Sure, some of the fans could be pushy sometimes. Some could be strange. There was the time, not long after the publication of the first book, when we were invited to a literary festival in Vermont. We were new at this, so I didn't check into it too much. Mother and I drove up to Vermont, all excited about going to a festival. We'd been booked into a local B and B for the night. Turns out there was no festival. No guests, no other authors. Just one woman who owned a B and B and wanted to meet Renalta and have her stay over in her house. Creepy. Mother tore a strip off me, let me tell you, for not investigating it. It was after that incident that we decided to hire our own publicist. The one at McNamara and Gibbons hadn't checked into this festival either."

"Kevin Reynolds."

"Kevin's only been with us for four months. Mother goes through publicists like Kleenex. They don't last long." Linda smiled without humor. "Her daughter's the only one who can put up with her for any length of time."

"You said your mother liked being an author," I said.

"She loved it."

"Yet I got the impression she was nervous about public speaking."

"Oh, yes. She was in great form talking to individuals or even small groups but suffered from a serious case of the nerves if she had to speak to a crowd in a formal setting. Like actors who after thirty years on the stage still throw up in the wings. And moments later they step out to dazzle the audience with their prose. We went to a psychologist who specializes in that sort of thing. She said Mother was subconsciously afraid that someone in the audience would stand up and denounce her as a fake and gave her a small routine to go through before speaking. It helped a lot."

"She might have loved being an author, but she didn't like being a writer, did she?"

Linda selected a plump purple olive. She put it on the cocktail napkin next to the uneaten cheese and cracker. She picked up her wineglass and twisted the stem in her fingers. Her fingernails were bitten down to the quick, and she had the small, nervous habits of a chipmunk investigating a pile of picnic crumbs. "My mother wasn't fond of the work part, no," she said without looking at me.

"She spent a lot of time in Cape Cod when she was a child. We came once or twice when I was little but haven't been back for a long time. Out of the blue, Wednesday night, she announced that she absolutely had to visit. Right now! Never mind the events Kevin and M and G had lined up for her over the weekend. She did everything on impulse. Which is a good part of the reason she could never keep a publicist. She drove poor Robert nuts too. He was beyond furious when she canceled this weekend's engagements. Of course, I, who had no part in the decision, took the bulk of his rage. He yelled at me over the phone. I finally told them both I'd had enough, handed the phone to Mother, and went for a long walk. When I got back, she said she'd do one signing in Cape Cod and ordered me to find something. So I called you first thing the next morning." Her voice drifted away, and she gave us a soft, sad smile.

"I like it here," she continued. "In West London, what little I've seen of it. I might consider moving here. Buy a small cottage with a view of the sea and a strip of beach."

"You'd be able to get a lot of writing done," I said.

"Yes, I would, and that—" She bit off the end of the sentence. Her intelligent eyes studied my face. I tried to look intelligent in return. "You know?" she said.

"I suspected."

"Suspected what?" Jayne asked. "What are you talking about?"

"Does anyone else know?" Linda asked me.

"I haven't told anyone. If other people guessed, I can't say. It was obvious, to me at least, that Renalta didn't know much about the Holmes canon. Even more obvious that you do. That in itself wasn't conclusive. You could have been an adviser. When you talk about the books, you say 'we' more than 'she.' *We were invited to a literary festival.* You refer to the author of the books as 'Renalta' but to the person doing author appearances as 'Mother.' You pointedly mentioned how much she loved being an author, but you've said not a word about her writing. Her talk at the Emporium about the writer's life was stiff, scripted almost. I thought at the time she wasn't telling us the truth, but put it down to wanting to make it sound more interesting than it was. Plus, of course, you mentioned that the psychologist knew she feared exposure as a fake."

"You're saying you wrote the books, not Renalta Van Markoff?" Jayne asked.

"Renalta Van Markoff wrote the books, all right," Linda said. "That's my pen name. My mother, Ruth Smith, just played her in public."

"Have you always written them?" The room was empty, aside from the bartender standing behind the bar, wiping glasses, but still I kept my voice low.

"From day one. My mother desperately wanted to be a writer. By that, I mean she wanted to *be a writer.* Not to write. She tried, and she wasn't totally awful, but she had no patience for the work part of it. She came up with a vague idea for a historical mystery about a female private detective, but she got no more than a rough outline done before she sat back with a glass of wine and waited for the muse to visit her."

"That blasted muse again, who, as Picasso said, only strikes when one is working."

"Precisely. So I tried my hand at it. The outline was okay, and her main character was worth exploring, but all in all, it was pretty mundane. The concept needed a spark. The BBC *Sherlock* series was on TV, and that gave me the idea for the Sherlock Holmes angle. I finished the book in six months, working nights and weekends. Some nights I wrote straight through until I had to get ready for work. It was a totally amazing time in my life. I called the book *An Elementary Affair,* and I landed the publishing contact with M and G soon after it was finished. I'm the exact opposite of my mother. I want to write, but I don't want to *be a writer.* I don't want the slog of public appearances, the book tours, the convention circuit, talking to people and trying to be charming." She gave me a sad smile. "I am not, as you might have noticed, charming."

"Plenty of authors aren't. Your mother's flamboyance, her excessive behavior, was a one-off. A personality like that isn't necessary for a successful book, you know."

"You can't say it hurt our sales."

"No, I certainly can't say that."

"Instead, it was responsible for it. Without my mother's public personality, I suspect my books would be struggling to stay in the middle of the midlist."

"Was that always the plan? For her to pretend to be the author?" I asked.

"It wasn't intentional at all. I was going to use my real name, but Mother insisted 'Linda Marke' was totally boring.

It needed more oomph. Something befitting the creator of Desdemona Hudson. My dad's family name was originally Markoff, and they changed it when they arrived in America, so I suggested that. Mother said Van Markoff had a touch of old-world aristocracy. Somehow in all the back and forth about names, my first name got changed to Renalta."

"Fancy that," I said.

"When I had to submit a photo of myself to M and G for the first time, absolutely nothing came out right. I looked like . . . well, I looked like myself. So Mother said, let's do without a photo on the jacket, and that was okay with M and G. The night of my book launch in Manhattan, I was sick, awfully sick. Nerves probably. M and G had pulled a lot of strings to get us . . . me . . . into one of the big bookstores for the launch. And there I was, throwing up all day. I was in no condition to go out in public, but I couldn't cancel, so Mother said she'd go and represent me."

"She did more than represent you."

"It happened, she said, by happenstance. She walked in the door, in her usual over-the-top flamboyant dress and manner, and the staff rushed to greet her. She was introduced to everyone as Renalta Van Markoff. McNamara and Gibbons had sent a junior publicist, and she gushed over Mother. She said that she'd read the book and Mother was exactly how she'd imagined her to be. Mother didn't correct anyone, and she went with the flow. The evening was a huge success, and the next day my book was the talk of the town in the New York book world. With Mother's picture accompanying it. And so it was done. From then on, Mother was the public face of Renalta, and I was the hardworking PA by day and author by night."

It sounded to me as though Ruth Smith had bullied her shy but talented daughter, badly. Whether she had gone to the book launch fully intending to pose as the author or if it truly did happen accidentally didn't matter now. I also wondered about Linda falling so ill on her big night and whether Renalta had done something to arrange that. But ultimately, Ruth Smith looked like someone named Renalta Van Markoff, and she knew how to play the room and generate publicity.

Obviously, her plan had worked.

People came and went across the lobby. A man shouted for his wife to hurry up. The restaurant hostess was busy showing people to their table or thanking them for coming. The rain had stopped and the evening sun bathed the windows overlooking the veranda in a soft orange glow. But in the bar, all was quiet and still. This was one of the few places left that had enough taste and consideration not to have a TV fastened to the wall. The bartender wiped glasses and probably wished there was a telly turned to the sports channel. He paid us no attention.

"The success of *An Elementary Affair* was totally unexpected," Linda said, "although my mother seemed to think it was simply her due. I thought we'd sell a couple of thousand copies, make a bit of money, but not enough that I'd be able to quit freelancing as an editor. The deception, if you want to call it that, worked well for the first two books. I got a kick out of sitting at the back row in a bookstore or library and hearing my mother talk about her exhausting writing schedule and where she got her ideas. Then it all started to go to her head. She began to believe her own press. She was the famous author, and I was nothing but the famous author's personal assistant and thus totally expendable."

"That had to be tough," Jayne said.

"She was my mother, and I always loved her. Sometimes I didn't like her very much, though."

"Is a new book under way?" I asked.

"It's close to being finished. Personally, I think it's going to be my best yet."

"That's great news," Jayne said. "I have to tell you, I'm a big fan, and I just about died thinking there'd be never be a resolution to that cliffhanger."

Linda smiled at her. "Thanks."

"Does Robert, the publisher, know you're the author?" I asked.

"Nope. I act as my mother's agent, so we don't have to worry about that. I surreptitiously took out the clause in which the signatory to the contract confirms she is the author." She looked me full in the face. "I trust you will keep my secret."

"I'm a bookseller," I said. "All I'm interested in is selling books. Who actually wrote them is immaterial."

"There you are!" Kevin Reynolds and Robert McNamara crossed the bar. They loomed over us, making no move to take seats.

"I've been calling you and calling you, Linda." Kevin put a hand on Linda's shoulder. "I was worried sick when you didn't answer."

"I turned off my phone," she said. "I don't want to talk to anyone."

"I've been fielding calls all afternoon," Kevin said. "Renalta's death is big news, but I'll do all I can to keep them away from you."

"What brings you here?" Robert asked me. "This doesn't seem like an appropriate time for a social call."

"I think it's very appropriate," Jayne said. "We've stopped by to offer our condolences."

"Why were you phoning me anyway?" Linda asked Kevin. "I told you I wanted some alone time."

"I was worried about you." Kevin put his hand under Linda's arm and guided her to her feet. "That interview with the police was very upsetting. If you'd told me you wanted something to eat, I would have gotten it for you. Come on, you need to rest."

"Thank you," Linda said to me, "for respecting my privacy. If I decide to buy a place on the Cape, I'll give you a call."

Kevin led her away. Robert didn't follow. Instead he leaned over and helped himself to the cheese and cracker that Linda had never gotten around to eating. He popped it into his mouth. "If you're trying to find out what's next for the Van Markoff books, I'm happy to tell you that the next one's almost finished. We'll be releasing it ahead of schedule. In honor of Renalta, of course. It's what she would have wanted."

In order to capitalize on the publicity surrounding her death, I thought but didn't say. "Brilliant. Have you seen it? Does it have a title?"

"I haven't read it yet. Renalta didn't write from an outline, and I accepted that. Her writing was as daring and spontaneous as her personality. I can always tell, you know, when I first read a new manuscript what sort of person the author is. Renalta could be counted on to deliver a very clean manuscript.

127

She once told me that Linda tidied up some of the inconsistencies and fixed typos for her so it would be as near perfect as possible when I saw it. She was very considerate that way."

"Quite."

"She told me only this week that the book's almost finished. I'm hoping to get it from Linda right away. We'll hire a ghostwriter to complete it and do the final polish."

"Why not get Linda to do that," Jayne said, "if she worked with Renalta on the earlier books?"

"There's a difference between writing and copyediting. We'll have the new book on your shelves by Christmas, Gemma."

"That is quick," I said.

"That's the modern face of the publishing industry. The old model of set deadlines and release dates a year from now is passé. We have to be proactive, ready to move at a moment's shift in the winds of the public mood."

"I feel myself shifting even as we speak."

He grinned at me. "I knew you'd understand. We'll talk later about doing a special promotion in your store for the release of the new book. Something in memory of Renalta's final signing." He walked away.

I picked up my glass and took a sip of wine. It was cold and crisp and delightful on my tongue.

"Is it just me," Jayne said, "or does he seem particularly callous?"

"Callous. Then again, I don't know if he and Renalta were at all close. Probably not considering he doesn't know she didn't write the books or even that her personal assistant is her daughter. He's making a business decision, and it's probably the right one. He has to get Renalta's last book out as fast as he can before interest in her wanes." I studied the food on the table. Other than a thin slice of Stilton, a single cracker, and one olive, it was untouched. "We might as well finish that cheese."

"That was interesting," Jayne said, "about Linda and her mom. What a weird relationship. But we didn't learn anything to help us with finding out who killed Renalta."

I scooped up a handful of nuts. "On the contrary, we learned a great deal."

"And what was that?"

I popped the nuts into my mouth and then leaned back in my chair and cradled my wineglass. I closed my eyes. Linda herself had unwittingly given me a motive for her mother's murder. How much, I had to ask, did she resent her mother taking all the credit for the hugely successful books? Did Linda want to come out from under her mother's shadow? Take her rightful place as the author of the novels? Maybe Linda wanted to take her writing in a new direction and Renalta refused. The Desdemona Hudson books were flamboyant and overblown, the writing occasionally veering dangerously toward purple prose. Much like Renalta, a.k.a. Ruth Smith, herself.

Had Linda decided she wanted to write more "serious" books? Something respectable. Literary even, whatever that meant. Had Renalta said no? Had they argued and Linda decided there was only one way to get out of her mother's shadow?

The afternoon of the book signing, Linda had emerged from the car clearly angry, and Renalta had spoken to her sharply. Unfortunately, I'd not heard what was said. Not difficult to assume they'd had an argument in the car or as they left the hotel. While Renalta gave her talk, Linda had stood against the counter, near the water bottle. She, more than anyone, would have known about Renalta's habitual consumption of great quantities of water.

Matricide is an exceptionally rare crime, particularly one committed by a daughter. But by Linda's own account, her relationship with her mother was nothing like the usual mother-daughter bonds, fraught though many of them might be. Notably, whenever Linda referred to Renalta, she said "Mother," never the more affectionate "Mom." Even I, who have a stiffer, more formal relationship with my parents than is the norm in modern times, call them Mum and Dad.

"I'm supposed to be meeting Robbie at seven thirty," Jayne said, "so I have to go."

I opened my eyes to see most of the cheese, all the crackers, and half of the nuts and olives gone. The leather folder containing the bill lay on the table.

"Sorry to interrupt," Jayne said. "What were you thinking about anyway?"

I took the receipt and placed money on the table. "I'm thinking that it's time for me to go home too. This is on me. A meeting with an author's PA is a business expense."

"Kevin seemed very concerned about Linda. Do you think they're an item?"

"He wants to be. He was quick to comfort her when her mother collapsed. I can't read what she wants though."

I dropped Jayne off at her place and drove home.

Chapter 9

First things first, I took Violet for her evening walk. The rain had passed, leaving the air crisp and fresh and full of the scent of salt from the sea. We took the road that runs along the crest of the hill. The sun was sinking in the west, and to the east the sky over the Atlantic Ocean was streaked pink and gray.

Not far from the shoreline, an enormous yacht drifted past. Yellow light gleamed from multiple windows above the waterline, the deck was strung with lamps, and I could see a swimming pool in the stern and even a helicopter pad. The sound of conversation and laughter drifted over the water. *Must be worth a fortune*, I thought.

A fortune. The Holmes and Hudson books were a publishing phenomenon. They would have earned the author a heck of a lot of money. Not enough to buy that yacht, but more than most people could dream of ever having.

Whose money was it? Ruth Smith, who pretended to be the author, or Linda Marke, who was?

Regardless, now that Ruth had died, presumably all she had would go to her only daughter.

Kevin Reynolds was handsome and charming. Linda Marke was plain and shy. Kevin appeared to be interested in Linda. She was harder to read.

Was that Linda's appeal to Kevin? Her mother's money? I sucked in a breath. Was it possible that Kevin killed Renalta, expecting Linda to inherit her mother's fortune? He did know the true nature of their relationship, that they were mother and daughter, after all. It would have been a heck of a risk to take, for an unassured outcome. Linda and Kevin weren't married; they didn't even seem to be a couple. Maybe Kevin had intentions toward her, but if he did, he didn't seem to be getting very far. Surely he wouldn't take the chance of killing the mother until he was safely wed to the daughter?

Unless something happened that forced his hand. How secure was his job with Renalta? He'd been working for her for a short time. He was but the latest in a long line of publicists. Maybe he was about to be let go. Without close access to Renalta, he might not get another chance to, as they say, "bump her off." Did Kevin know who wrote the books? Linda said he pretty much lived in their pockets, so it would have been hard for him not to.

Might it be Kevin, not Linda, who wanted the real author to get the credit?

"So, Violet," I said to the dog, "we have no shortage of suspects here."

She sniffed at a bush and didn't ask me to elaborate.

I cut our walk short and hurried home. I settled myself in my favorite armchair in the den with my iPad and opened the ever-faithful Google. First, I searched for "Kevin Reynolds." Unfortunately a fairly common name, and I got an overwhelming number of hits. Once I'd narrowed the search to "Renalta Van Markoff," I had fewer results. Like a good publicist should, he kept himself out of the limelight, but I learned that he was from New York City and had graduated from Columbia with a degree in English literature. He'd had several positions in publishing companies over the last five years, none of which had lasted longer than a year. Which meant, I deduced, that his financial situation wasn't comfortable and the Van Markoff job was important to him.

Next: Paige Bookman. She had a website. Her photograph had been professionally done, and it showed her against a plain dark background, unsmiling, chin resting on the back of her hand, looking extremely serious and author-like. The page had two tabs: one headed "Books" and the other "Contact." I clicked on "Books" and read that Paige was working on a novel that was sure to be a "huge international sensation." The description of the book was vague. A quote by someone I'd never heard of (possibly Paige herself) said it was a "groundbreaking cross between Harry Potter and the novels of Anne Perry with a touch of Wilkie Collins." Agents and publishers were invited to contact the author.

I continued searching the Internet, hoping to find some record of arrests or charges of disturbances at Van Markoff functions, but nothing came up.

"Linda Marke" had no hits at all. I found that significant in itself. Almost everyone has some mention somewhere in this age of information. She truly did lead a behind-the-scenes life.

At the signing, I'd overheard Nancy telling a woman she was the head of the Renalta Van Markoff Fan Club, New

England Chapter. The group had a Facebook page, but it was private. I asked to join, using my bookstore profile.

I'd briefly looked up McNamara and Gibbons Press in preparation for Van Markoff's visit to the Emporium, but I decided they warranted a closer look. The front page of the company's website was draped in a thick black banner, reminiscent of the Victorian habit of framing portraits of the deceased in black crepe. The author photo of Renalta was at the top, with her obituary underneath, followed (tastelessly, I thought) by a list of her books with buy links. The biography of the supposed author was brief. It said little more than what appeared on the back of the book jacket, none of it interesting, and all of it, as I now knew, lies.

Renalta Van Markoff was the only bestselling author McNamara and Gibbons had. They published thrillers mostly, standard stuff about rogue CIA agents and beautiful Russian spies out to save civilization as we know it, as well as a few works of historical fiction set in the South around the time of the Civil War. They also produced some nonfiction to do with North Carolina history and a line of cookbooks, with emphasis on traditional Southern cooking. Looking at the cover image of one of them, a plate piled high with glistening barbecued pork and creamy coleslaw, reminded me that I hadn't eaten anything but a handful of nuts since breakfast. Which seemed so long ago.

Violet snuffled and rolled over. She was sound asleep, but her legs moved rapidly. Chasing squirrels through her dreams, most likely.

I clicked on the link that took me to details about the people who worked at the publishing company. A publicist, the editor in chief, an assistant editor, an acquisitions editor, the publisher. Each had short bios and contact details but no photographs. Robert McNamara's biography was extremely dull. He'd gone to the University of North Carolina, where he earned an undergraduate degree in psychology. He was married with three children. His father started McNamara and Gibbons Press in 1977 as a publisher of North Carolina history textbooks for high schools, and when Mr. McNamara Senior retired, Robert took over and expanded the line into fiction and other forms of nonfiction.

Yawn.

About the only interesting thing about Robert appeared to be his wife. He had been, the web page told me, married to the photographer Janet McNamara for twenty-seven years. I clicked on her link, and the screen exploded with light and color. She had done a lot of work for *National Geographic*, starting when she was barely out of college (gorgeous scenes of towering redwood forests, gloomy Scottish Highlands, panoramic African savannas) and lately for publications such as *Martha Stewart Living* and *Architectural Digest*. I spent some time looking through a lifetime of her work. McNamara and Gibbons, I read, had brought out a coffee table book as a retrospective last year. Before I left the page, I studied the tiny self-portrait of the photographer. It was black and white and very arty, but I was confident I'd never seen the woman before.

I finished my prowl of the World Wide Web by reading up on Renalta Van Markoff. I learned little I hadn't known before Linda called the Emporium on Thursday morning. Critics ridiculed her books, Sherlockians despised them, and legions of dedicated readers loved them. One item of interest caught my eye: an online bookstore was offering a signed copy of *An Elementary Affair* for five hundred dollars.

I closed the iPad. One more task before bed. I called Donald.

"Hello?" said a very hesitant voice.

"Good evening, Donald. It's Gemma here. I'm just checking in."

"Have you discovered who killed her?" The hope in his voice was so strong, I hated to let him down.

"Sorry. No. Have you heard anything more from the police?"

"No. I don't know whether that's good news or bad. I thought you might be them, calling to say they were coming over to arrest me. Do you think I should seek legal counsel, Gemma?"

"I can't give you that sort of advice, Donald. You're the lawyer, not me."

"I was a family law attorney. Not criminal."

"I'm not even that. I'll talk to you tomorrow. Call me if you hear anything."

"Good night, Gemma."

Violet followed me into the kitchen, and I let her out for another sniff around the garden. I rummaged in the fridge, looking for something, anything, to eat. When Uncle Arthur's home, he does all the cooking. Good, hearty English stuff like sausages and mash, toad in the hole, shepherd's pie, a Sunday joint with three veg. When he's away, I forage in the tradition of our hunter-gatherer ancestors. I was in luck tonight and found half a roast beef sandwich I'd picked up earlier in the week from the tea room. Made with one of Jayne's fresh baguettes, locally made spicy mustard, garden-fresh arugula, and good brie, it was marvelous when new. Even now that the bread had hardened slightly around the edges, the arugula wasn't crisp, and the brie was hard and cold, it was tasty, if not absolutely delicious. I ate it standing at the sink. My mother would not have approved.

The moment I finished and was wiping my fingers on a paper towel, my phone rang. My heart might have lifted, ever so slightly, when I saw that the call was from Ryan Ashburton. Or perhaps that was just indigestion from gobbling down my dinner standing over the sink.

"Hope I'm not interrupting anything," he said.

"I'm enjoying a quiet dinner with Violet."

"And how's Violet doing tonight?"

"The neighborhood squirrels live in terror."

Ryan laughed. "Glad to hear it. I'm calling to let you know that the forensic people say they're finished at the Emporium. You can open for business at the regular time tomorrow."

"That's good to hear. Thank you."

"Gemma, I saw you heading for the Harbor Inn earlier."

"I know you did."

"I hope you weren't paying a call on Linda Marke and Kevin Reynolds."

"I offered them my condolences."

He sighed. "Gemma, please stay out of it."

"What did you think of the strange relationship between Linda Marke and Renalta Van Markoff?" I asked.

Eventually, he said, "Okay, I'll bite. What strange relationship? We didn't get much of a chance to talk to her.

Mr. Reynolds was being very protective of her. He insisted that she was in shock and needed to lie down. Understandable. I plan to talk to them both at greater length tomorrow. What do I need to know going in, Gemma?"

"Renalta Van Markoff is a pen name. The dead woman's real name is Ruth Smith."

"I know that. Reynolds told us that up front."

"Linda is Ruth's daughter. Her only child, in fact."

More silence. Then, "Are you sure?"

"Need you ask that, Ryan?"

"No. She told you this?"

"An elementary observation." I didn't think it worth mentioning that the news had taken me completely by surprise. Once I knew the truth, only then did I begin to observe traces of similarity between the two women, most notably in the shape of the chin. A serious oversight on my part. "And yes, she confirmed it."

"Did you . . . learn anything else?" The words came out as though they were being dragged across his tongue one by one.

I didn't tell him about the identity of the real author of the books. For now, I'd keep that little detail to myself. If Linda wanted to tell the police, she would. "A woman by the name of Paige Bookman was evicted from the Emporium shortly before Renalta collapsed. Have you spoken to her?"

"She was brought down to the station earlier as a person of interest." That must have been shortly after Jayne and I left Paige standing in the rain at the beach. I hoped she didn't think I'd called the cops on her. Again. "We had a long chat. She insists on her innocence, and I have no reason to consider her a more viable suspect than anyone else who was there. I've told her she's not to leave West London without my permission. She has a history of annoying Van Markoff, but charges have never been laid. We're looking deeper into her background to see if there've been other incidents with other authors or celebrities."

"You must know that Donald Morris didn't kill Renalta."

"I know no such thing. If you're getting involved in this out of some sense of loyalty to Donald, don't."

"What do you know about him? What are you saying?"

"I'm saying nothing, Gemma. Nothing except good night. Thanks for the tip about Linda." He hung up.

Violet scratched at the door to be let in, and we went to bed.

* * *

The irony about living in a place so marvelous that hordes of tourists flock to it is that I myself don't get much of a chance to enjoy it. I'd love nothing more than to grab Jayne, hop into the Miata, and take a couple of days to drive up Highway 6. Explore the historic lighthouses and open beaches of the National Seashore, poke around Truro and Provincetown, spend a night in a charming old B and B or a modern luxury hotel. Maybe make a day of it to take a whale-watching excursion out of Brewster, explore the shops in Hyannis, and have a late lunch or early cocktails in Chatham. But summer in Massachusetts is short, and it's the busiest time of the year, by far, at the bookshop, so I can rarely get away for more than a few hours. I cherished secret hopes that Ashleigh would turn out to be capable enough that I might be able to take a short getaway in the autumn. Dragging

Jayne out of her kitchen might prove to be a problem though, no matter what the time of year.

The Emporium opens at noon on Sundays, making it the one day of the week I can enjoy some time at the beach when the sun is up. I pulled shorts and a T-shirt over my swimming costume; slipped my feet into flip-flops; tossed my towel, my copy of *These Honored Dead*, and a bottle of sunscreen into a tote bag; and loaded the beach chair and umbrella into the Miata. In the off-season, I enjoy taking Violet for a walk along the shoreline, but when the beaches are crowded with tourists and locals enjoying a day off, that's not doable.

I hoped she didn't notice the beach apparel and thought I was just heading out for another day at work. Hard to tell, as she gave me sad, mournful gazes every time I left, even if I was only going as far as the mailbox at the end of the driveway.

This morning, I was one of the first to arrive at the West London Beach on Nantucket Sound. The sheltered waters of the Sound are considerably calmer and warmer than those of the Atlantic Ocean on the other side of the peninsula and thus where I go to swim. When I'm out for a walk, I like to wander along the ocean, wade in the surf while sandpipers scatter, and look east in the approximate direction of dear old England.

I found the perfect spot to set up my chair and umbrella. I swam up and down the shoreline for half an hour, and when I climbed out of the water, families were beginning to arrive. I toweled myself off, reapplied a thick layer of sunscreen (my complexion is what is called in romance novels an "English rose"), and dropped into my chair with my book.

I'd not slept well last night, disturbed by thoughts of the death of Renalta Van Markoff. I regretted telling Donald I'd investigate. About all I could do was talk to people, and if they didn't want to talk to me, they wouldn't. I didn't have the resources of the police, nor the authority.

I knew Ryan was a good detective, and he'd assured me that Louise Estrada was also.

I'd let them handle it. I opened my book and began to read.

Would Ryan and Louise realize that the value of Van Markoff books, signed ones, would increase substantially now that she was dead? Perhaps not. They were not booksellers; they had no involvement or interest in the world of book collecting. Last night, only hours after the woman's death, a signed copy of the first book in her series was going for five hundred dollars. I remembered Andrea proudly showing me her book, which had been signed and personalized not more than a few hours before the author died—before the author was *murdered*.

The value of such a book might go through the roof.

Donald, of all people, had bought a copy of *Hudson House* when he came into the Emporium on Thursday afternoon bursting with righteous indignation. He told me it was for "research" so he could see how bad it was. He hadn't brought the book with him on Saturday for Renalta to sign. The initial print run had been more than a hundred thousand. An unsigned book had no rarity value.

But signed books did. Would the worth of the book increase the closer to the time of her death that it had been signed? She'd autographed preordered books only minutes before collapsing. Including some for Grant Thompson. Grant had specifically told me he wanted Renalta to write the date in the books.

Was I now suspecting Grant Thompson of killing Renalta? I pushed that thought away. Any number of people had the opportunity. Andrea told me fans had surrounded Renalta before she left for the Emporium, and she signed books while Kevin waited impatiently. I had no way of knowing which of those people had then come to the Emporium, where they would have had access to the bottle of water. Ashleigh had taken pictures of the crowd, but she didn't get anywhere near everyone in attendance, and the pictures mostly showed backs of heads anyway. The backs of heads had a lot in common—gray hair either cut short or piled into a bun—as was the case at all our author events unless it was a children's or YA author visiting. When I got my camera back from Ryan, I could show the pictures to Andrea and ask if she recognized any of her guests, but what purpose would that serve? Presumably when the police took details from the attendees, they mentioned what hotel they were staying at if they didn't live on the Cape.

I closed my book. I looked out over the Sound. Sailboats drifted across the horizon, people swam in the warm water, and children filled colorful plastic pails with saltwater and sand. One laughing preteen girl was being buried in the sand by her brothers while her anxious mother fussed about.

Such a beautiful day. Such a beautiful place.

But I couldn't get murder off my mind. I packed up my things and headed home to get ready for work.

*   *   *

I planned to go into the tea room first, but my attention was caught by the mound of flowers, some wrapped in grocery-store cellophane, piled at the door of the Emporium. I bent over and plucked a card off one: *Renalta, forever in our hearts.* I groaned. What on earth was I supposed to do with all these? I couldn't leave them there; they were blocking the door. Maureen would report me to the bylaw officers for cluttering the sidewalk.

As I stood there, a weeping woman approached. She stopped at the shop and gently placed a teddy bear with a red ribbon around its neck next to the flowers. "So sad, Gemma," she said.

"Sad," I repeated.

She continued on her way. I went into the tea room.

"There's a pile of flowers and teddy bears outside the shop doors," I said to Jayne.

"Yeah, I saw them. We had some too. I didn't know if you wanted me to move yours." She was rolling pastry. Jocelyn dished up a bowl of tomato and red pepper soup from the cauldron on the stove, put it on a plate beside a fresh green salad, and carried the tray into the dining room.

I looked around the kitchen. No flowers. "What did you do with them?"

"I called Mom, and she took them to the hospital. The adult patients will love the flowers, and the kids can have the teddy bears. She'll take yours too, if you want."

"Thanks. I don't want to just throw them away. People have been thoughtful, but I can't leave them blocking the door."

I left Jayne with her baking. During the week, I like to enjoy a leisurely breakfast over a cup of tea, toast and marmalade, and the online newspapers, but on Sunday I treat myself to takeout from the tea room after my swim or walk with Violet. Today I bought a blueberry muffin to accompany a large cup of tea.

With great trepidation, I unlocked the door that joins the tea room to the Emporium. Moriarty had been confined in the office for the entire night. His physical welfare had been provided for in terms of adequate food and water and the presence of a litter box, but his dignity was likely to have been greatly offended. I stood in the doorway, clutching my late breakfast. All was quiet. I put my purchases on the counter and headed upstairs, making a great deal of noise as I went. Moriarty had the hearing of . . . well, of a cat, but I didn't want to surprise him. "Good morning!" I threw open the door.

A black ball streaked past me, heading for the stairs. I glanced around my office. It didn't seem as though too much damage had been done. Yes, litter was scattered everywhere, a suspicious yellow puddle was soaking into the papers in the middle of my desk, books had been knocked off the shelf, and the computer mouse was dangling from its cord, but the damage could have been worse. I checked the boxes of books. No sign of the cat's attention there. Even Moriarty knew not to endanger our livelihood.

I cleaned up and then headed back downstairs, where I found my teacup upside down on the floor and the bag containing my muffin shredded and squashed flat. The cat perched on the top of the gaslight shelf, tail slowly moving, narrow amber eyes glaring at me.

"Okay," I said, "now we're even."

Moriarty said nothing.

I returned to the tea room.

"Sorry, Gemma," Fiona said. "You got the last of the blueberry muffins. You must have really enjoyed the one you had."

I grumbled and asked for my second favorite, lemon poppy seed, as well as a fresh cup of tea.

As the hands on the clock above the sales counter touched the top of the big circle, I opened the doors, and the first customer of the day clambered over the flowers to get in.

This time I wasn't fooled.

"Hello, my darling." Nancy enveloped me in a huge hug and a tsunami of cheap perfume, followed by a peck on both cheeks.

I pulled away. She was once again in full Renalta mode. Swirling red cape, black wig, huge red glass ring, heavy makeup, dramatic gestures, and deep breathy voice.

"Such a tragedy. An unspeakable loss to the world." She used a lace handkerchief with a dramatic red *R* embroidered into the corner to dab dry eyes. "I was so hoping to have a nice private chat with Renalta when all the fuss and bother was over."

"Did that happen often?" I asked, knowing full well the answer.

"Not as much as we both would have liked. Her entourage can get overly enthusiastic about the performance of their duties sometimes."

Which I took to mean Kevin and Linda hustled Renalta away before she could be waylaid by excessively enthusiastic fans.

"We shared a mental bond, and that was enough." Nancy smiled at me.

Creepy.

"I own all of her books, you know. Every edition, hardcover, paperback, even some of the foreign translations. I once sent her a picture of my library. She wrote a lovely note thanking me."

"That was nice of her. A personal signed note?"

Nancy glanced to one side. "Well, no, not exactly. It was an e-mail. But from her personal address."

"Are many of your books personalized?"

"Oh, yes. Whenever she does an event in Massachusetts, I try to attend. I was planning to buy *Hudson House* on Saturday and have it signed. But that didn't happen. It will make a huge hole in my collection." Nancy pointed to the center table, which still contained the Van Markoff display. My first order of business today was to dismantle it. "Did she leave anything behind?"

"What do you mean?"

Nancy leaned in so close, I could smell the eggs she'd had for breakfast. Mixed with the perfume, it was not a pleasant scent. "An item she dropped, maybe? A pen, a piece of jewelry? I'll pay you well for it."

I stepped back. "If anything was found—and I'm not saying it was—the police have it."

"Just asking." She winked at me. "I'll be around for a few days, if you do come across something I might be interested in."

"How can I contact you?" Not that I planned on selling her the dust Renalta had stirred up when she took her last walk through the shop, but my investigative instincts were stirring.

"I'll call you and check in." She tossed her head and flung her cloak over her right shoulder in a gesture I'd last seen in a movie version of *The Three Musketeers*. "Dear Renalta had so many loyal fans. Just look at all those tributes at your door. None of them were so loyal as me, of course. I'm sure some of them would like to meet me now that she's gone. Knowing that the spirit of Renalta still lives will give them such comfort. I'm thinking of going on the lecture circuit to mystery conferences and the like. I'll talk about Renalta's life and her work and display some of my valuable memorabilia."

"Now that I'm thinking of it, I might have something you'd be interested in."

Her eyes gleamed.

The shop was empty, but I glanced behind me, as though someone might be eavesdropping. Moriarty leapt off the shelf and headed for his bed under the center table. "She bought a . . . a . . . coloring book. *Sherlock Mind Palace* coloring book. She told me it gave her a marvelous idea for a plot twist in her current manuscript. She left it with me while she gave her talk but wrote her name on the cover first."

Nancy gasped. "I have to have it."

"It's not here. I took it home yesterday. I didn't want it to be caught up in all the police activity. It might have gotten damaged. Or something." I was laying it on mighty thick, but I took the chance that Nancy wouldn't notice.

"You're not busy. Let's go and get it right now."

I shook my head sadly. "Sorry. I can't leave the shop unattended. Why don't I bring it around to your hotel later?"

"How much do you want for it?"

"Five hundred."

"That seems like a lot."

"It was signed only moments before her death. She . . . uh . . . put the date and time on it too."

"Okay," Nancy said.

If I was criminally inclined, I might be able to do a good business in forged Van Markoff memorabilia. Too bad Renalta hadn't asked to use my restroom. I could auction off the roll of loo paper.

"I don't think I got your surname," I said.

"Brownmiller. Nancy Brownmiller."

The chimes over the door tinkled, and a woman came in.

"Let me know if you need any help," I said to the customer.

"Thanks, but I see what I want." She headed directly for the center table and snatched up *Hudson House.*

"I can't talk now," I said to Nancy. "How about I come to your hotel after closing today? Where are you staying?"

"The West London Hotel."

"I know it. I'll be there around half five."

"I'll be waiting." Instead of leaving, Nancy moved further into the shop, heading directly toward my customer. "Hello, my darling. Fan of Renalta, are you? She might no longer be with us, but . . ."

I stepped between Nancy and the startled woman. "Off you go now. I'm sure you have things to do. All those conference engagements to arrange."

"You're right. I'll see you at five thirty. Uh, that is what half five means, right?"

"Yes."

She left. The customer looked at me. "I heard the author died yesterday, so I have to assume that wasn't her, was it?"

"A pale imitation."

"Takes all kinds, I guess. I'd also like to get a gift for my niece's birthday. She's going to be fourteen. Do you have anything you recommend?"

"If she hasn't tried the Agency series for young adults by Y. S. Lee, she might like to start. It's not Sherlock related, but it's about an all-female detective agency in Victorian London."

"Sounds good."

I rang up her purchases. Moriarty came out from under the table. She bent over to pet him, effusive in her praise of his handsome bearing. He threw me a self-satisfied smirk.

I had absolutely no intention of going to the West London Hotel at half five with a copy of the *Mind Palace* coloring book embossed with a fake signature. I'd pulled five hundred dollars out of thin air. If Nancy was prepared to pay such a ridiculous sum, either she had money to squander, she had such an overwhelming desire for the book that she was prepared to make sacrifices for it, or she had the expectation of shortly coming into funds.

I wouldn't go to the hotel, but I'd send someone else.

More customers began arriving, so I took my phone into the reading nook in search of a bit of privacy but still kept an eye on the shop. I called Ryan, but it went to voice mail. "Hi, it's Gemma. I have a pretty solid lead into a suspect you might not have considered for the killing. Give me a call when you have a chance."

I hung up and went back to work.

Jayne's mother, Leslie, pulled into the loading zone in front of the shop, and I went out to help her pile all the flowers and other gifts into her car. I kept one particularly nice bunch of red roses to display in the shop.

Ashleigh arrived at one. We were busy, but not extraordinarily so for a Sunday in summer. A few people asked about Renalta and expressed shock at her death, but I got the feeling that the more eager fans had been in the shop yesterday to meet her. I stuffed the excess copies of *Hudson House* into boxes and shoved them behind the counter. I had no doubt that I'd be able to sell them, but I didn't want to have a special display anymore. Some people might leap at the chance of taking monetary advantage of Renalta's death, but I wasn't one of them. I hadn't known the woman well, and I hadn't liked what I did know, but her memory still deserved to be treated with respect.

I left a few of the books in place but took away the posters advertising *Hudson House* and filled the rest of the center table with a selection of other new releases.

At three forty, I told Ashleigh I was nipping next door for my daily meeting with Jayne. And, not incidentally, to get something for a late lunch. Ryan hadn't phoned me back, so I called again to tell him about Nancy, but again it went straight to voice mail. If I didn't hear from him, should I keep my appointment at her hotel? If I didn't show, she might decide to leave town.

Most of the tables in the tea room were occupied as groups of women enjoyed their afternoon tea or cream teas. Looking totally out of place, three husky workmen in overalls and steel-toed boots sat in the window alcove, sipping fragrant tea out of rose-patterned china cups and nibbling on crustless sandwiches and dainty fruit tarts.

Fiona passed me carrying a three-tiered silver tray. "Jayne said you're to go into the kitchen. We're still busy out here."

I pushed open the swinging doors and entered Jayne's realm. She was scraping the leftovers into the garbage. Not that there were many leftovers. "Good day?"

"Typical summer Sunday. Delightfully overwhelmed. We're still serving the last of the customers, so I thought we'd be better talking in here. You?"

"Busy. A few crime scene tourists peering into the corners in search of blood spatter, but not many." I perched on a stool and pulled out my phone. "Give me a minute, will you. I have something I want to check."

Jayne gestured to a plate of pretty sandwiches. "I saved you some. Help yourself."

I opened Facebook. Along with a few inquiries as to our hours of business (which were clearly posted at the top of the page), several queries as to if I had *Hudson House* in stock, and one book collector looking for a first or good-quality second edition of *The Valley of Fear*, I had received a message from the Renalta Van Markoff Fan Club (New England Chapter) saying I'd been approved to join. I accessed the page and scanned it quickly. The banner had been updated since yesterday, expressing the group's shock and grief at the death of their idol. Many fans commented, clearly upset at the news. Scrolling down and thus moving backward through time, I found an announcement about the signing at the Emporium. A few people expressed their extreme disappointment at the last-minute cancellation of the Boston appearances, and before that the chatter was all about the imminent release of the new book. But nothing, old or recent, stood out immediately as worth my attention. Even the people upset about her canceling her appearances were at worst annoyed, not threatening.

I put the phone away and took a salmon sandwich. Cucumber is my favorite, and there were two of them, so I decided to save them for last.

"You're a big fan of Van Markoff's books," I said to Jayne. "As a reader, did it make any difference to you to find out who wrote them?"

"Not really. Then again, I love the books, yes, but I'm not what you'd probably call a fan of the author. I was excited about meeting her when she was here in town, but I wouldn't travel any distance to her book signings, nor did I care about her personal life. Some more ardent fans might think they've been cheated. Do you think it will matter if word gets out?"

"It might. Then again, they say there's no such thing as bad publicity." I popped the last bite of sandwich into my mouth.

"Do you have any more insights into who might have killed Renalta?" Jayne asked.

I finished chewing, but before I could answer, a voice from the doorway said, "Exactly the question I have." Detective Louise Estrada had not come in for tea and scones. She was not suitably dressed either for afternoon tea or for the weather in jeans, high black boots, and a black leather jacket over a black shirt with a white collar. She did not smile in greeting. "You have something to tell us, Gemma?"

"I called Ryan earlier."

"He's otherwise engaged."

"With what?"

"I ask the questions here," she snapped.

"Would you like a sandwich, Detective?" Jayne pointed to the plate on the counter in front of me.

"As long as it's not intended to be a bribe."

"We always have leftovers, even after the busiest of days."

Estrada selected a cucumber and cream cheese on white bread. I threw Jayne a glare I'd learned from Moriarty. Those sandwiches were supposed to be for me. The cucumber most of all.

"This is good," Estrada begrudgingly admitted. She then helped herself to the other cucumber one. I pushed the plate toward her.

"Detective Ashburton is talking to Ruth Smith's business associates and her . . . uh . . . daughter," Estrada said.

"Daughter?" I said innocently.

"Turns out the PA is actually her daughter."

"Imagine that," Jayne said.

"He's also investigating the background of other interested parties. I—that is, *we*—felt that in light of your previous relationship with Detective Ashburton, I'd be the best one to talk to you. What did you want to tell him?"

"A woman came into the shop this morning as soon as I opened. Her name's Nancy Brownmiller, and she is, to put it mildly, a huge Van Markoff fan."

"If you think that's a motive for murder, Gemma, I have a hundred suspects out there."

"Hear me out. This Nancy person dresses like Renalta, wears a wig that looks like Renalta's hair, puts on her habits and mannerisms. She wanted to speak to Renalta when she arrived for the signing. Kevin Reynolds recognized her and tried to chase her off."

Estrada did not look overly impressed by my revelations. She next selected an egg salad pinwheel.

"After that, Nancy came into the shop, where she stood, as I told you yesterday, against the counter near the water bottles. But more to the point, she's got some crazy idea of attending historical mystery conferences and literary events as a sort of Renalta Van Markoff replacement."

That got Estrada's attention. Her dark eyes flickered.

"I remember my mother talking about the killing of John Lennon," I said. "He was murdered by a fan so extreme, he'd come to believe he *was* the famous person. And as there can't be two of them, he had to get rid of the real one."

"I've seen stranger things," Estrada admitted. "I worked in New York City before coming here. Some of those celebrities really do need all the security they surround themselves with. I wouldn't have that life for anything."

"Nancy's staying at the West London Hotel. I happen to know she will be there at five o'clock. Just in case you want to drop by."

"Thanks for the sandwiches, Ms. Wilson," Estrada said.

Estrada left without thanking me for my assistance in this matter.

*   *   *

"Do you have plans for tonight?" I asked Jayne.

"Nope. Robbie's having dinner with his folks."

"Robbie has parents?"

"Yes, Gemma, he has parents. I haven't met them yet, though."

That, in my mind, was a good thing. If she hadn't met the family, then the relationship wasn't getting serious.

"Feel like an early dinner? Considering as to how I didn't get any lunch." I looked up hopefully as the kitchen doors swung open. Jocelyn came in with a stack of dirty dishes. Barely a crumb remained.

"Not tonight, thanks," Jayne said. "It's been a hard week, and all I want is to get into my jammies, open a bag of potato chips, and watch reality TV."

I shuddered at the thought. "I can lend you a good book."

"I have lots of good books. There's a time for books and there's a time for mindless entertainment."

"Not in my opinion. Nevertheless, I understand. I'm pretty bushed too." Like all the other shops along Baker Street, the Emporium closes at five on Sundays. Making it, like a morning trip to the beach, the only time I can enjoy an early night during the summer season.

"Why don't you see if Ryan's free?" Jayne suggested helpfully.

"And have Estrada complain I'm exerting influence over his investigation? He doesn't need that."

"Why not let him decide what he needs?"

Had Ryan sent Estrada in answer to my phone call? Or had Estrada complained to the chief, once again, about me and my supposed influence over Detective Ashburton? Heck, if I had any influence over that man, we'd be happily married with two point three children.

Just as well, I reminded myself for the umpteenth time, things hadn't gone that way. It wouldn't have worked out.

"See you tomorrow," I said to Jayne.

She gave me an impromptu hug. I hugged her back. Jocelyn joined in.

"What was that for?" I asked when we'd separated and Jocelyn had gone out front to clear the last of the tables.

"Just a reminder that I love you, Gemma."

I smiled. "Thanks."

Seeing as to how I had no plans for my evening and I still had unanswered questions about the death of Renalta Van Markoff, once I was back in the bookshop, I called Linda Marke.

Kevin Reynolds answered the phone in her room. I told him who I was and asked to speak to Linda.

"Why?" he asked.

"I thought she might be in need of some company. Maybe we could have a drink in the hotel bar this evening. Dinner if she's free."

"She's not in need of company."

"Why don't I ask her?"

"I don't want her to be disturbed, Ms. Doyle. The autopsy on her mother is being done right about now. You must realize how upsetting that must be."

"I do. So I thought it best she not be alone. May I talk to her?"

"She's resting."

"Okay. What about you, Kevin? Fancy a drink?"

"No." He hung up on me.

Okay, so that line of inquiry was temporarily closed. I considered calling Robert McNamara, the publisher, next, but I didn't really want to spend my free evening in his company.

I phoned Grant Thompson.

*   *   *

"Like most collecting," Grant said, "the only value books have is what people are willing to pay for them. And the best determining factor in that is rarity."

We were at McGillivray's Pub in West London. I'd decided not to even bother trying to get into the Blue Water Café without a reservation, so I suggested Grant meet me at the pub. Like most so-called pubs in North America, something was seriously out of kilter at McGillivray's. Maybe it was the lack of a crush at the bar, the absence of an open fireplace (they did have a gas one), and no wet, smelly dogs snoozing under the table. Or maybe it was the table service and the fact that the pretty young waitresses were dressed in short kilts. The evening sunshine pouring in through clear windows, rather than a steady driving rain or thick drizzle, might have had an effect on the atmosphere also. Nevertheless, it was a warm and friendly place, in the fine tradition of the best of British pubs. They also served excellent food, which the best of British pubs were increasingly doing these days.

"Cheers." Grant lifted his pint of Guinness. He'd lived in England when he studied at Oxford and had learned to love a rich, hearty beer.

I saluted him with my wineglass. I've never been a beer person. "Therefore," I said, "books dated the day of the author's death would be rare and thus worth more."

"Yup. Good thing I have three of them." He read my face. "I didn't kill her to increase the value of three books, Gemma."

"I didn't think for a moment that you did." That wasn't entirely the truth. I had thought it and quickly dismissed it. "The same might be said of me. I had her sign some for store stock. I'm torn about what to do with them. Normally, I'd put an 'autographed by the author' sticker on them and put them on display in a prominent place. Readers like signed books, and it's always a good selling point. But in this case, I'm wondering if I should hold on to some of them and hope to sell them for more than cover price eventually. I know it seems mercenary, but I also have a business to run."

The waitress arrived with our meals. Steak and kidney pie for me and a hamburger and chips—what Americans call fries—for Grant.

"How much are we talking about?" I asked once we'd savored the first welcome bites. My pie came with canned peas and a mountain of mashed potatoes drenched in thick gravy. Exactly the way I like it.

"Not as much as you might think," Grant said. "Renalta was very popular, yes, but not among"—he put down his burger and made quotation marks in the air—"'people who matter.'"

I snorted.

"Right. She was a genre writer. What might have once been called pulp fiction, and she was also a"—quotations marks again—"'woman writer' who wrote for 'women readers.'"

I snorted again.

"Thus," he said, "her books are not worth spending a lot of money to collect, probably even in death."

"You mentioned rarity. She didn't sign many books because of the arthritis in her wrist, certainly not by the hundreds, even thousands, which some popular writers do. Would that help?"

"Minimally. Most of her signed books would have been personalized. *For Mary, Enjoy.* Nice for Mary to own, but that would only decrease the value to a serious collector, not increase it. I specialize in Victorian and Edwardian detective fiction, Gemma. I know a bit about the market for contemporary books, but not a lot. I can talk to one of my acquaintances, if you'd like."

"Probably not worth going to any trouble over," I admitted. "I can't see that being a reason for her murder. The monetary value for any contemporary book is simply not enough. If it were, more famous authors than Renalta Van Markoff would be dropping dead all across America."

"The news at five was noncommittal," Grant said. "The chief made a statement about an arrest being imminent, but he gave no details."

"Imminent is code for *we don't have a freakin' clue.*"

Grant chuckled. "What are your police friends saying?"

"Nothing to me."

"I've heard that Donald Morris is, as they say, 'in the frame.'"

"They're clutching at straws. All they have is a threat. A threat spoken in public in front of a hundred or so people is meaningless. But it is enough to have poor Donald worried." I'd come up with better suspects than Donald: Paige Bookman, Nancy Brownmiller, Kevin Reynolds, even Linda Marke. "I don't suppose you noticed anyone acting suspiciously around the bottle of water, did you?" I asked.

"So that's true then? Poison was in the water? The police aren't coming right out and saying so, but that's the rumor going around. Anyone who was close to her when she died saw her take that drink, and the police are asking a lot of questions along that line. I gave them my statement, Gemma. I didn't see the bottle, although it was apparently near to where I was standing while Renalta gave her talk. I didn't see anyone handling it either."

"The only one anyone did see handling it was me," I said around a mouthful of mashed potatoes and gravy. "I picked it up off the counter and gave it to her."

"The rumor says cyanide."

"I haven't heard the autopsy or lab results, but that's almost a certainty. How's your burger?"

"Good. But this talk of poison is threatening to put me off my food."

"It shouldn't. Cyanide isn't something the average person comes across in their daily life. Whoever put it into that water bottle had to know what they were doing and had to have decided to do it a long time before. Cyanide isn't a natural compound. It has to be made or purchased and then transported, and that means Renalta's murder was premeditated."

"Is there any chance the water was intended for someone else?"

I shook my head. "I can't see it. Renalta was accustomed to drinking a good deal of water at her public appearances. It helped calm her nerves. The killer was taking a chance that someone else wouldn't pick up the bottle and take a drink. But the risk of that was minimal, so he or she clearly considered it worth taking."

"You think so?"

"These days people don't help themselves to other people's glasses or bottles, so the likelihood of that happening was small. If the attempt had been made in a less public place, then the number of possible suspects would have been fewer also. It was a rather clever plan."

"You aren't saying you admire this person, are you, Gemma?"

"Admire?" I said. "Not in the least. Murder is never something to admire, and particularly not in such an underhanded way as this one. I can, however, respect the intelligence and planning that went into it."

Grant gave me a sideways look as he ran a chip through ketchup.

"What?" I asked.

"Nothing. You're an unusual woman, Gemma Doyle."

"I don't think so."

He grinned and popped the chip into his mouth.

We talked about more pleasant things while we finished our meals and ordered another round of drinks.

"Can I walk you home?" Grant asked once we'd wrestled over the bill and eventually agreed to each pay our own share.

"That would be nice."

We said little on the walk. It was a gorgeous night, and the warm air carried the scent of salt, sand, and flowers. Lights from the harbor glowed in the distance. We turned into Blue Water Place, and Grant took my hand. I left it there.

He cleared his throat. "I have to ask . . ."

"Yes?"

"Is there something between you and Ryan Ashburton?"

"There was. Once. It ended."

"Are you sure it ended?" We walked up the front path, illuminated by the dying light of the day and the dim glow of the lamps over the sidewalk. Violet sensed our approach and let out one welcoming bark. The motion detector over my door came on. Grant gazed down at me. His eyes were dark and serious. His five-o'clock shadow was thick, sharp cheekbones prominent in the lean face.

"Am I sure?" I reached up and touched his face. I ran my fingers lightly across his cheek. "These days, Grant, I'm not sure of anything."

"In that case, Gemma, I'll say my good-nights. But I hope, when you do decide, you can find a place for me."

He walked away, and I let myself in.

Chapter 10

On Monday mornings in summer and autumn, Violet and I change our routine, and rather than walking the usual route through our neighborhood, we head into town. It's market day in West London, and I love little more than poking around the farmers' stalls. It was early in the season, so not a lot of fresh local produce was available, but I filled my woven basket with a variety of lettuce and arugula, an abundance of yellow and purple beans, green onions, and snap peas. I chatted to the farmers and craftspeople as I browsed, and people stopped to admire Violet.

"No tomatoes yet?" I said to a teenage girl taking money at her family's farm stand.

"Couple of weeks still to go. You can't rush a tomato."

"I know, but I'm getting very impatient."

"The warm spring has helped, and everything's looking good so far."

I could almost taste a deep-purple, bright-yellow, or cheerful-red cherry tomato on the tip of my tongue. Some things in life are worth waiting for. A locally grown heirloom tomato in season, eaten warm from the sun, is one of them.

I handed over my money, but before I could move on, a woman came up to me. "I can't believe what happened on Saturday. Renalta Van Markoff, dead. They're saying she was murdered. Is that right, Gemma?"

She was a regular at the Emporium. I struggled to remember her name. I knew she had a huge crush on Martin Freeman, that she watched the Jeremy Brett version of *The Adventure of the Blue Carbuncle* every Christmas, that she loved dark and gritty historical novels and had most recently purchased *Wishful Seeing* by Janet Kellough, that her kitchen was full of mugs inspired by the BBC *Sherlock* series, and that she dried her dishes with Benedict Cumberbatch's portrait. I also knew that her husband was having an affair with a friend of a friend of Jayne's mother. All that, and I couldn't remember her name. "So it seems," I said. "You were there on Saturday, weren't you?"

"Yes. Renalta was so interesting. I enjoyed her talk, and I was excited about getting a book signed by her. Such an over-the-top personality, wasn't she? A true original."

"I wouldn't have thought her books were to your taste. You usually like more realistic novels."

"Who wouldn't love Renalta? And having met her, who wouldn't love her books? They were so like her, weren't they? I bet she took inspiration for the character of Desdemona Hudson from her own life."

Bored of this conversation, Violet tried to wander off. I gently tugged on the leash to pull her back. "Did you speak to the police about Saturday?"

"A young officer came around to the house and took my statement. I wanted to help, but I couldn't tell them anything. I didn't see anyone acting suspiciously. Did you?"

"No, I didn't." Violet was straining at the leash now, urging me to get a move on. "Gotta run. We're getting in some new Sherlock jigsaw puzzles. I'm expecting them by the end of the week."

She clapped her hands in delight.

I never did recall her name.

*   *   *

The autopsy on Renalta Van Markoff was scheduled to have been done Sunday afternoon. The lab analysis of the contents of the bottle I'd saved from spilling all over the Emporium floor should be available soon. It was highly unlikely the police would share the autopsy and forensic results with me ahead of releasing them to the press, and try as I might, I couldn't think of any way to trick them into giving me the information. I was 99 percent sure I'd smelled cyanide in that water bottle, and Renalta's symptoms at the time of her death were consistent with a strong, instant-acting poison. But I didn't like that missing 1 percent.

Irene Talbot came into the Emporium shortly before noon carrying a takeout latte and a sandwich. We said the same thing at the same time: "Have you heard anything?"

We laughed.

"I'll go first," Irene said. "No."

"I'll go second," I said. "No. The autopsy was yesterday afternoon. Have the results been released?"

"Not a peep. I got a quote from our chief for this morning's paper. I'll save you the trouble of reading it: 'We are confident that an arrest is imminent in the tragic death of blah blah blah. Residents and visitors to West London are assured blah blah blah.'"

"I consider myself assured," I said.

She grinned. "The company that manufactures the Riviera brand of water has issued a press release, claiming the strictest and most up-to-date methods of quality control. The police took every bottle off the shelves of the convenience store and are testing them all. They've also asked anyone who bought a bottle and hasn't yet consumed it to turn it in."

"They won't find anything."

"No chance this was a random crime?"

"Perish the thought. That would kill tourism to West London." Not to mention business in my shop. "That's always a chance but so unlikely as to be not worth considering."

"You're probably right, but poor Freddy is lamenting a severe drop-off of business."

"Who's Freddy?"

"The convenience store owner."

"Oh, right. I'm sure you've been asked about it, Irene, but you were standing by the water bottle during Renalta's talk. Did you see anything?"

Her story was the same as Grant's. She hadn't even noticed the bottle on the counter, much less seen someone interfering with it. "I did some research into cyanide," she said. "Not something you keep on a high shelf in the garage in case you have an infestation of rats."

"No. Potassium cyanide, also known as KCN, isn't even normally available in its poisonous form. The ingredients, hydrogen cyanide and potassium hydroxide, have to be mixed.

And the person mixing it has to know what they're doing if they don't want to risk killing themselves."

"How do you know so much about cyanide, Gemma?"

"I hope you're not accusing me," I said. "I know about a lot of things."

"I'm not accusing you. Sometimes you seem to know what others do not, that's all. I'm glad you're not my enemy."

"Whatever that means, I won't ask."

She toasted me with her latte. "Cheers. I'm off." Her phone buzzed with an incoming text, and she read quickly. "The chief has scheduled a press conference for six o'clock. Probably the autopsy results. Two press conferences in two days. He must be hoping to get his picture in the Boston or national papers, maybe even on TV. I bet he'll be at the barber shop this afternoon. I might lie in wait and try to get an exclusive. See you later."

"Let me know if you hear anything significant, will you, Irene?"

"Sure."

As she walked out, my phone rang. I checked the display. "Good afternoon, Donald."

"Gemma!" he screeched. "They're here!"

"Calm down, Donald. Who's where? Where are you?"

"I'm at home. I'm looking out the front window. Police cars are pulling up outside. Two of them. No three. The detectives are getting out. Uniformed officers are with them. Oh, no. She has a piece of paper in her hand. They're ringing the bell. Gemma! I need you!"

"Calm down, Donald. I'll be right there. You might want to call a lawyer."

"No time. Now they're knocking. They'll break the door down if I don't answer." Silence.

A few more bouquets had appeared outside the Emporium. I ignored them, locked the front door, and flipped the sign to "Closed." I ran into the tea room, pulling the adjoining door shut behind me. I shouted to Fiona behind the counter, "I need a car, now. Can I take yours?"

She blinked. "Sure. I guess. Why?"

"Where are your keys?"

"My purse is in the computer desk off the kitchen. Second drawer on the left."

I found them and ran out the back way. "Back soon. Can't stop to explain," I shouted to a startled Jayne. I unlocked Fiona's battered dust-and-rust-covered Dodge Neon and jumped in. The engine coughed, and for a moment I feared it wouldn't start, but it struggled to life, and I sped out of the parking lot, kicking up dust and gravel as I went. Uncle Arthur and I had once been invited to a party at Donald's home on the occasion of Sherlock Holmes's birthday. Yes, that is a thing. Sherlock's birthday is January 6 and is much celebrated by his devotees. It had been a surprisingly enjoyable event. The twenty-two guests had dressed well but had not gone overboard with period costumes or accessories. Jayne had made the cake, a towering affair of four chocolate layers decorated like a book with *The Complete Sherlock Holmes* written in icing on the top. The conversation was all about Holmes, of course, discussing and arguing over the minutiae of the canon. A conversation my uncle Arthur can engage in with the best of them, although the details far exceed my knowledge or interest. At the end of the evening, talk veered into disparaging all the modern imitations. I disagree—I think some of the pastiche works are very clever and faithful to the spirit of the original—but I refrained from commenting, not wanting to get into an argument.

As I drove I thought about what might be happening at Donald's house now. He was right to be panicking. If the detectives came around to his home with more questions, that would be one thing. But three cars? Uniformed officers? Carrying a piece of paper that was quite likely a search warrant? The autopsy must have found something that incriminated Donald.

Was it possible Donald had killed Renalta after all?

No value in speculating without facts.

Donald's small 1950s-era house is tucked into a grove of oak, aspen, and pine on the outskirts of West London. The driveway was crowded with police cars, so I parked on the street. I jogged up the path to be greeted by Officer Richter standing at the open front door with his arms crossed over his chest and a scowl firmly on his ruddy face.

"No entry," he said. It wasn't a particularly hot day and a light breeze blew, but sweat dripped down his chubby red cheeks.

"I have been summoned by Mr. Morris." I peered down my nose and spoke in my snootiest British accent.

"Let her in," Ryan called.

Richter stepped aside. I gave him a friendly smile as I slipped past him.

It was unlikely this house had been renovated since it was originally built. The entranceway was wrapped in gloom, the bulb in the single light mounted in the ceiling wasn't up to the job, and brown curtains over the narrow windows on either side of the door were firmly shut.

"Why does she keep appearing?" Estrada said.

"Mr. Morris called her instead of his lawyer," Ryan said. "Since we're only here for a friendly, informal chat, she can stay."

Estrada harrumphed. Donald gave me a sickly grin. It was early afternoon, and he was dressed in a moth-chewed brown bathrobe and tatty bedroom slippers. Strands of thin hair stood up on either side of his head as if in a failed attempt to sprout wings.

"Let's sit down, shall we?" Ryan said. "Mr. Morris?"

Donald went into the study as I knew he would. It was by far the nicest room in his house, and the only one into which he invited guests. Birch logs were laid in the large open fireplace, and a stack waited in an iron basket for the first touch of winter. The mantle was covered with brass candlesticks, a magnifying glass, several glass vials (seemingly empty), and a pipe and matches in a box, although Donald didn't smoke. A small side table held a bronze, life-sized bust of a hook-nosed man with a thin face and sharp cheekbones. A metal pipe was clenched between his lips and a bronze deerstalker hat perched on his head. The walls were covered in heavy red-and-gold paper into which had been shot a "patriotic" *VR*. I knew from my previous visit that a hammer and bolt had been used to make the initials, not guns and bullets as Sherlock Holmes had done in his rooms at 221B Baker Street. Estrada studied the pattern. She shook her head, clearly not getting the reference. I didn't bother to enlighten her.

One wall consisted of a floor-to-ceiling bookshelf. The books were either the canon, in one edition or another, scholarly works on Sherlock Holmes, or biographies of Sir Arthur

Conan Doyle. Donald's large desk was made of solid oak, circa 1960s, covered with papers and magazines and an out-of-place sleek white MacBook Pro. Also out of place was the hardcover copy of *Hudson House* resting on top of a pile of magazines in the center of the desk.

"You are not under arrest at this time, Mr. Morris," Ryan said. "But we do have a search warrant. We're authorized to search your house and property for anything to do with the production of chemicals."

"You won't . . ." His voice broke, and he cleared his throat. "You won't find anything like that here." I believed him. Donald was no actor. The relief on his face when Ryan mentioned they were searching for chemicals was palpable.

"And any other items that might be of interest in our investigation," Estrada added.

"I would help you if I could." Donald threw me a pained look. "But I don't know what you want from me."

I slipped quietly into a chair, thinking I'd try to keep myself inconspicuous.

"Now that we're all here," Estrada said, "why don't you take a seat, Mr. Morris?"

"I don't see . . ."

"Sit down, please." Estrada shoved a stack of papers aside and perched on the edge of Donald's desk. Donald balanced on the edge of a tattered chintz-covered armchair, the cheerful red pattern long ago faded to a dusty pink.

Ryan wandered casually around the room. He scanned the bookshelves, studied the decorations on the mantle, eyed the bronze head, and flicked idly through the papers on the desk.

"You practiced as a lawyer," Estrada said to Donald.

"That's right." He glanced at me again. I nodded in what I hoped was a supportive manner. Ryan appeared to be paying not the least bit of attention, but I knew he would be taking in every word that was spoken—and many that were not.

"I practiced family law for twenty years," Donald said. He relaxed fractionally and settled back into his chair. He even crossed his legs at the ankles, displaying lower legs as frail as the fallen twigs in the woods around his property. I wanted to tell him not to get too comfortable; the police had to have had something to take to a judge to be granted a warrant to search Donald's house. Estrada would get to the point, soon enough. "I was fortunate to inherit a small amount of money on the death of my father, and that combined with my savings was sufficient to allow me to retire to West London. I live simply but comfortably. I don't see why you're asking me this."

"Tell us about your education," Estrada said.

"Harvard Law."

"Impressive," she said.

Donald preened. That was a mistake. She wasn't asking idle questions. This was leading to something.

Ryan picked the copy of *Hudson House* off the desk. He opened it and read the blurb on the inside cover flap. The casual observer would have thought Estrada's questions were boring him.

"Before Harvard Law," Estrada said, "what was your degree in?"

Comprehension dawned, and Donald's eyes opened in something approaching panic. I had no idea what she was getting at, but he clearly did. "Science," he mumbled.

"Science," Estrada said. "Science covers a lot of ground, Mr. Morris. Physics, biology, astronomy. Can you be more specific?"

He said nothing.

"Let me remind you then—you have a PhD in chemistry from Yale." Estrada couldn't help throwing me a quick triumphant glance. I kept my face impassive. It wasn't easy.

Donald let out a strangled laugh. "That was so long ago, I'd almost forgotten. Pure research wasn't to my liking, so I switched to law. I found that not to be to my liking either, but a man has to work at something. Opportunities to make a living as an expert in the Sherlock Holmes canon or the life of Sir Arthur Conan Doyle are unfortunately few and far between."

I'd maintained all along that the average person wouldn't know how to obtain or use cyanide. It would appear that when it came to chemistry, Donald Morris—*Doctor* Donald Morris, *PhD*—was not an average person.

"Knowledge is one thing," I said. "Intent and production of a substance is entirely another. If that's all you have to go on . . ."

"Interesting book you have here, Mr. Morris." Ryan held up *Hudson House.*

"Plenty of copies of that book are in my shop," I said. "I've sold a lot of them. It's very popular."

"True," he said. "My niece has one. I bought it for her myself. But not everyone adds their own comments to the text."

"I was upset," Donald said. "I didn't mean it."

I got to my feet and approached the desk. I held out my hand. Ryan didn't give the book to me, but he held it out for me to see. He had it open at about the halfway mark. Dark, angry lines were drawn through a paragraph. I read enough to understand that in this scene, Sherlock and Desdemona were sharing an intimate moment. Someone, and I could guess who, had scrawled "An outrage!" in the margin. Ryan flicked the pages. More slashes, more handwritten notes. More exclamation marks. He stopped near the end. The entire page was covered in lines of black ink so deep, the page was torn in several places.

"A highly involved reader," I said weakly.

Ryan turned to the back. No slashes marked the last page. Only neat handwriting:

It's time someone put a stop to this outrage! Once and for all.

Estrada took the book from Ryan. She read the final page and then flipped forward.

The three of us looked at Donald.

"I didn't mean," he said in a low voice, "that someone should kill her. I only wanted to reason with her."

"Oh, yeah," Estrada said. "Looks perfectly reasonable to me."

"Idle threats," I said. "That means nothing."

"Your fingerprints were found on Ms. Van Markoff's bottle of water, Mr. Morris," Estrada said. "Can you explain that?"

"I—" I said.

"Yours were found too," she said. "Fortunately for you, everyone in the room saw you carrying it, and you never denied it."

"I might have touched it," Donald said. "Now I remember. It was sitting on the counter next to where I was standing, and I bumped it with my elbow. I moved it aside so I wouldn't knock it over."

"Donald Morris," Louise Estrada said, "I am arresting you for the murder of Ruth Smith, a.k.a. Renalta Van Markoff."

As she said the warning, Ryan avoided my eyes. His face was set into hard lines, and I could tell he didn't approve of what Estrada was doing, but he wasn't prepared to argue with her in front of us. I could do nothing but stand by and listen. When she finished, Ryan said, "Time to bring in the boys and girls in the white suits. Tell them we're interested in traces of chemicals and evidence of threats made to the dead woman."

"And as this is now an official arrest," Estrada said, "your presence, Ms. Doyle, is no longer required nor permitted. Get out."

*　　*　　*

Estrada ordered Richter to ensure that I left the property. Under his watchful eye, I marched down the driveway, head high, steps firm, and turned into the street. I then sneaked into a patch of overgrown shrubbery and crept back. I didn't have long to wait until they came out of the house. Estrada and Ryan had Donald Morris between them. He'd been allowed to change and was wearing faded blue track pants and a loose T-shirt with "The Game's Afoot" printed across the chest. I wished he'd taken the time to find something more appropriate to be arrested in. His head was down, his face was pale, and his hands were cuffed behind his back. He was loaded into the back of a cruiser for the drive into town. As I'd been rushed out the door of his study, I'd shouted over my shoulder to Donald to call a lawyer.

I hid behind a bush and watched the cruiser drive away. Estrada went with Donald, but Ryan stayed behind to give instructions to the forensics people.

I crept forward, keeping myself hidden in the thick overgrown bushes, giving thanks to Donald's lack of gardening skills. The woman Ryan was talking to said, "You got it, Detective," and walked away, leaving him momentarily alone. He sighed heavily and rubbed at his chin.

"Pssst."

He whirled around. "Oh, for heaven's sake. I should have known. Can't you ever do what you're told?"

"No, I can't." I pulled a twig out of my hair. I made no move to leave my place of concealment. I didn't want officers reporting to Estrada that I'd hung around. Although it wouldn't do Ryan's reputation any good if he was observed engaging in conversation with an untrimmed shrub. "This is meaningless. The man scribbled in a book. You should be calling the library police, not arresting him yourself."

"He scribbled threats in a book, Gemma, and that gives us a pretty good window into his mind. Who knows what else we'll find in that ridiculous Sherlock-imitation library of his when we give it a good going-over. The degree in chemistry isn't incidental, not to mention that his fingerprints were found on the bottle."

"No one has ever claimed that the bottle was kept secured," I said. "It was on the counter, in plain sight of everyone in the store, for almost half an hour. His story of moving it out of his way is perfectly reasonable. You found other prints on the bottle, didn't you? Mine and . . ."

He didn't finish my sentence. I have to admit that it had been a clumsy attempt to get him to tell me what they'd found.

"I know Donald," I said. "He's passionate about Sherlock Holmes, and I'll agree that he takes it a mite over the top on occasion, but he isn't a killer."

"I'll continue to keep other avenues of inquiry open."

"Did Estrada give you my tip about Nancy Brownmiller, who's now thinking she's going to be able to take Renalta's place at her public appearances?"

"She did. I spoke to Ms. Brownmiller."

"What did she have to say for herself?"

"That she didn't kill Ruth Smith or anyone else. That she loved and admired the woman so much, she's devastated at her death. I told her she could go home but that I might have further questions later. She said she's waiting for you to bring her some comic book."

"Coloring book."

"Whatever."

"And then there's Paige Bookman, who accused Renalta of stealing her ideas. Not to mention . . ."

"Gemma," Ryan said firmly, "stay out of this." He walked away.

I dragged myself back to the Emporium. I tried calling Ashleigh to ask if she could come in for the rest of the day, but it went straight to voice mail. No doubt she was enjoying a pleasant day at the beach.

I called Linda again, and this time she answered her phone herself. "Did you hear the news, Gemma? Detective Estrada phoned me to say they've arrested someone for my mother's murder. It's that crazy man. The one in the Sherlock Holmes getup who yelled at her at the signing."

"I heard. They have to build a case though, and I don't think that will be easy. Do you have time to meet for a drink later? My shop closes at six tonight, so I could come to your hotel. Say six thirty?"

"That would be lovely, thanks. I just want to go home, but the police still won't tell me when I can have my mother's . . . body." She swallowed. "I have things to arrange. So many legal details to sort out."

"Is Kevin staying here with you?"

"Of course. He's being so supportive."

Between now and half six, I'd try to think of a way of oh-so-casually asking whose name is on the royalty checks for the Hudson and Holmes books. Linda, the author, or Ruth Smith, the pretend author. Those checks would be substantial. And where there is money, there is motive for murder.

Ryan had assured me he'd continue investigating other possible suspects, but I feared that, even if he wanted to follow my advice, he'd be told to concentrate on building a case against Donald. Ryan had been reluctant to place Donald under arrest. I don't know if that was because he didn't like charging someone he knew or if he had his doubts, although Estrada had seemed convinced they had the right person. Renalta Van Markoff was a celebrity of sorts, and her murder had made the national papers. No doubt some political pressure had been put on the detectives to get the case solved, and fast. Ryan didn't care about political pressure, but Estrada might.

"I'll meet you in the bar," Linda said. "Six thirty."

A few minutes later, Jayne's head popped into the Emporium. "The police arrested Donald. I can't believe it."

"How do you know?"

"Jocelyn heard it from her sister, whose best friend is dating one of the cops."

"Not exactly a reliable source, but in this instance, the gossip is correct. It only happened half an hour ago."

"It's all over town already. Do you think he did it, Gemma?"

"No, I don't. The evidence, from what I've seen, is flimsy. So flimsy, I suspect he'll be granted bail. I'm meeting Linda for a drink tonight after the Emporium closes."

"Are those details related?"

"Donald and Linda? Yes. If Donald didn't kill Renalta, someone else did. I don't know enough about Renalta and her relationships to form any conclusions about other suspects. I'm hoping to learn more."

"I'd love to come with you, but I'm seeing Robbie later." Jayne wiggled her fingers at me and drifted back into the tea room.

*   *   *

My plan to subtly interrogate Linda as to the financial relationships she had with her mother came to naught.

She was seated in the bar when I arrived. Kevin, I was not happy to see, was with her. He gave me a smug grin as he stood up to greet me. I smiled, took a seat, and ordered a glass of wine.

Every time I tried to approach the topic of the owner of the copyright of the books, Kevin steered me away. Finally, tired of beating about the bush, I said, "Do you think you'll continue working for Linda now, Kevin? If she doesn't keep up the busy speaking schedule Renalta did, she might not need a personal publicist."

They smiled at each other. Kevin picked up one of Linda's hands and kissed it. She said, "We're going to take things slowly." She'd changed ever so subtly since I'd first seen her. A bit of blush on her cheeks, a touch of light-pink lipstick on her lips, her hair loosened and brushed to a shine. Her clothes were of the same type as previous, brown pumps, pantyhose, knee-length brown skirt, white blouse, but the top button was unfastened, and a small gold-and-diamond necklace shone at her throat. Even her voice was different. It had deepened slightly, and her speech wasn't broken by so many ums and ahs.

"Linda has a lot of decisions to make," Kevin said. "I intend to be by her side to help her make them."

They continued smiling at each other.

Alrighty then.

Kevin finished his beer and waved to the waiter for the check. "We'd love to have dinner with you, Gemma, but we've got plans already. A boring business meeting. How's that for good timing? Here he comes now."

Robert McNamara hurried into the bar. He spotted us and headed over. "Great idea, folks. I could use a drink right about now." He plopped himself down. "I'll have a beer," he said to the waiter.

"Sir?" the waiter asked Kevin.

"Might as well," he said. "Another round for us too."

"Not for me, thanks," I said.

"Detective Estrada called me this morning," Robert said. "She had some questions about Renalta. If we, as her publishers, had ever received any threats directed at her, that sort of thing. I told her we got the occasional crank complaining about her books. Like that guy at the bookstore Saturday, dressed up like Sherlock Holmes and prepared to take Renalta on." He let out a bark of a laugh. "That never ends well. Not for them. Renalta loved nothing more than being challenged by that bunch."

The waiter put the drinks in front of us.

Robert picked up his glass. "To Renalta."

We drank.

"That crank," Kevin said, "was arrested for the murder this afternoon."

Robert's eyes widened. "Is that so? Glad to hear it. Now you can get on with your life, Linda. Detective Estrada told me you're Renalta's daughter, is that right?"

Linda dipped her head, and a loose lock of hair fell over her eyes.

"Can't say I was surprised." He reached across the low table and patted her hand. "Anyone could tell how devoted you were to her. And she to you, of course."

I glanced at Linda. She pulled her hand away and picked up her wineglass. "Devoted" was not the word I would have chosen. For neither mother nor daughter.

"Keep it in the family is what I always say. My dad started McNamara and Gibbons Press, and we worked well together for years. When he passed, I was able to slip easily and comfortably into the saddle." Robert cleared his throat. "I still can't believe she didn't use Dropbox."

"What's Dropbox?" Kevin asked.

"Cloud storage," Linda said. "A way of sharing documents between computers or backing up files off-site."

"Renalta didn't use it or anything else, it seems," Robert said.

"Why is that a problem?" I asked.

"Robert wants to see the latest manuscript," Linda said. "And he wants to see it now."

"Of course I do." He threw up his hands. "We have to see if it's viable. She told me the new book's almost finished, but who knows how much work still has to be put into it to make it publishable. If she used cloud storage, Linda could give me her password and I'd have my people pull it up."

"It's viable," Linda said. "I told you. I've seen it. Only the last couple of scenes need to be written and then given a light polish."

"Didn't she have a computer with her?" Robert asked. "In case she felt the urge to write or something?"

Linda stared at her hands, folded neatly on the table in front of her. "Miss Van Markoff never wrote when she was touring. She claimed she needed all her energy for meeting her fans." That was true enough: Ruth Smith never wrote when she was touring as Renalta Van Markoff. She never wrote at any time. Linda wasn't lying, but she was dissembling, and she appeared to be comfortable doing so. Very interesting.

Linda had told me she liked to write at night. In that case, it was highly possible, probable even, that she'd brought the manuscript with her to work on. I studied her face. It showed not a hint of deception, but that might not be significant: she and her mother had been playing this game for years. It would be second nature to her by now.

"Look, Linda," Robert said in a soothing, father-knows-best tone, "I know all this must be very difficult for you, but I need you to understand my position. The sooner I can get the manuscript to a ghostwriter, the sooner we can release the book. I promise you, no expense will be spared. I'll get the very best people working on it. It will be a tribute to Renalta. It's what she would have wanted."

"Linda told you . . ." Kevin said.

"I can speak for myself, Kevin, thank you." Linda sat up straight in her chair. "I am not leaving until I can take Renalta . . . my mother . . . with me, Robert. And that's final. You will have to wait."

"Okay, so we don't have the manuscript here. That shouldn't be a problem. Give me the keys to her apartment and the password for her computer, and I'll send someone to get it."

"No," Linda said. "I told you already that's not going to happen. I won't have strangers poking through her files until I have had time to sort them out."

"Then I'll go," Robert said. "I'm no stranger. She and I had a long, close working relationship. We were as much friends as colleagues. Or you can send the Boy Wonder here."

"I won't leave Linda alone at this difficult time," Kevin said.

Robert held his hands out. "Look, all I'm asking is for you to see where I'm coming from. It's in all our interests that I get ahold of that manuscript as soon as I can." He smiled at Linda.

She did not smile back. For the first time, I saw a touch of steel in her spine. "You can't have it now. And that's final. Whether or not I have access to it at the moment is irrelevant, because I don't intend to hand it over to you unfinished. I will work on it myself."

"Be reasonable, Linda. You might be Renalta's daughter, but you're only the PA, remember. Leave the business decisions to me."

"I don't work for you, Robert, and I never have. I work for . . . with . . . my mother."

"Which is kinda the point here," he said. "As your mother is no longer—"

"Enough," Kevin said. "This is all very upsetting to Linda."

She didn't look upset in the least to me. She looked like a woman prepared to do battle and confident that she would win. She sipped her wine.

Quite a transformation from the nervous, twitchy woman who'd come into my shop for the first time only four days ago. Ruth had cast a long, deep shadow over her daughter; it had now been removed. I wondered if Linda even knew how much she'd changed so quickly.

Robert took a long drink of his beer, and then he put his glass down with careful deliberation. "Okay, I get it. You want a little something to help you get things sorted out. I'm prepared to chip in to help with your expenses. We won't even take it off the advance for the new book or royalties for the others. I assume you're your mother's heir. Perhaps we can talk about upping the advance this time around." His words were clipped. He was trying hard to keep a lid on his annoyance. "Once I have the manuscript, that is."

"I'll have to think about it," she said.

"There is nothing to think about," Robert said. "Help me here, Kevin. We're all in the same boat here. We want to get that manuscript finished as quickly and as professionally as possible. If you don't hand it over, Linda, I might have to reconsider my options. I can decide not to publish it, you know."

I don't know how I expected Linda to react, but leaning back in her chair with a roar of laughter wasn't it. "Don't be ridiculous. The only thing keeping McNamara and Gibbons afloat is the Hudson and Holmes books. According to the terms of my mother's will, I am not only her heir but also her literary executor. That means I am empowered to make all the decisions around the books. You'll have it when—and if—I'm ready to hand it over. Not before." The small diamond at her throat caught the light as she moved.

"Speaking as your publicist," Kevin said, "not to mention your friend, Linda, you do not want to get into a contract war. Neither of you do."

Robert glared at Linda. She gave him a soft smile. With considerable effort, he forced his expression into a smile in return. "You're so right, Kev. We all want the same thing here—to do the very best we can to honor Renalta's memory." He turned to me. "I hope we haven't bored you too much, Gemma. Just another day in the publishing world."

"Not bored in the least," I said.

Robert waved for the waiter. "Now let's forget about it and get some dinner, why don't we? More boring business, Gemma. You won't find it at all interesting."

I was about to reply that I expected to find it very interesting when Linda stood up. "Oh, I'm sorry, Robert. Didn't I say? Kevin and I want to have some private time tonight. I'll be in touch." She walked away. Kevin scurried to follow.

*　　*　　*

I'd considered going to the chief of police's press conference (if they'd even let me in) but decided my time would be better spent talking to Linda. And it had been. I found the conversation (more of a verbal battle) between her and Robert highly interesting. Not so much in what was said but in the way Linda handled herself. Smooth and calm and confident. She'd been released from her mother's shadow like a butterfly coming out of the cocoon. I wondered when she was planning to tell him that she was the real author of the books. That would make him a happy man indeed.

Irene called me as I was putting together something to eat. I'm not much of a cook, but in New England in the summer, anyone can throw together a quick, delicious, and highly nutritious meal with little effort. I put the phone on speaker and talked while I cooked. I threw a seasoned chicken breast onto the Foreman grill and tossed together everything I'd bought at the market on Monday: lettuce, beans, peas, spring onions. When the chicken was cooked, I chopped it into chunks, added it to the bowl of greens, and stirred in a vinaigrette dressing.

The press conference, Irene told me, had been so well attended, not everyone could fit into the media room at the West London police station, so the chief gave his statement outside on the steps. "He looked very natty with a fresh shave and new haircut. He must have been up all night ironing his uniform."

"Or his wife was," I said.

Irene laughed. "All the trouble he went to was worth it. There were a lot of out-of-state newspapers and even a TV station from Boston. Renalta Van Markoff was a dramatic figure. Suitable, I guess, that her death was dramatic also."

"What did you learn?"

The autopsy, Irene told me, confirmed that Renalta Van Markoff had been poisoned by cyanide contained in her water bottle. Donald Morris, resident of West London, had been arrested and charged with her murder.

"Do you think he did it, Gemma?" she asked.

"No."

"The chief did say they were pursuing other avenues of inquiry."

"I hope so. It's easy for them to become fixated on one suspect, to the exclusion of others. Did he say anything about fingerprints on the water bottle?"

"I asked that question. The bottle appears to have been wiped down, but they were able to get some prints off it. The water in the second bottle was not tampered with. Louise Estrada was there, looking highly pleased with herself. I didn't see Ryan. What's that banging noise?"

"I'm cooking."

"I didn't know you could cook."

I stirred the contents of the big bowl in front of me. "Anyone can prepare a simple and delicious meal, Irene. You should try it sometime."

She laughed. "That's what restaurants are for. I learned to cook from my mother. She always said what she made best in the kitchen was reservations."

"Thanks for this."

"Any time, Gemma. Any time."

I ate my dinner, washed up the dishes, and yelled, "Walk!" to Violet. She leapt to her feet and ran into the mudroom. I took the leash off the hook, fastened it to her collar, and we set off. While she sniffed under bushes and followed trails only she could see, I thought about the case. I didn't see what more I could do. I'd identified Nancy and Paige to the police as people with strong motives. I'd tried to find out what I could about the financial affairs of the bestselling books but had run smack into a dead end. Grant had said he'd keep his ears to the ground and let me know if he heard about anyone selling a signed-on-the-day-of-her-death Van Markoff for an excessive amount of money, but nothing so far.

I had one thing in my favor in this case: the range of suspects was fixed. Only someone who had quick access to the water bottle would have been able to add the cyanide without anyone noticing. Ashleigh had bought the water and broken the seals, but I could see absolutely no reason for her to kill Renalta. After the unfortunate circumstances with my last employee, I'd checked Ashleigh's references very, very carefully. She was precisely what she'd told me she was: a young woman from Nebraska seeking a change in her life.

Ashleigh had bought the water, broken the seals, put two on the speaker's podium and two on the counter where they'd been left unattended and unwatched for a short period of time.

That left me (and I knew I hadn't killed Renalta), Grant, Paige, Nancy, Linda, Kevin, Robert, Irene, and Donald as the only possible culprits.

I dismissed Irene, as she, like Ashleigh, had no reason to kill the author. I shouldn't dismiss Grant because I liked him and because I knew he liked me, but I did on the grounds that a signed Van Markoff wasn't worth killing over.

I didn't know what else I could do. I needed financial information, but I was not with the police. I had no way of finding it, save hacking into the bank's computers. I could try that, if I had to, but I didn't even know which bank handled the Van Markoff affairs.

My phone rang. Donald Morris, said the display, and I was glad to see it. "Donald, where are you?"

"I'm at home, Gemma. I was granted bail."

"Thank goodness. You found a good lawyer?"

"I hated every minute I spent practicing law, and I was glad to leave it all behind me. Fortunately, I kept in touch with a few colleagues who also have an interest in the Great Detective, and I was able to engage the services of Margaret Hastings."

"Should I know who that is?"

"You remember the case two years ago of that major league baseball player who killed his wife's female lover when he caught them *in flagrante delicto?*"

"I certainly do remember. It was a news sensation. He got off scot-free. A lot of people were outraged at the verdict. I was one of them. Wasn't his barrister named Hastings?"

"My old friend and law school classmate Margaret. I was able to do Margaret a small favor a year ago and put her in the way of a pristine first-edition *The Valley of Fear* signed by Sir Arthur himself before it was put up for auction. Sadly, the cost of the volume was far beyond my limited means."

"Margaret returned the favor today and got you bail."

"She dispatched an underling, but the very mention of her name was enough to have the judge quaking in his boots. I'm home now. I am under orders not to leave the town limits of West London, and I have no intention of doing so. How is your investigation coming, my dear? Can I be confident that an arrest—of the true killer, that is— is expected shortly?"

"Uh," I said.

"Glad to hear it. By the way, Detective Estrada came to my bail hearing. She was forced to admit that the presence of my fingerprints on the bottle is evidence of nothing, as the bottle was in a public place and surrounded by people. I have to warn you that she is not happy. She managed to corner me outside the courtroom and told me to tell you that if she finds you meddling, she'll arrest you for interference."

"Let her try," I said with more confidence than I felt. "I'm doing my duty as a concerned member of the public."

"I'm glad you're on my side, Gemma."

"Good night, Donald."

"Good night."

"Oh, joy," I said to Violet. "Estrada's been humiliated in court, and now she's on the warpath against me. How do I get myself involved in these things?"

Violet did not have an answer.

Chapter 11

The West London Police Department pays its employees through the Regional Bank of New England. I gained that tidbit of knowledge when Ryan and I were together. Thus I was surprised on Wednesday afternoon to see Louise Estrada going into the West London offices of the First Bank of New York shortly before the branch's three o'clock closing.

I was outside the Emporium deadheading flowers, watering plants, and watching the traffic pass by. Across the street, next to the bank, Maureen peered through the windows of Beach Fine Arts, no doubt hoping to catch me in an infraction of the bylaws. I waved cheerfully, and her face disappeared from the window.

There is, of course, absolutely no reason Detective Louise Estrada might not have personal affairs to conduct at First Bank.

I took the basket of dead blooms and the watering can inside the bookshop. "I'm going out for a couple of minutes," I called to Ashleigh.

"Have you considered my idea?" She'd come to work today in a Mrs. Hudson's Tea Room uniform: a stiff white apron with the Mrs. Hudson's logo worn over a plain black dress and black tights, flat shoes, and hair tied back into a tight bun.

"No," I said.

"Franchising is the big thing these days, Gemma. I'm thinking a branch of the Emporium in Boston for sure—they love history in Boston—then maybe another in . . ." First thing upon arrival at work today, Ashleigh had verbally presented me with the beginning of her business plan. That I had not asked her to draw up a business plan for me seemed to be of no consequence to her.

I had to wait a few minutes before crossing as a long line of motorbikes were coming down Baker Street, engines roaring. Most of the drivers, male and female, were showing a lot of gray hair beneath their helmets and bandannas. A few drove those three-wheeled bikes that remind me of tricycles. But some of the drivers were stone faced and hard eyed in leather jackets bristling with patches, and they revved their powerful machines to scream at pedestrians to get out of the way. A big classic rock concert was scheduled to be held in the town park tonight, featuring a variety of cover bands. Gray-haired groupies and excessively tattooed bikers had been pouring into town all day.

Once they'd passed, I dashed across the street. The First Bank of New York occupies a stately old building, a West London original. Painted a fresh, gleaming white, with four Greek-style pillars and a wide staircase, it looks every inch a place of business. The bank sits between Beach Fine Arts and Fun and Frolic, a woman's casual clothing shop. I stood at the store window studying the display. A sleeveless, calf-length summer dress in various shades of blue would suit me, I thought. Or maybe the red-and-white-striped T-shirt and capris with red stitching on the pockets.

I had examined every inch of the clothes, studied the jewelry, and was onto an analysis of the cleaning streaks on the windows when Louise Estrada emerged from the bank. A portly man wearing a midrange suit about ten years out of fashion opened the door for her. She paused on the top of the steps to send a quick text and put her sunglasses on, giving me time to head her way. I timed it so I arrived at the bottom of the steps at exactly the moment she stepped onto the sidewalk.

"Good afternoon, Detective," I said.

"What are you doing here?" she said in her usual friendly manner.

"I work here." I pointed. "Across the street. I thought Fun and Frolic might have some things on sale so came to have a look. They have nice clothes, don't they? Do you ever shop there?"

"No."

She was wearing her habitual black jeans, black shirt, and black leather jacket. She studied me through opaque sunglasses.

"Do you bank here?" I asked. "Are they any good? I've had a few problems with my business accounts, and I'm thinking of changing banks."

"This wasn't a personal call. I'm working."

"Is that so? Any developments on the Van Markoff case?"

She glanced to one side. "Nothing you need to know, Gemma."

"It occurred to me," I said, "that Ruth Smith's bank accounts might need looking into. I'm a bookseller, remember, and I know the kind of numbers her books sell. In the hundreds of thousands of copies. That means they earned a lot of money. It would be worth knowing what financial arrangements she had with her daughter and who stands to inherit."

As I spoke, Estrada's eyes twitched. She rested her left hand on her hip, over her jacket pocket. She was right handed. If she'd gone for her right side, I might have suspected she was considering pulling out her handcuffs and arresting me. I smiled at her.

"As pleasant as this chat is, Gemma, I have to go."

A car pulled up to the curb beside us, Ryan Ashburton driving. Estrada jumped into the passenger seat. Ryan gave me a long look before he pulled away.

I waved after them.

As I waited for another convoy of motorbikes to pass, my phone rang: Donald.

"Good afternoon, Donald."

He didn't bother exchanging greetings. "Estrada has been here," he said. "To my home! Again!"

"As you are phoning me, I assume you weren't rearrested. What did she want?"

"I've been betrayed."

"What does that even mean? Calm down and just tell me what she had to say."

Deep, calming breaths came over the phone line. "Okay, I'm calm," he squeaked. "One of my colleagues in the Baker Street Irregulars—Estrada wouldn't give me a name—contacted the WLPD to say that I had made a threat against Renalta Van Markoff."

"What sort of threat? And did you make it?"

"I . . . uh . . . might have. On Friday evening, I participated in a conference call with various members of the Irregulars. The conversation was about *A Scandal in Bohemia*. Specifically, if Conan Doyle, through Holmes, was making a comment about the corrupting power of—"

"Never mind the plot of the story, Donald. What did you say about Renalta?"

"That I had . . . uh . . . skimmed through her latest tome and found it a disgrace to the memory of Sir Arthur and that . . . uh . . . someone might have to . . . uh . . ."

"Someone might have to what, Donald?"

"Assume the role of Professor Moriarty."

"Oh, for heaven's sake, Donald. I find that almost impossible to believe!"

"I'm glad you agree with me, Gemma. That one of my colleagues would repeat a private conversation to the police is . . ."

I meant, of course, that he'd care so much about Renalta and her books. But he did, so there was no point now in berating him about it. "Keep me posted if there are any new developments."

"Good-bye," he said.

I hung up and studied my phone. A vague threat such as that one on its own wouldn't have much value as evidence. But combined with the case the police were building against Donald, this didn't sound good.

Before going into the shop, I made a quick call.

"Come to my house at ten tonight."

"Why?"

"Because I need you to."

"Are you going to give me a hint?"

"No. Wear black."

Jayne groaned. "I don't like the sound of that."

"And come alone," I said.

* * *

Back in the shop, I found Nancy Brownmiller waiting for me. She was dressed, I was pleased to see, like a normal person today, not a cheap imitation of her favorite author.

She dropped the book she was flipping through onto the table. "You never came to my hotel, Gemma, so I thought I'd pop in and pick it up myself. I'd like to stay in town longer to be close to the police investigation into the murder, but the prices at that hotel are going up, and I just can't afford it anymore. I'll take it with me."

"Take what with you?"

"You can give it to me now."

Confused, I looked at Ashleigh. She shrugged. "Give what to you?" I said.

"The coloring book, of course. You were going to bring it around to my hotel on Monday evening. The police called me while I was waiting. I was so excited about being interviewed about Renalta's death that I forgot all about meeting you. I wrote it up on the Facebook page. I see you joined our group. That's great. You can let us know as soon as you have word about Renalta's next book. Everyone says there's another one out there."

"Oh, right. The coloring book."

"Five hundred dollars seems a bit steep, don't you think? I can pay you one hundred."

"I'm sorry, Nancy, but . . ."

"Okay, a hundred and fifty. That's all I can afford."

"I don't have it."

"Two hundred then."

I sighed. "You aren't listening to me, Nancy. I don't have it anymore. Sorry. My . . . uh . . . my assistant didn't realize it had been signed by Renalta and gave it away as damaged goods."

"What!" Nancy whirled around. Ashleigh's eyes opened wide.

"Not her," I added quickly. "My other assistant. The not-any-good one. I've been thinking of firing her . . . uh . . . him."

"What's the name of the buyer? I can get it back."

"He didn't get it. They paid cash."

Nancy's face crumpled. "I so much wanted to own it."

"Sorry," I said again, but I didn't mean it. I was doing poor Nancy a favor. If she couldn't afford another night at the West London Hotel, she shouldn't be offering two hundred dollars for a scribbled-on coloring book. Even if such a thing existed. I wondered how high she'd have gone with the bidding if I'd encouraged her.

"If you find it or anything else Renalta might have touched, you'll let me know, right?"

"Sure," I said. I didn't bother to ask for her contact details.

*   *   *

Jayne arrived at my house promptly at ten. She knocked on the mudroom door, and I let her in. As instructed, she was dressed all in black. Short black skirt, black leggings, black T-shirt. The black stilettos, however, were not exactly what I had in mind.

I had on trainers, dark jeans, a black T-shirt, and a black cardigan far too heavy for the weather but full of pockets.

I went into the kitchen and began filling those pockets.

"I don't like the look of this," Jayne said. "What are those?"

"Lockpicks." Into my pockets they went, along with a miner's light and a tiny digital camera. My larger camera was still with the police, but I needed the small one tonight anyway.

"I don't want to know why you own a set of lockpicks."

"They belong to Uncle Arthur."

"That I want to know even less. Why the camera?"

"In case of the need to take pictures of the documents I'm after. I don't want traces of them to be found if my phone is confiscated and searched."

Jayne sat down. "I'm not going anywhere until you tell me what's going on here."

"I need to know who gets the checks for the Van Markoff books, Ruth or Linda."

"Why?"

"It can be motive for the murder, but only if Ruth had the money. If it went directly to Linda, then there would be no point in killing Ruth."

"Suppose the killer didn't know Linda's the author of the books and thus assumed Ruth is the one who gets paid for them?"

"Then we have an entirely different set of circumstances. I don't know how all this ties together, Jayne. But I'm missing a vital piece of information, and I can't act without it."

"Gemma, I will not help you break into a bank."

"You'll be relieved to know we're not going anywhere near a bank."

"Thank heavens."

"The information we need is in the police station."

"What?" Jayne's screech so startled Violet, the dog lifted her head and howled.

"Estrada visited First Bank this afternoon. I spoke to her when she left, and she admitted she was there on police business. Clearly they were discussing Van Markoff's financial affairs. Mr. Jefferson, the bank manager, walked her to the door."

"The police deal with more than one case at a time, Gemma. It might have been something entirely different."

"It might, except for the tell when I asked her about Van Markoff. She has this way of shifting her eyes to one side when I'm getting close. I've been in the police station before, and I know the layout of the detectives' office. I'm acting on the assumption that Estrada put the statements in her desk drawer. If it's locked, I should be able to pick it."

"She might have put it into the evidence locker."

"I'd be reluctant to break into that, I have to admit. I wouldn't want to compromise any other ongoing investigations. No, I'm pretty sure she'll have put it in her drawer. It isn't original evidence so doesn't have to be protected."

"Gemma, at long last you've gone completely nuts. So she went into the bank and spoke to the bank manager. He would have shown her a page on his computer and e-mailed her a copy."

"As we talked, she instinctively touched her jacket pocket as if checking that the information I'm interested in was still there, safe and secure. Another distinctive tell."

"Have you forgotten that police officers have been known to hang around the police station, even at night? We'll be caught."

"Don't you remember what's happening tonight?"

"What's happening tonight?"

"That classic rock concert at the park. They're expecting thousands of people to attend. This isn't the symphony or a visit by the Metropolitan Opera. Some classic rock fans can be, shall we say, boisterous. I saw a pack of motorbikes heading into town this afternoon. The concert ends at eleven, I checked, and I'm confident West London's finest will be out in full force to ensure the audience disperses calmly and peacefully."

"Gemma, I am not breaking into the police station."

"You don't have to. I need you to stand watch while I do." Jayne threw up her hands.

It wasn't as farfetched a plan as Jayne seemed to think. I'd spent some time in the police station and knew the layout. The detectives' office is at the back of the building, on the ground floor. The rear of the police station backs up against a tiny park and is not visible from the street. A window, conveniently located next to a nicely trimmed hedge, opens onto the corridor next to the office. The window is small, only wide enough to admit a nine-and-a-half-stone woman with good dexterity. Admittedly, I'd last noticed the window a couple of years ago, and it might have been alarmed since. But the cops rarely considered that someone might want to break *into* the police station. I'd checked the weather report earlier, and it was expected to be cloudy all night. That plus police attention on the concert should ensure I could get in and, more importantly, out undetected.

If I was found creeping about the police station in the dead of night with a flashlight, a camera, and a set of lock-picks, I'd have some fast explaining to do.

"You're certifiable," Jayne said.

"Are you coming with me?"

"Someone has to watch your back. Might as well be me."

"Put your phone on vibrate and let's go." I gave her a smile of encouragement, and we headed out. Violet wanted to come, but I didn't think her watchdog skills were up to tonight's task. "Guard the house," I told her.

I'd asked Jayne to drive to my house tonight. In case I needed to make a quick getaway, we'd take her car. The Miata is far too conspicuous.

I got into the passenger seat. Jayne turned the engine on, switched on the headlights, and threw the car into gear. She glanced over her shoulder to check behind her and shouted, "Whoa!" The brakes slammed with such force I almost hit the windscreen.

"What's going on?" I said.

"A car's parked behind us."

At that moment, headlights from another vehicle lit up the interior of our car. I threw open the door and jumped out. I couldn't see anything. I lifted my hand to my eyes in an attempt to block the strong lights.

A large black shape got out of the car blocking us. "Bit late to be heading out for a night on the town, isn't it?" Ryan Ashburton said.

*   *   *

I plunked the teapot in the center of the table. I didn't need tea, but preparing it gave me something to do with my hands. As well as time to organize my thoughts.

Ryan had moved his car out of my driveway, and Jayne fled into the night without giving us so much as a good-bye.

We'd watched the red glow of Jayne's rear lights disappear down the hill, and once they'd gone, Ryan walked to the back door of my house. He stood there, not saying a word, while I unlocked it. He was greeted by Violet, overjoyed to have a late-night visitor. After giving the dog a few moments of attention, Ryan sat at the kitchen table while I fussed with the tea things.

"Empty your pockets," he said.

"No."

"Gemma, I'm not playing games here. Empty your pockets."

I placed my mobile phone on the table, followed by the tiny camera, the flashlight, and lastly the lockpicks. He put the picks into his own pocket. "I won't ask where you got these."

"Tea?" I asked.

"Gemma, I can't imagine what you thought you were going to accomplish. I can only assume you had some half-baked idea of searching Louise's desk."

"My ideas are never half-baked. I won't say you're right, but what makes you come to that conclusion?"

"Louise went to the bank this afternoon with a warrant for Ruth Smith's and Linda Marke's accounts. Coming out, she just happened to run into you. She told me you were asking questions about what she'd learned. Most of the account information was sent to us electronically, but she was given a summary on paper. I assumed you knew that and wanted to see the paper. I couldn't imagine that even you would consider breaking into the police station, but I thought it might be wise to keep an eye on you. I was parked around the corner when Jayne drove up, dressed like an adult-movie interpretation of a second-story woman. You're not a whole lot better, I might add. Aren't you hot in that sweater?"

I sat down and poured the tea. After taking off my cardigan. "Linda Marke is Ruth Smith's daughter."

"I know that. You told me yourself, and she confirmed it."

"She is the author of the books. Ruth didn't write a word, she just played the part in public."

He leaned back in his chair. "Okay, I'll grant you one point. That's news to me."

"I consider it relevant to our investigation . . ."

"Our investigation?"

"As to who was aware of the situation, the state of the women's finances might tell us who knew and who did not."

He studied my face for a very long time. Violet rested her chin on his leg, and he idly scratched the top of her head. Then he let out a long breath. "Okay, Gemma. You'd be a valuable asset to the police, but neither my chief nor my partner agrees with me. It doesn't endear you to Louise that you openly mock her."

"Then she shouldn't be mockable."

"My point exactly. Try to be nice, please."

I gave him my sweetest smile.

"Louise is a good, competent detective. She's new, and she rushes into things sometimes. She takes stuff on face value more than I would like. She jumps to conclusions and then has trouble backing down. All that will change with time and experience. It doesn't help when you goad her. The case against Donald is so flimsy, he should never have been arrested."

"Proven by how quickly he got bail."

"Exactly. I wasn't going to contradict Louise's decision to arrest him in front of you and Donald. That's not to say he's in the clear. Even in my mind. We found no trace of any chemicals or any sort of lab in his house. Which doesn't mean he didn't get, or make, the cyanide elsewhere. He has it all, Gemma. Means, motive, and opportunity."

"In that case, why do you think there isn't much of a case to be made against him?"

Ryan held out his hand and pressed the index finger down. "Means. He has the knowledge to make the poison, but we have no evidence of him having done so." Next finger. "Motive. I admit I'm no Sherlockian, and I've thought Donald and his cronies take it too far sometimes, but even so, I can't see an argument over the plotline of a book being a motive for murder for anyone in their right mind. And Donald is, except for the Sherlock stuff, in his right mind." Ring finger. "Opportunity. Plenty of people were near that bottle. Including you."

"Including me. What did the fingerprint analysis show?"

"The unused bottle clearly showed Ashleigh's fingerprints on top of several unidentifiable ones, which we can assume came from it being handled prior to her purchasing it. But the bottle Renalta drank out of, the one that killed her, had been wiped down. In this weather, anyone wearing gloves would have stood out like a sore thumb, pardon the pun, so whoever did it had to use a handkerchief, the edge of their shirt, or something similar. Your prints are clear, indicating that you picked up the bottle after it was tampered with. Same with Renalta. Other than that, we did find a couple of smudged partials. Donald Morris's is one. Ashleigh's is another."

"We know Ashleigh bought the bottles and broke the seal. Only one bottle was poisoned?"

"That appears to be the case," he said. "The unused bottle contained nothing it shouldn't."

"Any sign of the container that was used to carry the poison?"

"No. We searched your shop thoroughly but came up with nothing. It would have been small, so I can assume the killer simply walked out with it in their purse or pocket. We didn't search everyone."

"Whoever it was must have had nerves of steel."

"Yup. Let's hope that self-control shatters before too much longer."

"Are you going to tell me what you learned at the bank?" I asked.

"As it would appear you are prepared to go to great lengths to find out, I guess I have to. You didn't hear it from me, Gemma."

"Understood." Ryan had gotten into trouble before for listening to me about an investigation. It meant a lot to him—and to me—that he was sharing information with me now.

"She was making a heck of a lot of money from those books. Twice a year she got a direct deposit from McNamara and Gibbons Press. Don't writers use agents?"

"Most do, but Renalta didn't have an agent when she was first published so they decided to keep it that way. Linda had worked for a literary agency at one time, so she supervised their contracts."

"The account was in the name of Ruth Smith. Not Linda."

I cradled my teacup. "Meaning that even the publisher doesn't know who wrote the books." Also meaning that Linda might have negotiated the contracts, but she didn't receive the income as is the standard arrangement between publishers, agents, and authors.

"So it would seem," Ryan said.

I'd been present when Robert McNamara had argued with Linda about him getting his hands on the new manuscript. At the time, I hadn't thought he was pretending not to know the author's identity, but it was a possibility. Now that detail was confirmed. "Did Renalta—I mean, Ruth—pay Linda a salary?"

"Every two weeks, money was transferred from Ruth's account to Linda's. The sum was slightly more than what you'd expect a successful author to pay her personal assistant but nowhere near what the books were earning. Ruth also paid the mortgage on Linda's apartment and her car payments."

"Have you seen Renalta's will?"

"Everything went to her only daughter."

And that, I thought, opened a whole world of possibilities.

Chapter 12

Linda Marke zoomed directly to the top of my suspect list. Again, I had to ask if she resented her mother taking all the credit (and most of the money) for the hugely successful books that she herself was writing. Had it seemed like a lark at first? Let the flamboyant Ruth pretend to be Renalta Van Markoff, get the attention of the adoring fans, pose for pictures for the papers and the book jacket, and be the one doing TV and radio interviews and appearing on panels at literary festivals and mystery conferences. While Linda not only wrote the books but did the business side of it too, including acting as the author's agent.

Had Linda decided enough was enough? Did she want out of the arrangement? Did she want the credit for her work? Had her mother, who had been totally committed to the persona of Renalta Van Markoff, objected?

Or had Linda simply wanted the money? Money she had earned but her mother controlled.

Speculation is wonderful, but proof is another thing altogether.

Ryan said on his way out the door, "You're a superb observer of people, Gemma, and you have insights I can't even begin to understand. But you are not a police officer, and you are certainly not a trained detective. You charge in like a bull in a china shop and rub everyone the wrong way."

"I can't help it if—"

He lifted one hand. "Talk to me if you learn something. I'll share with you what I can and let you mull things over. But that's all I want from you. Don't interfere with the investigation, and above all, please don't interfere with Louise. You do not want her as your enemy."

It was probably too late for that, but I said nothing and wished him a good night. I crouched in the doorway to the mudroom, my hand on Violet's collar, and watched Ryan Ashburton drive away.

* * *

Shortly before noon the day following my aborted raid on the police station, I called Linda. "You haven't been to Mrs. Hudson's Tea Room yet. Would you like to be my guest for afternoon tea?"

"Thanks, Gemma," she said. "I'd enjoy that. I'm sick and tired of hanging around this hotel, nice as it is."

"The police haven't released your mother's body yet?"

"No. I suppose I could go home and come back later, but . . . well, I just want to be close to her. For as long as I can." Her voice broke, and for a moment, I felt bad for suspecting her.

I reminded myself that more than one killer had regretted what they'd done when the enormity of it settled in. "One o'clock? Early for afternoon tea, but we can call it lunch."

"Great. Thanks."

"I'll make a reservation for two for one o'clock." I hung up before she could reply, hoping she got the hint that Kevin wasn't invited. Before I could get distracted and forget to reserve our table, I hurried next door.

"We're booked pretty solid, Gemma," Fiona said. "But as it's just for two, I can probably fit you in."

* * *

At five to one, I told Ashleigh I'd be out for a while.

She sighed heavily, and I felt a pang of guilt as I realized that I was leaving a lot of the workload to her. When I got back yesterday from observing Estrada at the bank and then talking to Donald, the shop had been packed. A lineup waited impatiently at the cash register while Ashleigh struggled to answer a customer's vague questions about which Conan Doyle books she should read to best understand the nuances of the Benedict Cumberbatch series.

The look on Ashleigh's face when I came in and took over speaking to the customer was one of pure relief.

I needed an assistant because the shop was too busy in the summer months for one person to handle, so I'd hired her, and then I'd left her to it. What else could I do? I'd committed myself to helping Donald clear his name. Right now the best chance of proving his innocence was to find the guilty party. And that couldn't be done only in off-business hours.

If she dressed according to her mood, Ashleigh's mood this morning must have been gloomy: gray Bermuda shorts bagging in the knees and the seat, a gray golf shirt, black socks in hiking shoes, hair pulled into an untidy ponytail, and a pair of thick-rimmed black glasses perched on her nose. She'd never worn eyeglasses before. When I peered closely at them, I could tell that the lenses were plain glass.

"I'm sorry," I said. "It's not usually like this around here. We're still busy because of the Van Markoff visit and what happened with that. And, well, I'm trying to do what little I can to help Donald."

"I don't mind," she said with another sigh that indicated she minded very much.

As if he knew I was about to be criticized, Moriarty jumped onto the counter to hear better.

"It's just that I don't know all that much about Sherlock Holmes. I've been trying to learn. I've been reading those books you loaned me, and I watched the TV show and some movies on Netflix, but some of the questions people ask are really weird."

"I have an idea to get you some help. Right now, I have to pop next door," I said. "Won't be long. When I get back, you can go for your lunch. Tell Fiona it's on me."

"Gee, thanks," she said.

Fiona showed me to a table for two. I pulled out my phone while I waited for my guest and texted Uncle Arthur. *How's your trip?*

The reply was almost instant: *Fell out with sister of RN chap. Kicked off their boat. Heading for Key West.*

I didn't bother to ask what sort of a "falling out" that might have been. *Key West? Isn't Florida hot in summer? Why not come home?*

He replied, *Am I needed?*

Super busy in shop. Keen interest in SH. Could use your help. SH was, of course, Sherlock Holmes. If that didn't get Uncle Arthur back to West London, nothing would. He didn't work out very well as a shop clerk, being more inclined to pull up a chair and discuss details of the canon and its numerous offshoots with the customers than try to sell them things, but if Ashleigh needed help with the "weird questions," no one was better equipped than Arthur Doyle to answer them.

On my way.

I imagined him leaping into the Triumph and speeding out of the parking lot of wherever he happened to be and put my phone away with a smile.

Linda had not gotten the hint and had brought Kevin with her. They came into the tea room holding hands. Kevin grabbed a chair from another table and dragged it over. I pasted on a frozen smile as we squeezed around the table for two.

"This is so charming," Linda said. "I love afternoon tea and all the formality around it. There's something about tea that inspires tradition, isn't there, Gemma?"

"That's certainly true, and in cultures as varied as England and Japan. You don't have to stay, Kevin, if you have something else you'd rather be doing."

"I'm good," he said.

"Would you like menus?" Fiona asked us.

"How about the basic afternoon tea for three?" I suggested. "Darjeeling for me, please."

Linda said she'd also have Darjeeling, and Kevin asked if he could have coffee instead. I repressed a grimace of disapproval.

"I wasn't happy to hear that the man they arrested got out on bail," Kevin said. "Bail on a murder charge. Ridiculous."

"The evidence is nothing but circumstantial," I said. "And barely even that."

"Should Linda be worried, Gemma?" Kevin asked. "Might he come after her next?"

"Donald Morris? Goodness no." That was something I hadn't considered. If Linda hadn't killed her mother, then might the killer now be after her if he (or she) learned the identity of the real author?

Kevin put his hand on Linda's, and she left it there. They hadn't shown any sign of affection in front of Renalta. Was that because I'd only seen them with her when they were conducting business or because Renalta didn't know of their relationship—or if she did know, didn't approve? I'd thought Kevin had an interest in Linda but didn't see signs of it being returned. Now freed from her mother's disapproving influence, did Linda feel able to express herself? Then again, might this be an entirely new development? Had the death of Renalta been the catalyst to bring Kevin and Linda together?

Again, I had to ask myself if the handsome Kevin might have decided to hurry things along. Today Linda was wearing a flowing dark-blue tunic over calf-length black leggings and sporty sandals. Small gold hoops were in her ears, and the same necklace she wore yesterday was around her throat. She'd added a touch of pink lipstick and a swipe of blush and combed her hair out. The change from when I'd first met her wasn't dramatic, but it was noticeable. Was this, I had to ask myself, the real Linda, and the dowdy but efficient PA nothing but an act she took on the road? Or was the real Linda only allowed to express herself by the death of her domineering, bullying, overly flamboyant mother?

Fiona placed a large teapot on the table as well as a small jug of milk, a sugar bowl, a plate of sliced lemon, and two cups and saucers. She dropped a mug of coffee in front of Kevin.

"What a beautiful tea set," Linda said. The pot and cups matched: roses of pink and pale blue on fine white china trimmed with gold. "May I pour?"

"Go ahead." I leaned back to allow Fiona to place the three-tiered silver tray in the center of the table along with pots of butter, strawberry jam straight from the kitchen of a West London woman, and proper clotted cream.

Ignoring any pretext of good manners, I snatched one of the cucumber sandwiches before my dining companions could get it. We'd also been served salmon, roast beef and arugula, and curried egg salad. The middle level of the tray held scones plump with raisins and on the top layer tiny perfect strawberry and lemon tarts nestled beside miniature coconut cupcakes piled high with buttercream icing.

"I try to have at least one scene involving afternoon tea in each of my books," Linda said. "It gives Desdemona and Sherlock a chance to get together and talk over what they've learned."

I refrained from mentioning that I couldn't imagine Sherlock Holmes, man of action, pipe tobacco and lover of a seven percent solution, enjoying a cream tea.

"One thing about this forced idleness," Linda said, sipping her tea, "I'm getting a lot of work done, and that helps to get my mind off my mother's death."

"So it wasn't true, what you said to Robert? That the manuscript is locked in a computer back in New York?"

"Of course not. Consider it a little white lie. I'm not going to lay all my cards on the table, am I? We'll be renegotiating contracts now that circumstances have changed. I trust you remember that you promised to honor my confidence, Gemma?"

"I remember, and I have no intention of breaking that promise." I had told Ryan, but I didn't feel at all guilty: the matter might be critically important in determining the motive for the killing of Renalta. "How far along is the book?"

"Almost finished."

"As a bookseller, I'm glad to hear it. I put in an order this morning for more stock of *Hudson House* as well as the backlist. The new book should do extremely well."

"Robert wants to hurry it up," Kevin said. "Take advantage of the publicity around Renalta's death."

Linda grimaced, and I said, "That's putting it a bit bluntly."

"It's business," Kevin said. He slathered butter and jam on a scone and added a huge dollop of cream.

"I understand that," Linda said. "Robert's worried about his investment now that the apparent author has died, but I won't have him shouting orders at me." A single salmon sandwich sat on her plate, uneaten. "He wants me to hand over the unfinished manuscript so he can hire a ghostwriter to finish it. Obviously, that's not necessary."

"Why haven't you told him the truth? I expect he'll be thrilled. That means there will be more Hudson and Holmes books."

"He might be happy. He might not," Kevin said. "More books is good, but speaking as a publicist, I can tell you that people don't like being tricked. All those Renalta fans won't be pleased to hear that the woman they fawned over, whose every word they hung onto when she talked about her writing routine and where she gets her ideas, didn't pen so much as a word or have a single idea."

"I need time to think, Gemma," Linda said. "And time to mourn my mother. I won't be rushed into any rash decisions by people wanting to take advantage of Mother's death." Tears welled up in her eyes, and she fumbled in her purse for a tissue. She found a packet, took one out, and wiped at her face. "Sorry."

"Don't apologize," I said.

She blew her nose. "People like that horrible woman who wants to take over the public appearances."

"What horrid woman?" I asked, although I was pretty sure I knew.

"Nancy Brownmiller. She's a pest. She was a pest when Renalta was alive," Kevin said, "and now she's proving to be even more so. She showed up at the hotel last night, lurking in the lobby like some sort of giant spider, and ambushed us when we were coming in after dinner. She wants us to hire her to impersonate Renalta at fan events." His expression showed what he thought about that idea.

Yesterday afternoon, Nancy told me she was going home because she couldn't afford to continue paying for a hotel. Instead, she'd hung around town waiting to talk to Linda. I tucked that piece of information into the back of my mind, where I was accumulating a rapidly growing folder labeled "Suspects' Movements." "Tasteless," I said. "But assuming she doesn't know Renalta was Linda's mother, it's not downright offensive."

"Offensive enough," Kevin muttered.

"Anyone mind if I have the last cucumber sandwich?" I asked. "They're my favorite."

Kevin shook his head, and Linda said, "Go ahead."

I did so. Delicious.

"What do you intend to do now?" I asked Linda.

"Take Mother home when the police let me. Settle her affairs. Finish the book. I know what I want to do with the nearly finished manuscript, but after that, I haven't decided."

"We'll do all those things together," Kevin said. She gave her eyes another wipe, smiled at Kevin, and put the used tissue into her purse. The packet remained on the table.

The restaurant was full. Fiona and Jocelyn bustled about with laden trays and empty dishes while Lorraine served take-out customers. People chatted over their tea and scones at the tables, and others lined up at the counter for coffee, sandwiches, and pastries. Groups milled about outside, patiently waiting for tables to come free.

"I'm still thinking about buying a place in West London," Linda said. "Something on the water with a private beach would be nice."

A house on the ocean would be very expensive. I couldn't help glancing at Kevin. If he married Linda, he might be coming into money. *Had he helped that fortunate set of circumstances along?*

"Excuse me, excuse me. My party is already seated." I glanced up to see a woman pushing her way through the patrons clustered in the doorway.

"Incoming," I said. "No time to hide."

"I thought I might find you here." Paige Bookman arrived at our table. She stood over us, feet apart, hands on hips. "I went around to your hotel, but they said you'd gone out." The table for four beside us had recently been vacated, and Jocelyn was collecting used dishes and gathering stray crumbs. Paige grabbed a chair and flipped it around. She dropped into it and attempted to wiggle herself between Linda and me.

"Go away, Paige," Kevin said. "This is a private meeting."

"Good. I've arrived in time. Have you considered my proposition?" She helped herself to the lemon tart.

"Proposition?" Linda asked.

"Didn't he tell you?" Paige glared at Kevin.

"No, I did not," he said. "It's not worth wasting Linda's time over."

"I'll be the judge of that," Paige said.

"You're not in the position to be the judge of anything." Kevin jumped up. He took hold of Linda's arm and half-lifted her to her feet. "We're leaving. Thanks for the tea, Gemma. Your restaurant is great, but some of your patrons are not." His voice was loud and angry. Heads began to turn.

"It's a good idea!" Paige shouted. "Hear me out, Linda. I can continue the series. I'll keep it faithful to Renalta's vision. It's really my vision, but I'll give her some of the credit. I'll make sure they keep her name on the cover. Under mine, of course."

"You're a nutcase," Kevin said. "The sooner you're locked up, the better." He almost dragged Linda out of the tea room. Startled patrons watched them go. Someone murmured, "Renalta's people," and someone else snapped a picture.

"I've written to McNamara and Gibbons!" Paige shouted after them. "I'm confident they'll agree, but it would be nice if we had Renalta's family's official approval." The door swung shut. Paige turned to me. "I'm just trying to be considerate. I was thinking of hiring Linda to work for me because she managed Renalta's schedule and things, but I'm certainly not going to do that now. Are you going to have that last scone?"

"Help yourself."

"Thanks. I'm running low on funds, I don't mind saying. Everything's so expensive here in the summer, isn't it? I'm expecting a hefty advance soon, and that'll help."

"I'm sure it will. What advance is this?"

"For the next Hudson and Holmes book, of course. It's quite common now, isn't it? For new authors to take over popular series when the original author dies."

"It's been known to happen. Will you look at the time? I'd better get back at it."

"How about I do my first signing at your store? Can we arrange something now?"

"Call my secretary." I pushed my chair back and stood up. Linda had left her tissue packet behind. I scooped it up.

I considered telling Fiona to present Paige with the bill, but my better nature took over. I left her with the last sandwich and her dreams of literary grandeur.

*   *   *

"That was a long lunch," Ashleigh said.

"Your turn," I said.

I took a quick glance around the shop, noticing that seven copies of *Hudson House* had been sold in my absence, along with five of the earlier books in the series, one copy of *House of Silk* by Anthony Horowitz, one of *Jewel of the Thames* by Angela Misri, a set of Sherlock coffee mugs, two packages of playing cards, a complete set of the Jeremy Brett DVDs, and two jigsaw puzzles.

The chimes over the door tinkled, and Grant Thompson came in. He gave me a smile. Moriarty hurried to greet him, and he leaned over to give the cat an enthusiastic pat. When he straightened up, he said, "I've learned something you might find of interest." He glanced at two women browsing the gaslight shelves.

I led the way to the reading nook in search of some privacy. "What?" I asked.

"A copy of *Hudson House* has come on the market. It's signed by Renalta and dated Saturday."

"The day she died."

"Yup."

"Is there something particularly special about this book? Other than the speed with which it's being sold."

"There is. It's personalized, which is normally not a good thing, but in this case it might be worth something. 'For my darling Kevin. With thanks for all the marvelous things you do for me.'"

"That is interesting."

"I thought you'd think so. Surely Kevin is Kevin Reynolds, the publicist?"

"Plenty of Kevins in the world," I said. "But not many men are fans of Renalta, and the meaning of the inscription is obvious. How much is the seller asking for this book?"

"A thousand bucks. Unlikely he'll get that, but it works as a starting point. He might end up getting a couple of hundred."

"Hold that thought," I said. A customer was ready to complete her purchase so I hurried to the counter to help her. Grant wandered over to the collectors' bookshelf where we carried second and later editions of Sir Arthur Conan Doyle's books and those of some of his contemporaries. He pulled a thin volume off the shelf. *Miss Cayley's Adventures* by Grant Allen.

"Have you read this?" he asked me when I was free again.

I shook my head.

"It's so quaint, it's quite charming. The female protagonist is a cyclist, and he loves describing her 'ankle action.'"

I laughed.

"No euphemism intended."

Chimes tinkled, and a large group came in. Judging by the number of store bags they carried, they were serious shoppers.

"Thanks for telling me," I said to Grant. "I'd better get back to work."

"Anytime," he said. "I can pretend to be an interested buyer, try to find out if the seller really is Kevin Reynolds."

"I'd appreciate that," I said.

Kevin had now zoomed to the top of my suspect list. It was getting very crowded up there. Had Kevin and Linda acted together to get rid of her mother?

Only one way to find out.

As soon as Ashleigh returned from lunch, I placed a call to Ryan.

"You've caught me on the hop, Gemma," he said. "I've just left a meeting with the chief to update him on the Van Markoff case."

"How did that go?"

"I have no comment suitable for the general public. What's up?"

I'd promised to keep him apprised of anything I learned. I hadn't actually learned anything, but I could tell him my suspicions and about Kevin's attempt to sell the book.

"That's interesting, Gemma," Ryan said when I'd finished summarizing my thoughts. "Although, I can't see the opportunity to earn a couple of hundred bucks on a signed book as a motive for murder."

"Agreed," I said. "But there is the hand of the fair Linda to consider. I don't know if Kevin and Linda were an item before Linda's mother died, but they are now. Kevin might have kept his intentions secret, fearing that Ruth would forbid Linda from seeing him."

"Linda Marke is thirty years old, Gemma. She doesn't need her mother's permission to date anyone."

"True. But Ruth was highly domineering. Bossy even."

"When I spoke to Linda, I found her intelligent and competent although grief stricken. Does she strike you as a woman so submissive, she'd let her mother rule her love life?"

I thought. "Hard to say. I only ever saw them together in the role of author and assistant. Her mother bullied her, and Linda appeared to let her do so, but that might have been only because she didn't want an argument in public. However, considering the metamorphosis she's appeared to have undergone since Renalta's death, I don't think it was entirely an act.

"I assume you've been investigating all the parties. Have you learned anything significant?"

"We never know what's significant until it becomes significant. Linda Marke has no police record of any sort, whereas Kevin Reynolds is known to the NYPD."

"Do tell."

"He was fired from a previous job for embezzling."

"Wow!"

"Nothing major. Less than a thousand dollars, so he got off with a warning and no jail time."

"If he'd risk his job over a sum like that, then we have to ask what he'd do for a lot more. What about their educational backgrounds? Do any of the people in question have a degree in chemistry, or have any of them spent time working in some sort of lab?"

"You mean like Donald Morris?"

"You were pretty quick to point the finger of suspicion at Donald for that very reason."

"That and others, Gemma. To answer your question, we've found nothing even remotely like that."

"Doesn't mean he or she is not an enthusiastic amateur."

I was standing at the rear of the shop, with my back to the room, but a woman coughed lightly behind me. I turned to see one of my regular customers smiling at me.

"Gotta run," I said to Ryan. I stuffed my phone into my pocket and gave my customer a smile.

"Sorry to interrupt, Gemma. But I was out of town on the weekend and asked you to get Renalta Van Markoff to sign a book for me. I heard she died, and it seems rather crass now, but I do want to read the book. Do you have it?"

"Let me get it for you."

* * *

At three thirty-eight, I called to Ashleigh that I was going next door for my business meeting with Jayne. She waved good-bye.

My favorite table in the window alcove was free, so I settled into the chair looking out over the street. I'd had afternoon tea earlier, so I asked Fiona to just bring me a pot of Lapsang Souchong. I was in the mood for something exotic and flavorful. Outside, traffic moved slowly as visitors eager to get an early start on their summer weekend poured into town and classic rock fans departed. A steady stream of pedestrians popped in and out of the shops along Baker Street.

"Another good day." Jayne put a tray on the table. My pot of tea, another pot for her, and a plate of tea sandwiches. "I'm cautiously optimistic that this is going to be a great summer for the business."

"It's hard for me to say what's regular traffic and what was brought to my doors by all the news around Renalta Van Markoff and her new book," I said. "But I have to agree with you."

"No one's being put off by the shop being the scene of a murder?" Jayne asked.

"Not so as I'd notice, although I am getting tired of cleaning up flower arrangements every morning."

"The hospital's happy to have them, Mom says."

"Always a silver lining. Tell me, Jayne, theoretically speaking, if you were rich, I mean moderately wealthy, not billionaire status or anything, and a friend of yours suspected your new lover was only interested in you for your money, would you want your friend to tell you?"

She peered at me over the top of her Sherlock-themed cup, decorated with a pipe and deerstalker hat. I thought the set—cups and saucers, sugar bowl and cream pitcher, teapot—hideous and tasteless, but Jayne's customers loved it. Who am I, of all people, to tell our patrons they can't have Sherlock Holmes accessories? "What brought this up?"

"Just wondering."

"You never just wonder about anything, Gemma. Everything you do has a purpose."

"You say that as though it's a bad thing."

"Whatever. Yeah, I'd want my friend to tell me, for sure. I hope I'd be smart enough to figure out that the guy didn't love me for myself, but it's easy to be fooled in matters of the heart, isn't it?"

I considered making a comment about the ever-unemployed Robbie. But once again, who am I to judge? Look at my marriage. Even I, supposedly so observant about people, hadn't recognized the signs that my husband was having an affair with the newest of our part-time shop clerks. Willful blindness, probably. One of the older clerks had taken me aside one afternoon, after my husband and the woman in question left to have a "coffee" together. She told me straight to my face, in no uncertain terms, that I was being made a fool of.

I was angry at first, of course I was, angry at the person who'd told me most of all. But I soon realized she'd done it because she cared about me, and I left the cheating rat shortly thereafter.

Now here I am in West London, Massachusetts, happy in my new life, enjoying a cup of tea with my best friend. "You're right," I said. "Love makes fools of us all."

"That's a good thing, Gemma."

"Is it?"

"What would we be without love? Look at Sherlock Holmes. Has anyone ever suggested the great Sherlock was at all *happy*? No, he was nothing but a thinking machine."

"He loved Irene Adler. In his own way."

"For all the good it did him. He spent the rest of his life looking at a photograph in a drawer. He could have gone after her, chased her across Europe, swept her into his arms and vowed undying love. I liked the way they did it in the TV show better, where he saved her from being killed by terrorists in the desert."

I smiled at her. "You're such a romantic, Jayne."

"And you should be too, Gemma. You don't keep a photograph of Ryan in your top drawer, I hope."

"What's that mean?"

She sipped her tea and avoided my eyes. "Nothing."

"It had better mean nothing. I don't like the way this conversation has moved from Sherlock Holmes to me. I'm nothing like him, man of his times that he was, but I will admit that we have one thing in common: I'm finished with romance. It addles the mind. Speaking of romance, have you talked to Andrew lately?"

"No. Why do you ask? Do you think Robbie might take me to the café for dinner one night? My birthday's coming up, but he can't really afford it right now. I suggested he paint some nice Cape Cod pictures to sell to the tourists. Maureen might take some on consignment at Beach Fine Arts, and maybe we could hang some in the tea room . . ."

I suppressed a shudder.

". . . but these days he's experimenting with a different form of art. Brutal realism, he calls it. I had to tell him we couldn't hang paintings of disembodied heads on the light-house grounds in a tea room. He said he understands, but he has to remain true to his artistic muse."

I was about to let Jayne know that I thought Robbie should worry about being true to his bank account, but before I could say so, Fiona came to our table to tell me that I had a phone call in the shop.

Thus ended the day's business meeting.

*　*　*

I took Linda's packet of tissues out of the drawer where I'd held it for safekeeping. I'd been planning to give her a call and tell her to pick it up next time she was passing, but I changed my mind.

"You left an item in the tea room," I said when I got her on the phone. "How about I pop around to your hotel with it? Are you there now?"

"What did I leave?"

"A packet of tissues."

"Oh, that. It's not worth anything, Gemma. You can keep it."

"Oh, no. I insist. It's your property, and I want to return it."

"I don't . . ."

"Are you at the Harbor Inn now?"

"Yes, but . . ."

"Brilliant. I can be there in ten minutes. It's no bother at all. We British people believe in the proper care and storage of possessions. I'll come straight to your room. What number is it?"

"Two-ten, but . . ."

"Cheerio." I hung up.

If Linda Marke now believed that the British were obsessively concerned with individual ownership of dollar-fifty packets of tissues, so be it. We are a nation of shopkeepers, after all.

"I'm heading out. Won't be long," I called to Ashleigh.

"Not again!" she said. "I was hoping we could talk about my franchise ideas."

Moriarty yawned, and I shoved down my guilt at once again abandoning my business.

The Harbor Inn isn't far from Baker Street so I didn't have to go home for my car. This time, if Linda called Kevin to tell him I was coming over and he insisted on joining us, I'd have to equally insist that he left.

"Good afternoon," I called to Andrea as I sailed across the lobby. Then I had a thought, and turned around abruptly. "I hope the change in the Van Markoff party's situation hasn't upset your booking arrangements too much."

Andrea grimaced. "Always something in the hotel business, Gemma. Keeps me on my toes. The regular rooms and smaller suites are pretty much booked solid right through to August, but fortunately the largest suite wasn't reserved for the next few days, so I was able to move Ms. Marke into what had been Ms. Van Markoff's room. I've told her she has to leave by Friday morning. I have annual visitors coming then, and no way can I put them into smaller rooms."

Her phone rang, and I left her to answer it.

I didn't wait for the elevator but took the steps two at a time. I knocked on the door of room 210, and it was promptly opened by Linda herself. She gave me a forced smile. "Thanks for coming, Gemma. I'm sure you're busy, so I won't keep you." She held out her hand. For a moment, I wondered why she'd done that—it wasn't in the position for a shake—and then I remembered I was ostensibly here to return her tissues.

"I see you've got one of the nicest rooms," I said, slipping past her. She could have blocked me, stopped me from entering, but like most people, she was just too darn polite. "I came on a tour of the hotel when they had the grand opening. They've done a marvelous job with this place, haven't they?" We were in the sitting room, sofa and chairs arranged around a coffee table and a desk tucked into a corner. Crystal vases of carefully arranged fresh flowers sat on the table and desk, and the art on the walls was original. The door to the bedroom stood ajar, and I could see a huge four-poster bed covered in a red-and-gold duvet about a yard thick, piled high with matching pillows. The rooms were decorated in period style, as matched the age of the house, with red wallpaper below a thick band of wooden wainscoting, cream walls, and foot-high baseboards. Sunlight streamed in through French doors opening onto a spacious balcony. In the distance, the ocean sparkled in the sunlight.

She saw me looking around and said quickly, "They moved me in here when my mother died. All the other rooms had been booked."

The sandals she'd worn earlier lay on the floor beside the bed. I peeked into the bathroom. A single makeup bag sat on the counter. A beige summer cardigan had been tossed over a chair in the living room, and a laptop was open on the desk. It would appear that Kevin Reynolds hadn't taken up residence. "Did Kevin have to move out of the inn?"

"They were able to find a room for him for a couple more days," she said. "Robert checked out yesterday. He's gone home."

I settled myself onto the sofa. Linda took a chair.

"Why have you not told Robert you're the real author of the books? He has to find out sometime."

"No reason, really, maybe just stubbornness. Obviously, we did almost all our business over the phone or by e-mail, but on the occasions when we met in person, he gushed and fawned over my mother and treated me like the hired help."

"Which you pretended to be."

"True enough. Maybe I resented it more than I thought I did. Anyway, Kevin and I think it's a good idea to keep the news to ourselves for a while, until the dust settles and I decide what our best course of action is."

"Speaking of Kevin"—I leaned back, crossed my legs, and attempted to sound nonchalant—"did your mother not approve of your relationship with him, or did she not know because you kept it secret?"

"What?" Linda jerked forward.

"I had a bad marriage. I should have listened to my mother. Mum warned me not to rush into things." That hadn't actually happened. My mother had been picking out china patterns for us the day she met him. She'd adored the cheating rat and still phoned me regularly with updates (he'd broken up with the part-time shop clerk) and not-very-subtle hints that he'd take me back if I asked. "Mothers can be highly perceptive about their daughter's boyfriends."

"Maybe you and your mom are close, but I never had that sort of relationship with mine. Kevin and I wanted to keep things discreet until we decided it was the right time to tell her."

"Discreet?" I asked. "Or secret? There's a difference."

"I don't see what business this is—"

"You're about to come into a lot of money, Linda. I hope you'll take this bit of advice in the spirit of friendship in which it's intended and think about Kevin's motives."

"If you must know, the advances and royalties from the books came to me, the author. I paid my mother a salary out of it." If I hadn't known that was a lie, the way she lifted one hand to fiddle with her hair and shifted uncomfortably in her chair would have been sure giveaways.

I gave her a friendly, just-between-us-girls smile. "I'm glad to hear that. I wouldn't want to think he was only attracted to you for the money."

"I'm not a total dog, you know," she snapped.

"I . . . uh . . . don't know what that means."

"It means that despite what you seem to be implying, I can get myself a boyfriend on my own merits. Not every man's attracted to simpering idiots with a bigger bra size than IQ."

I might have thought she was making a dig at me except that my bra size was nothing to brag about, and when I'd had my IQ tested in primary school, the researcher had concluded that the test didn't seem to be working properly.

"Are you aware he's offering a book signed by your mother for sale? At a highly inflated price owing to the date of the signature?"

"Where did you hear that?"

"I'm a bookseller. I hear things about bookselling."

"Yes, I knew." She tucked a loose strand of hair behind her ears, and she stared past me. The painting above my head was of a typical Cape Cod scene: sandy beaches, open ocean, splashing children, colorful umbrellas. Very nice, painted by a local artist, but not worth the amount of attention Linda was currently paying it. "Why shouldn't he make a bit of extra money when he can? My mother . . . I mean me . . . I mean *I* don't pay him all that well."

I smiled. "So he's in need of funds."

"I do not know why you think any of this is your business. Now if you'll excuse me, I have things to do."

"Are you aware that he was fired from a previous job for embezzlement?"

She blinked, but her face remained steady. "How do you know that?"

"No matter. You don't seem surprised."

"I'm not. He had a dispute with a previous employer over his pay, which they were withholding for no reason, so expecting he was about to be cheated out of it, he helped himself to a portion of the money owed. He was never charged. And by the way, he was not fired. He quit because he wasn't being paid. That was all discussed at his interview for the position with us."

"Fair enough," I admitted.

"I hate to rush you, but it's time you were leaving."

I didn't move. "In mystery novels, they always ask *cui bono*— who benefits? Who benefits from someone's death? I'm thinking Kevin has a lot to benefit from the death of Renalta."

She leapt to her feet. Her fists were clenched, and a fire burned in her eyes. "How dare you."

"I'm trying to be helpful," I said helpfully. "I want to make sure you're aware that Kevin might not be entirely aboveboard."

"Get out."

"What?"

She pointed a shaking finger in the direction of the door. "I said, get out. I know what you're doing. You're trying to shift suspicion from your creepy friend by throwing it onto Kevin. Well it won't work. If you tell anyone about this stupid fixation you have, I'll sue you for everything you have."

"That's not very much." I stood up. "I'd hardly call it a fixation. I thought you'd want to know."

Her finger didn't move. "I don't need you to tell me anything about the people in my life. Good-bye."

I didn't mention that if Kevin didn't kill Renalta, then Linda herself was back at the top of my suspect list. Instead, I crossed the room and opened the door. As I was doing so, Linda's phone rang. She pulled it out of her pocket and checked the display. "Robert, hi. Give me a minute. I have an unwelcome visitor I have to get rid of."

I stepped into the hallway. "If you want to talk things over, I—"

The door slammed in my face.

Andrea greeted me as I crossed the lobby. "Everything okay, Gemma?"

"That didn't go exactly as planned," I admitted.

Chapter 13

I headed back to the Emporium with my tail tucked between my legs, trying to figure out where my chat with Linda had gone wrong. If someone loved me only for my money (not that that's a possibility), I'd want to be warned. If it was possible they'd murdered my mother to get at my inheritance, I'd want to be warned even more. Jayne has sometimes told me I need to be slightly more circumspect when talking to people about intimate or private things. I wondered if this was an example of what she meant. Clearly, some people simply can't handle a frank exchange of information.

I might have offended Linda, but I had discovered something that might prove significant. Kevin knew that Linda wrote the books, but it was unlikely he believed—despite what Linda told me—that she was the one being paid for them. Case in point: Ruth was given the nicest suite in the inn, not Linda. Did Kevin decide Ruth had to be taken out of the picture? Linda would not only inherit her mum's money but could now continue to write the books under her own name—and get paid for it—rather than receiving a pittance of a salary.

I reached the bottom of the hill and turned into Baker Street. The thick, leafy branches of the old trees lining the street closed over my head, the canopy stirred in the breeze, and it was delightfully cool.

I thought about the call Linda had received as she was showing me the door. Robert was almost certainly Robert McNamara, the owner and publisher at McNamara and Gibbons. I hadn't given Robert much consideration as a suspect. Judging not only by the record of payments made from McNamara and Gibbons to Ruth but also by the way Robert fussed over Ruth while treating Linda like a hapless—and disposable—PA, he wasn't aware Ruth wasn't the author. No way would Robert kill the goose that was laying him so many beautiful golden eggs.

I reached the entrance to the Emporium and placed a quick call before going inside. "Everything okay there, Donald? Have you had any more visits from the police?"

He sighed heavily. "Estrada came around again this morning. She asked the same questions, and I gave her the same answers."

"Chin up," I said.

"Are you getting anywhere with your investigation, Gemma?"

"I . . . uh . . . might be." I didn't have the heart to tell him I was getting nowhere fast.

"Glad to hear it. I've been receiving calls and e-mails from Sherlock aficionados all across the country. They're congratulating me on doing something about that 'offensive woman.' Their words not mine."

"What did you say to them?"

"That I had absolutely nothing to do with it. I'm sorry Miss Van Markoff is dead, Gemma. Really I am. Whoever killed her deserves to be punished with the full force of the law. But I have to say, I am pleased we won't have to put up with any more of those dreadful books." He barked out an awkward laugh.

I didn't want to be the one to break the news to him that a new Hudson and Holmes book would be on the shelves shortly. And perhaps many more to come after that. I told him to keep in touch and hung up.

That was an angle I hadn't considered. Could it be possible that a Sherlock fanatic, unknown to me, had slipped into the book signing, done the deed, and slipped out again before the police secured the door? If so, they could be on the other side of the world by now. A single murder is surprisingly easy to get away with, provided the killer has no obvious relationship with the deceased, has never come to police attention before, makes no attempt to get cocky and replicate the deed, and (probably most important of all) resists the temptation to brag about what they have done. If that was the situation here, we might never find out who killed Ruth Smith, a.k.a. Renalta Van Markoff, and the dark cloud of suspicion would lie over Donald Morris until the end of his days.

Not to mention that this person or persons might then come after Linda when he or she found they hadn't killed the author after all.

I called Donald back. "I have a job for you."

"Anything. What do you want me to do?" The hope in his voice was almost too much to bear.

"You say people are congratulating you on getting rid of Renalta. It might be possible that one of your fellow Sherlockians killed her for the same reason they think you did it."

"Heavens, Gemma. We're a respectable group. I'd say the average IQ of our band of brothers and sisters is far—"

"Into every group, it is possible someone bad might fall. Or something. Poke around on the Holmes message boards, pay attention to what people are saying. Find out if someone seems particularly interested in the killing and if they drop little hints that they might be responsible."

"You want me to be your Dr. Watson, Gemma. A wonderful idea."

"I'd rather you didn't phrase it like that," I said.

"A modern version of the situation when Holmes sent Watson to Baskerville Hall in his stead to keep an eye on Sir Henry while Holmes supposedly had work to attend to in London, but in reality—"

I cut him off before he could relate the entire plot of *The Hound of the Baskervilles*. "You know these people, or at least the circles in which these people move."

"I will attempt to get the guilty party to confess."

I imagined him rubbing his hands together in glee and tossing his Inverness cape over his shoulder. Subtlety is not one of Donald's virtues. "All I'm asking you to do is listen in. Please, please don't try to trap anyone into confessing. Remember what happened after your conference call with your Irregular pals."

"Oh, yes, that."

"It's possible the police have the same idea as me and they have someone monitoring the boards. That's more likely to bounce back on you than trap anyone."

"Discretion is my middle name," he said.

Another cheap supermarket bouquet had been laid at the door of the bookshop. I scooped it up with a sigh on my way inside.

*   *   *

For the rest of the day, I tried to put aside all thoughts of the murder and attend to my shop. Ashleigh finished work at six, and almost as soon as she left, I had a rush of customers. I smiled and chatted and rang up purchases and reminded myself that I really do love owning this business.

By the time I'd flipped the sign on the door to "Closed," switched off all but the lights in the window and behind the sales counter, checked that sufficient food and water were in the cat bowls in the office (not that Moriarty ever thanked me for my attention to that detail), I had a kink in my back and my shoulders were stiffening up.

I needed a swim.

I walked home through the darkening streets. It was after nine, and the shops along Baker Street were closed, but the bars and restaurants overflowed with music and laugher. The lights in the harbor moved gently as boats rose and fell on the incoming tide. Long lines formed at the ice cream and candy booths on the boardwalk, and patrons waited patiently outside the Blue Water Café for a table on the deck to come free. The fourth-order Fresnel lens of the West London Lighthouse flashed its steady rhythm. I turned off the boardwalk at Blue Water Place and headed up the gentle hill to my saltbox. The light of the setting sun was a pink glow in the western sky, and the first of the stars were coming out. The night air was warm, but the heat of the day had broken, and there was no humidity. It was a nice night to take Violet for a ride in the car. I'd have my swim and then let her romp on the beach for a while.

I collected the day's post—flyers advertising fast food restaurants and a postcard from my parents on holiday in Scotland—from the box at the end of the drive and went around to the back of the house. I let myself in through the mudroom, and Violet was there to greet me, as she always is. She yipped, and I rubbed her favorite spot at the top of her head. I tossed the mail onto the counter, refreshed her water bowl, and poured kibble into the food dish. While she dined, I went to my bedroom and slipped out of my work clothes and got ready for the beach.

By the time I returned to the kitchen, Violet had finished eating. I said, "Car," and she dashed to the door. I took the leash and the car keys off the hook, and we set out.

The streets were busy with evening traffic as people returned to their summer homes, rental properties, or hotels. I turned off the main street and headed toward the public beach. Large houses on spacious grounds surrounded by neat woods line the road to the shore, and I paid no attention to the handful of cars on the road.

A few cars were parked in the public lot of the West London Beach. It's a popular spot for late picnics and for those who like to walk on the sand or swim at night or who, like me, don't have time during the day. The area is regularly patrolled by the police, so it's not a gathering spot for the wilder of high school partiers. The lot's well lit, and the beach is close enough to town that the glow of civilization breaks the darkness of the night.

I left Violet in the car, promising to return. I locked my handbag in the trunk, put the keys into a plastic container on a lanyard and slipped it around my neck. A narrow path leads from the pavement through a line of low dunes and scruffy vegetation toward the beach. A group of chairs were gathered in a circle around a roaring bonfire about a hundred yards from where I emerged. Red sparks leapt into the night, the music was turned up, and people laughed. A young couple passed me, holding each other close. We murmured greetings.

I kicked off my flip-flops at the edge of the water. The sand retained the last vestige of the heat of the day. The tide was nearing its highest point, washing over tidal pools in the rocks.

I took off my shirt and shorts and laid them along with my shoes on my towel, and then I waded into the water. It was warm enough not to be shocking but still crisp and refreshing. The ground here slopes gently, and I had to wade out a long way before I could dive forward and plunge beneath the gentle waves. I only wanted to work out the kinks, so I didn't swim for long. No one else was in the water, although a few couples and the occasional single person waded in the surf. Eventually, I flipped onto my back and floated, arms stretched out. Stars were popping out in the sky above. I identified the most noticeable constellations and watched the steady beam of a satellite pass overhead. Closer down, a jet was heading east, toward the vast expanse of the Atlantic Ocean. I thought of England and my parents. They were promising (threatening?) to come for a visit at the end of summer.

Finally, I clambered out of the water. I dried myself off with my towel as best I was able and put my clothes back on.

Flip-flops in hand, I walked across the sand. I stopped where the sand ended and the path to the parking lot began to put on my shoes. The scent of flowers in the bushes surrounding me was strong, mingling with wood smoke drifting from the bonfire and the smell of hot dogs roasting over the open fire. I dropped the flip-flops to the ground and wiggled my right foot into place, trying to get the thin strap between my toes.

Behind me a branch broke, and I was aware of someone standing far too close. I started to turn.

Pain streaked through my head, and all went dark.

Chapter 14

An airplane zoomed overhead. It was flying too low over the water. My mum and dad were in it. They were coming to visit me, but they were going to crash into the sea! I had to get help. I had to swim out to warn them.

I couldn't move; something held me down. A cloyingly sweet scent filled my nose, a strong light was in my eyes, and soft but firm hands were on my arms. I yelled and thrashed against them.

"Stay still," a voice said. "Don't try to get up. Are you okay?"

I groaned. "I'm . . . I'm . . . I can't see."

The light moved. Two faces peered into mine. Two angels, surrounded by brilliant white halos.

I was in heaven. I sighed happily.

"We've called nine-one-one," a woman said.

I blinked and struggled to sit up. The hands tried to keep me still, but I said, "I'm okay. Let me up."

"If you're sure." The pressure eased off.

Not heaven but West London, Massachusetts. I could be excused for getting them mixed up.

"What happened?" My head spun.

"Someone attacked you," a woman said. "We saw it, didn't we, Jason?"

"A sucker punch," a man said. "He got you from behind. Pow. You went down like a ton of bricks."

"You . . ."

The girl giggled. "We were in the bushes."

"Help me up," I said.

Jason gripped my right arm and pulled. He held the flashlight so it illuminated the scene but didn't blind me. They were young, probably in their midteens. She was short and thin and very pretty with a halo of curly hair, smooth coffee-colored skin, and huge dark eyes. He was bigger. A heck of a lot bigger, with a darker complexion and a rock-solid head. I took a guess as to what had been going on in the bushes.

I heard a siren getting closer. Red and blue lights washed the parking lot.

"Over here!" Jason called.

Beams of light from a police-issue Maglite bounced down the trail.

Adrenaline was slowly draining out of my body. My legs felt weak, my head began to pound.

"Careful there." Jason grabbed me. I leaned up against him. It was like leaning against a brick wall. So safe. So solid.

"What's going on here? Did you call this in?" I recognized Officer Johnson. "Gemma, is that you?"

"The one and only," I said.

"And thank heavens there is only one of you," she said. "What happened here?"

"She needs to sit down," the girl said.

"I'm sorry," I said. "I didn't get your name."

"Jolene."

"Nice to meet you, Jolene. I'm Gemma."

Lights began coming up from the beach, and voices called out.

"An ambulance is right behind me," Johnson said.

"I don't need an ambulance. I'll be fine." My head swam. "In a minute or two." I touched the back of my head. My hair was wet. Fair enough, I'd just come out of the water. "My dog's in the car waiting for me. I . . ." Jason's arms gripped me, and I felt no more.

*   *   *

When I next woke up, I was in a brightly lit white room, lying on a small, hard bed. A tinny disembodied voice called for Dr. Fitzpatrick. I smelled Lysol and blood and fear. Someone was pounding at the inside of my head with a mallet.

Louise Estrada perched uncomfortably on the edge of a plastic chair checking her phone.

I'd gone to hell.

She heard me groan and glanced up. She put the phone away. "Glad to see you're awake, Gemma."

Not hell but the West London Hospital. I'd heard that some people got those mixed up.

"What happened?" I asked.

"You had a heck of a blow to the back of your head," Estrada said.

I reached up and lightly touched the spot in question, momentarily afraid of what I'd find. I felt only clean dry bandages and short hair.

"They tell us you'll live," she said.

"Violet."

"What?"

"My dog. She was in the car, waiting for me, at the beach."

"You had your keys on you, and we know where you live, so we arranged to have someone take the dog and your car to your house. Are you up to answering some questions?"

"Yes." I struggled to sit. My head hurt like the blazes, but I was fully aware of all that was happening around me.

"I'll get Detective Ashburton," she said. "He's with the doctor now."

She left me, and a nurse, plump and cheerful in pink scrubs, came in. Jayne followed her, looking as though she'd been called out of bed in a hastily thrown-on yellow T-shirt and white shorts, hair mussed and face scrubbed clean. With her thin frame and lack of height, it gave her a charming, innocent, almost childlike appearance. She threw her arms around me. My head jerked back under the force of her affection, and I muffled a moan. "Oh, Gemma," she cried. "I've been so frightened."

"What are you doing here?" I mumbled into her soft, warm chest.

"Ryan called me. He said you'd been taken to the hospital. He said you'd be okay, but I was afraid he was lying to me." She pulled away and stared into my eyes. "You are okay, aren't you? How many fingers am I holding up?"

"Twenty-seven," I said.

"You two can chat in a minute," the nurse said. "Let me have a look at her."

Jayne stepped away and let the nurse fuss. "The doctor says you can talk to the police if you feel up to it." She took my pulse. "Do you?"

"Let 'em at me," I said.

At that moment, Ryan and Estrada came in.

"I'll be nearby if you need me," the nurse said.

"Jayne, would you wait outside, please?" Ryan said.

She planted a kiss on my cheek and slipped out.

Ryan studied my face. His own face was set into tight lines, and the stubble on his jaw was thick. His expressive blue eyes had gone dark, and for the briefest of moments, I thought they might be wet. But that had to be a trick of the light. He rubbed at his face. "Can you tell us what happened?"

"I went for a swim. I was heading to the car to get Violet and take her for a short walk on the beach when I heard someone coming up behind me. And that's it. Next I knew, a nice young couple was shining a light in my face. Jolene and Jason they said their names were. What did they tell you?"

"They're with a church group from Boston here on vacation," Estrada said. "They were having a bonfire on the beach, and some of the kids went for a walk. Jason and Jolene were taking a shortcut through the bushes next to the path . . ."

"A likely story," I said, and Ryan grinned.

"Whatever was going on," Estrada said, "you can be glad it was. They heard you cry out. When they peeked out of the bushes, they saw you lying on the path and someone standing over you. He had a rock in his hand, and it appeared as though he was about to hit you again."

I shuddered.

"Jason doesn't look like the sort to be trifled with," Ryan said. "He yelled and stepped out of the bushes. Your attacker took one look at him and ran."

"Can Jason or Jolene describe him?"

"They say no," Estrada said. "They said it was dark and that it all happened so fast. They aren't even sure if it was a man or a woman. He or she was dressed in loose clothes with a hood pulled over the head."

"Did you notice anyone, Gemma?" Ryan asked. "A car following you when you left your house? Someone watching you while you were swimming? Anything at all?"

I thought but came up blank. "It was almost full dark when I left home. Plenty of cars were on the road, but I paid them no mind." When I did look in the rearview mirror, all I'd seen were headlights. "I had my swim and left the beach. I heard a footstep behind me and started to turn, but I didn't see who it was. I wish more people smoked these days."

"What has that got to do with anything?" Estrada asked.

"The scent of tobacco follows a smoker like a cloud. I smelled nothing like that, so we can conclude our attacker doesn't smoke. I know almost no one who does, not anymore." A memory tugged at the back of my mind. I struggled to remember. Estrada opened her mouth to say something—probably to order me to confess—but Ryan put up his hand. Then I had it. "Oh, yes. Paige Bookman. I remember now—she lit up when Jayne and I . . . uh . . . happened to run into her the other day. Unlikely she was my attacker, although it is possible to disguise the scent of stale tobacco with a shower, a hair wash, and clean clothes. I did smell something distinctive and individual, cloying and sweet, but it turned out to be Jolene's perfume. Somewhat liberally applied for a shortcut through the bushes."

"You had time to notice all that while you were under attack?" Estrada said.

"Of course I did. Isn't that normal? Some say the senses are heightened when one is in danger."

"Some say the moon is made of blue cheese."

"Green cheese."

"What?"

"The moon is made of green cheese. Not blue." I glanced at Ryan. His face was twisted into contortions. I wondered what he was finding so funny.

"I don't care what color the moon supposedly is," Estrada snapped. "You'll be pleased to hear, the doctor confirmed that it would have been impossible for you to hit yourself with sufficient force to cause an injury in that spot on your head."

"You suspected I might have knocked myself out? And presumably also hired a couple of kids to say they'd chased my attacker off. Are you crazy? Because I can assure you, I am not."

Estrada bristled. "We're investigating all possibilities, like good police officers do. Those not influenced by personal friendships."

I bristled back. "I wouldn't expect—"

"We're having casts made of the footprints in the area," Ryan interrupted. "But that's a well-traveled path, not to mention you and the young couple and all their friends, plus the responding officer and then the paramedics."

"The rock?"

"We're looking for it, and it might be possible to identify it as the weapon if it has blood traces on it . . ."

My injury emitted a jab of pain.

". . . but Jason thinks the attacker was wearing gloves, so no fingerprints."

"It's possible, likely even," Estrada said, "that he took it with him. Or her."

I leaned back and closed my eyes. I'd had a lucky escape. I had to find Jason and Jolene and thank them. Perhaps I could treat them to afternoon tea at Mrs. Hudson's. I had an image of one of Jayne's bone china teacups clasped in Jason's massive hand.

"I'm glad you're amused, Gemma," Estrada said.

I opened my eyes. "All's well that ends well, Louise."

"Except that this might not be over," Ryan said. "Can you give us a moment, please, Detective?"

Estrada threw me a look but left without argument.

Ryan pulled up a chair and sat down. He took my hand in his. He said nothing for a long time.

"Can I go home?" I asked.

"Check once again with the doctor, but as long as you have someone to look in on you in the night, it should be okay."

"Will you look in on me in the night, Ryan?" Whatever the doctor had given me must be lowering my defenses.

He lifted my hand to his lips. "Tonight, I think I'd be better put to trying to find who did this. I'm sure Jayne will agree to stay with you."

"You don't think this was a common-or-garden assault, do you?" I made no move to take my hand back. It was safe and warm wrapped in his.

"Do you?"

"No. It has to be connected to the Van Markoff killing."

"I agree," he said.

"Which proves Donald didn't do it."

"How do you reason that?"

"Donald wouldn't hurt me, Ryan. He asked me for my help."

"A double cross maybe. A triple play."

"Donald is simply not that devious."

"I want you to stop asking questions about this, Gemma. You sometimes might think I'm giving you a nudge and a wink when I say that, but this time I'm serious."

"I must be getting close. I've clearly put a fright into the killer."

"You've put a fright into me. Gemma, listen to me. If I find you snooping around . . ."

"I don't snoop."

". . . interfering with this investigation, I will personally have you charged with obstruction and tossed into jail. If that's the only way I can ensure you're kept out of danger, I'll do it. I'll do it because—"

We weren't in a proper hospital room, just a curtained alcove in the ER. Estrada burst in saying, "Oh, one more thing . . ." Ryan dropped my hand as if it had burst into flames. Estrada's dark-brown eyes studied us both. I coughed lightly and politely patted my mouth. My face felt as though it were on fire.

"Did you tell anyone you were planning to go to the beach tonight?" Estrada said.

"No. It was a last-minute decision. I was stiff and tired after work, and a nice relaxing swim seemed like a good idea."

"Not so nice and not so relaxing." Ryan got to his feet. "I'm going back to the beach, see if they've found anything. It's probably too late tonight to make calls, but first thing in the morning, I'll be checking some people's whereabouts earlier this evening. Gemma, if the doctor releases you, you're to go home with Jayne and stay there."

"I have to go to work tomorrow."

"See how you feel in the morning. It should be all right if you're up to it. But that's all. The store and home. You've riled someone up, Gemma. Next time a young couple might not be necking in the bushes. I'll send Jayne in." He stalked out of the room.

Estrada gave me a parting shot: "Stop interfering in police business, Gemma."

Stop interfering? Someone had attacked me. I'd only just begun.

Chapter 15

A rmed with a bottle of prescription pain killers, I left the hospital. Jayne fussed and bustled about as she loaded me into her car, drove me home, and then tucked me into my own bed.

"You don't have to stay," I said, sinking into the soft mattress. "I'll be fine. Just leave that pill bottle immediately to hand."

"Of course I'll stay." She pulled the duvet over me and tucked it around my shoulders. "I've set my phone to wake me every two hours so I can check on you. I'll be right here beside you if you need anything."

"I won't . . ."

When I woke, sunlight filled the room. My head throbbed, but it wasn't screaming in pain. The pillow beside me was dented and the sheets tumbled, but Jayne was gone.

"Good morning, Gemma," said a cheerful voice.

I slowly rolled over. Leslie Wilson, Jayne's mum, stood in the door holding a tea tray. "When you started to stir, I thought it might be time to put the kettle on. How are you feeling?"

I performed a quick mental inventory of myself. Other than a sore head and aching right knee, everything seemed in proper working order. "Better than might have been expected. Why are you here?"

"Jayne called me last night to tell me what happened. She had to go to work—that bread won't make itself, you know—and asked me to stay with you."

Violet put her paws on the edge of the bed and peered into my face. I rubbed her nose.

"I fed the dog." Leslie put the tray on the night table. She arranged my pillows and helped me sit up. She then poured a cup, added milk and sugar, and handed it to me. I accepted it gratefully. My throat felt like someone had crawled in there to sand it down. I don't usually take sugar in my tea, but Leslie had already added a generous amount. I drank it gratefully, knowing I needed the rush of energy.

Leslie pulled the curtains back, and sunlight flooded into the room. "I'll be in the kitchen if you need me," she said.

I cradled my cup, letting the welcome warmth sink into my hands. Violet had trotted after Leslie, no doubt hoping a second breakfast was about to appear. I finished the tea and pushed the bedclothes aside. My right leg was badly scratched and the knee swollen from where I'd fallen on the rocky path. Movement brought a jolt of pain into my head. I glanced at the pill bottle on the side table but decided against taking any more: today, I needed a clear head. I climbed out of bed, taking care to move slowly.

I had to twist myself into pretzels to check out my injury in the mirror. A white bandage was stuck to the back of my head. A large patch of hair had been cut away to allow the doctor to work.

By the time I'd showered (taking care to keep my head dry), dressed, and staggered into the kitchen to find Leslie preparing a boiled egg and toast, I was feeling almost human. She told me to take a seat, and I did so. Fresh tea was in the pot, and a single place had been set at the table alongside the butter dish and a jar of marmalade. She cut the toast lengthwise into four sections, making what English children call soldiers, and put the plate in front of me.

"Will you be my mum, Leslie," I asked, "and make me breakfast every morning?"

"I'd be happy to, my dear, except that now my own children have flown the coop, I'm enjoying the carefree single life." Jayne's dad had died some years ago. "You look like you're dressed for work. Jayne said I was to try to keep you at home, but I suspect that's a lost cause. If you insist on going in, I've been instructed to drive you."

"I don't need a lift."

Leslie had been smiling, cheerful, and bubbly. Now a dark cloud settled over her face, so much like Jayne's. "Until the police find out who attacked you and why, you are not to be left alone."

I smiled at her. "When I said I wanted a mum, I meant to fix me tea and soldiers. Not someone to give me a curfew."

Leslie laughed and poured another cup of tea.

*   *   *

I arrived at the Emporium sharply at ten and was surprised to see that the shop was already open for business. Ashleigh leaned on the sales counter, chatting to Moriarty. They both looked up as I came in. Neither of them seemed pleased to see me.

"Shouldn't you be home in bed?" Ashleigh said.

"I am perfectly well, thank you for asking. What are you doing here? You aren't scheduled to start until noon."

"Jayne called me first thing this morning and said you weren't coming into work today."

"How'd you get in?"

"Jayne unlocked the store. It's no problem, Gemma. I've got this." Today she was dressed almost like a normal sales clerk in black capris and a loose white cotton blouse that fell to her hips. Her hair was brushed to a shine and folded lightly around her shoulders. The unexpected summons to work early must have meant she didn't have time to put together today's costume.

"Thanks," I said.

"Jayne said you'd been in an accident."

"Of a sort." So as not to have to answer questions all day as to what had happened to my head, I'd put on a big blue sun hat. "I'm going next door for a minute. Carry on!" I waved and went into the tea room.

"Jayne in the kitchen?" I asked Jocelyn.

"Yup." She paid me no particular attention as she arranged a tray of fresh bran muffins in the display cabinet.

Jayne's domain was in its usual state of controlled chaos. The room was hot from the ovens and full of the delicious scent of rising bread, warm pastry, sugar, and cinnamon. Jayne stood over an industrial mixer whirling individual ingredients into batter. She switched the machine off, took it out of its stand, and dumped in a bowl of blueberries.

"Those look good," I said.

She turned. "I was hoping you'd stay home in bed."

"I'm okay."

"Of course you are. And if you weren't, you'd never say so. The hat's a nice touch. How's the head?"

"Fine."

"Do you have the pain killers the doctor gave you?"

"Yes." No, I'd left them at home so as to avoid temptation.

"What are you going to do about your hair?"

"Wear a hat until I can go for a cut. It's due for a trim anyway."

She burst into tears. I crossed the room and wrapped her in my arms. "It's okay. My hair grows really fast."

She choked out a laugh. "Oh, Gemma. I was so worried." She dropped onto a stool.

"I didn't have time to be worried. It was all over before I realized what was going on."

"You didn't see who attacked you?"

"Not a glimpse."

"Couldn't you . . . uh . . . deduce anything?"

"Afraid not."

"I hate to think it's not safe to go to the West London Beach in the evening."

"It's perfectly safe, Jayne. This was no random attack."

"I figured that was why Ryan and Estrada were at the hospital. Ryan would come anyway, because it was you, but not her. You think someone was trying to warn you off the Van Markoff case?"

"I'm sure of it. Unfortunately, it's not helping me narrow down the suspect list at all. The young couple who scared my attacker away couldn't even tell if it was a man or a woman. It wasn't random, meaning whoever it was didn't happen to come across me out at night and decide to get rid of me. He or she had dressed for it in loose dark clothes, a hood, and gloves. They must have been lying in wait for me outside the house."

Jayne shuddered. More tears welled up in her eyes. "Hey! Why are you standing and I'm sitting?" She jumped to her feet and guided me to the stool.

"I'm not an invalid," I said.

"No, but you did have a nasty crack on the noggin. Good thing your head's so thick."

"We English have thick skulls. Comes from all those years of bashing each other with axes."

We smiled at each other. She touched my arm. "What are you going to do now?" she asked.

"That's the question, isn't it? Ryan told me not to pursue the investigation."

"Good for him."

"I have no intention of following that advice. Clearly, I have someone worried. Now all I have to do is figure out who I have worried and how I managed to accomplish that. From this point on, I'll take care to be more observant of my surroundings." I almost smacked myself in the head, but fortunately I remembered in the nick of time that that would hurt. "Uncle Arthur!"

"What about him?"

"He's on his way home. I spoke to him yesterday and told him he's needed in the shop. I'm worried that I'm leaving Ashleigh alone too much."

"Is that a problem? Arthur, I mean, not Ashleigh."

"If someone's out there intending to do me harm, I can't have Uncle Arthur in the way. You know what he's like. He thinks he's hale and fit, and he is—for a man who's almost ninety. The days when he could defend himself and his mates in a bar brawl in Manila or Southampton against another pack of sailors on shore leave are long over."

"When do you expect him?"

I'd called him shortly before one yesterday to suggest he come home. If he was somewhere between the Outer Banks and Key West, he wouldn't make it to West London until this afternoon at the earliest. More likely tomorrow. Perhaps even the day after. He's not as young as he used to be, although he pretends he isn't aging, and he can't drive for long hours at a stretch. "Possibly this afternoon or tomorrow."

"Call him back. Tell him not to come."

"What am I going to say, Jayne? That he can't come home because I'm in danger? That'll have him breaking every speed limit in a rush to get here."

The timer over the oven dinged. Jayne opened it to take out a tray of pastries, and a wave of intense heat hit us. "A fire," she said.

"A what?"

"A fire in the kitchen at your house. Nothing major. Just something in the wiring. You're safe. Violet is safe. No serious damage. You're staying with me until the insurance company confirms everything is okay."

"A brilliant idea. I'll suggest he continue his vacation until we get the all clear." When Great Uncle Arthur eventually arrived home, he'd want a full inspection of the damage and an interview with the insurance inspector and would probably demand we have the entire house rewired. By then it would be safe to confess my deception. "Thanks for sending your mother around this morning. She looked after me as though I were her own daughter. She brought me tea in bed. It was heavenly. I haven't been spoiled like that since I was home sick from school." And not often then either. My mother was a big one for letting her children get on with things. Somehow, we usually did.

"Isn't that what friends are for?" Jayne said. "So we can share mothers. My mom and I used to go at it something crazy when I was a teenager. Our fights would get so bad, Jeff and Dad would flee the house. Rascal—that was our dog—hid under the bed with his paws over his ears." She laughed. "Funny how as soon as I finished high school, Mom matured. Now we're really close, friends even."

Friends. Mothers. My mother and I never actually fought, as in yelling and throwing things (my mother was far too well bred for that), but we certainly had our arguments. Mother and daughter. It's a complex, difficult, marvelous bond. What had Linda said to me? *You might have had that sort of relationship with your mother, but I didn't.*

When I first met Linda, I'd not paid her much attention. She was the flunky, the small planet orbiting around the star of the famous, flamboyant author. When they arrived at the bookstore for the fateful event, Linda had been angry. I'd noticed it at the time, dismissed it as nothing to do with me or the shop, and then forgot about it with all the drama that followed.

Had Linda and her mother been fighting? Had the argument been abandoned, unfinished, when it was time to go to the bookshop? Had Linda decided to finish it herself? Once and for all?

Had Linda Marke killed her mother? Either alone or with Kevin Reynolds? Had one of them been at the West London beach last night?

I needed to find out if they had alibis for the time of the attack on me, but I couldn't exactly phone them and ask. I couldn't call Ryan either. He'd made that perfectly clear.

"I recognize that look," Jayne said. "And I don't like it. What are you thinking?"

"I'm thinking it's time to eliminate the impossible and thus discover the improbable."

"That makes absolutely no sense."

"It will in due course." I hopped off the stool. "Thanks for calling Ashleigh in. She's working out okay. It's time to give her a set of keys to the shop."

"Gemma," Jayne called after me, "remember, Ryan said you're not to go out alone."

I waved to her over my shoulder.

"I'll be in my office," I called to Ashleigh.

Moriarty followed me upstairs. He settled himself in the center of my desk. My first call was to the West London Hotel. "Nancy Brownmiller's room, please."

"One moment, please." Computer keys clicked. "I'm sorry, but Ms. Brownmiller has checked out," said the receptionist.

"Oh, dear. We have an appointment, and I'm going to be very late. I wonder if she's on her way. Do you know what time she left?"

"Yesterday."

"Thank you." I hung up. Check-out time at the hotel is noon. It was possible Nancy'd hung around town until the evening, planning to ambush me, but it was unlikely. If she checked out, it was probably because she'd finally decided to go home.

I looked up her phone number on 411.com. She'd mentioned in passing that she lived near New Bedford. I found one "N. Brownmiller." Fortunately for me, some people still had landlines at their homes. I dialed.

It was picked up on the second ring. "Hello?"

"Good morning, Nancy. It's Gemma Doyle here."

"Hello." Notably she didn't gasp. "You're still alive!" Instead she said, "You've found the book! Fabulous. Look, I'm a bit short of funds right now, but if you send it to me, I'll pay you as soon as I can. Better use a courier service; that's safer than in the mail."

"Book?"

"The coloring book Renalta signed. The one you promised to me but then foolishly let be sold. You have found it, haven't you?"

"Oh, that book. Sorry, no, still not located."

"Then why are you calling me? Do you have something else of Renalta's?"

I didn't want Nancy rushing back to West London in pursuit of some piece of junk dropped by her idol. "Nothing to do with Renalta, sorry. I'm calling to let you know the book you ordered has arrived. One copy of *The Sherlock Holmes Handbook* by Ransom Riggs."

"I didn't order anything like that."

"You didn't? But I have a note right here."

"Wasn't me. Sorry. You know what I'm interested in. Call me if you find it." She hung up.

Nancy Brownmiller had not attacked me last night. Assuming—and how could I assume otherwise?—the person who followed me to the beach was also Renalta's killer, that person was not Nancy Brownmiller.

I tried the same trick with the Ocean Side, and the receptionist immediately put me through to Paige's room. No one answered. I studied the phone in my hand. Moriarty washed his whiskers. "What do you suggest I do now?" I said to the cat. "Smoker or not, Paige is still in the frame, but I don't have her mobile phone number." He yawned.

My phone rang as I was heading downstairs to help in the shop. Ryan. "'Morning, Gemma," he said. "I hope I've caught you at home resting in bed."

"Are you thinking of coming over if I am?" I teased.

"Don't tempt me. How are you feeling?"

"Better than I deserve to be. Jayne sent her mom around, and I woke up to tea and toast. It was quite delightful." I sidestepped an answer as to my present location.

"Glad to hear it. I'm afraid I don't have anything to report. We brought out a K-9 unit last night, and the dog followed a trail to the parking lot. He lost the scent there, meaning the perp almost certainly got into a vehicle and drove away. The lot's paved, and it hasn't rained for several days, so no tire tracks."

"Did you think to ask any of the people involved in the Van Markoff case for an alibi?" I asked.

"I did. I've just been around to the Harbor Inn. Kevin Reynolds and Linda Marke had dinner last night in the hotel's restaurant. They finished shortly after nine. They say they then went to their separate rooms. Meaning neither of them can account for their whereabouts after that time. They both claim they didn't go out again."

"Are you sure of the time?"

He laughed. "Absolutely positive. The restaurant called nine-one-one at eight fifty. A certain Ms. Paige Bookman was arrested for causing a disturbance."

I sucked in a breath.

"Paige arrived at the restaurant and sat herself down, uninvited, at Linda's table. When Paige was asked to leave, she refused. She started yelling about some book she'd written and demanding that it be published. The whole place heard her. Kevin Reynolds told the responding officer he'd finally had enough of Bookman and he wanted her charged. Ms. Bookman spent the rest of the night in the cells. She was released this morning, under a restraining order to keep away from Linda Marke."

"That definitely eliminates Paige from the attack on me. You can't get a more cast-iron alibi than that."

"No, you can't. I told Linda that I've ordered Ms. Smith's body to be released later today. Her daughter will be allowed to take her home."

Once everyone had scattered, I'd have precious little chance to bring all this to a conclusion.

"What are your plans for today, Gemma?" Ryan asked.

"I might spend some time in the shop. I won't overdo it. If I tire, I'll go home for a nap."

"Glad to hear it."

"Oh, before you go, one thing. Can you ask Jason or Jolene to contact me? I'd like to thank them for helping me last night. They quite literally might have saved my life."

"I can do that, but be warned, they're in mighty hot water."

"Why?"

"They're here for a few days with their church's youth club. A bunch of the teens went for a walk along the beach while the fire was getting started, and Jolene and Jason snuck away for some private time in the bushes. The group leaders are not happy about that."

"I was going to invite them for tea at Mrs. Hudson's. I might extend the invitation to the group leaders. Can you ask one of them to call me?"

"Sure."

I folded my hands over my chest, leaned back in my chair, and closed my eyes. I went over the entire conversation, parsing every detail of what Ryan had said.

My eyes flew open.

I turned to the computer. A minor detail had been sticking in the back of my mind, and it was time to shake it loose. I went back to the web pages I'd reviewed recently, gathering information on the people in Ruth Smith's life. And there it was. The telling detail.

I called Linda.

"Not you again" was her greeting.

"Me again. I don't know if you heard, but I was attacked last night."

"Oh. I'm sorry. No, I take that back. I'm not sorry. You're obviously well enough to continue annoying me. So that's why Detective Ashburton called on me this morning and asked what I was doing last night. I don't have to tell you, but I will anyway—I was alone in my room from nine o'clock onward, writing. I always write at night, sometimes straight through until early morning. I was not creeping down darkened alleys after you with what Desdemona Hudson would call a 'cosh.'"

"As would Dr. Watson," I said. "And modern-day detectives like Inspector Rebus too." Interesting that Linda mentioned darkened alleys. Not a path leading up from the beach. Meaning Ryan had not told her where and what had happened, fair enough, but also meaning she probably didn't know the location. Unless she was craftier than she appeared to be.

Which, if she had the nerves and the wherewithal to kill her own mother and try to get away with it, she would be.

"That's not why I'm ringing," I said. "I need to talk to you, Linda. I'm sorry I offended you the other day. I was honestly trying to help. My friend has been accused of this dreadful crime, and he's asked for my help in clearing his good name. Doing so is my sole intention."

She sighed. "Kevin loves me. And I love him."

"I'm happy for you. Really I am."

"Thank you. In that case, I accept your apology. Detective Ashburton told me I can take my mother home. I've booked us a flight tomorrow afternoon. When the funeral's over and the legal necessities settled, Kevin and I will be announcing our engagement."

"Congratulations."

"When the new book comes out, I'd like to do a signing at your store."

"You'd be very welcome."

"'Bye, then," she said.

"Wait. I need to talk to you, Linda, and it would be best in person. Are you free now?"

"No. Kevin and I are going to the police station shortly. We have paperwork to do so they can give me my mother."

"Lunch?"

"Gemma, I—"

"Please. Let's have lunch."

"I have an appointment with a realtor at one thirty." Her voice softened. "I saw a lovely place for sale yesterday, and I want to have a proper look at it. I'm serious about moving to West London. Seriously considering, anyway. I should be finished by three. How's that? A drink on the patio?"

"See you then. Invite Kevin and Robert too. They'll be interested in what I have to say as well."

I put down the phone, full of thought.

Dare I say it? The game was most definitely afoot.

Chapter 16

B y twelve o'clock, I had to admit to myself, although I never would to anyone else, that I was flagging.

My headache wasn't too bad—a low, steady throb that I treated with a couple of aspirin I found in the back corner of the cabinet in the staff restroom, but my knee was acting up. I'd taken advantage of a momentary lull in customers to dash behind the counter and pull up the leg of my trousers. I'd worn jeans today, although I rarely do to work. I wanted something long to cover the injuries and something dark colored in case one of the cuts reopened. The scratches were clean and turning a healthy pink, but my knee was a variety of shades of yellow and purple and about twice its size. Good thing I don't like skinny jeans; if my knee swelled any more, I'd have to cut them off.

"That looks bad." Ashleigh peered over the counter.

"Looks worse than it feels."

"If you say so. I notice you're limping a bit."

"It's just stiff."

"If you say so."

"I do say so!"

A customer came through the tea room doors, and I rolled the leg of my jeans quickly down.

By one o'clock, I could no longer pretend to have any energy or not to be in pain when I walked. Unasked, Ashleigh went next door and came back with a takeout cup of tea and a ham and cheese sandwich. She passed her purchases to me.

"Thanks for the tea," I said, "but I'm not hungry."

"You might not be hungry, but you need to eat. If you won't go home, at least go upstairs. Take a break and put your leg up. I can handle the store."

I didn't argue. I would have crawled up the stairs had my knee not hurt too much to put any weight on it.

I sat down at my desk and took the top off the tea. It smelled wonderful. Moriarty jumped onto the back of my chair. He swatted at my head. He's never playful, at least not with me.

"Stop that," I said.

He whacked me again. I gathered loose tendrils of hair and tucked them under my hat. He hit the rim of the hat.

I took the hat off and then reached around and plucked him off the chair. "Are you trying to annoy me?"

He hissed.

I put him on the floor.

I was settling back, cradling the warmth of the mug in my hands and breathing in the scent of hot sweet tea, when Morality dug his claws into my jeans, right about the level of the deepest of the scratches.

I screeched. Tea sloshed everywhere.

A black ball of fur streaked across the room and out the door.

* * *

The floorboards in the hallway creaked, and my eyes flew open.

"Sorry to disturb you," Jayne said. "I didn't mean to wake you."

"I . . . I wasn't asleep." I wiped sleep out of my eyes.

"Ashleigh was worried when you didn't come back down, and she asked me to check on you."

I put my hand on the cup. Stone cold. The little man with the mallet had once again started work behind my eyes. The clock, the one Uncle Arthur had given me when I took over management of the shop, said it was two forty.

"I must have lost track of the time." I pushed myself to my feet. I gripped the edge of the desk for support. "I have to go out. I'm meeting Linda Marke for a drink at three."

"You don't look too well, Gemma."

"I'm fine."

"I don't think you should be drinking."

"I'll have tea."

"You should eat something."

"Not hungry."

"Eat something, Gemma. You've had a blow to the head and then a fall. You're on pain killers. Eat that sandwich!"

I stuffed it into my mouth and ripped a hunk off with my teeth. I chewed and swallowed. "There, satisfied?"

"Partially. I doubt you're going to see Linda for a friendly drink. You're still investigating."

"She'll be leaving tomorrow. Ryan's released her mother's body. I know who killed Renalta and why. This will be my last chance to end it."

"Why is it up to you to end it? Tell Ryan what you know. Let him handle it."

I shook my head. That was a mistake. "All I have is speculation. I'm meeting her in a public place in broad daylight. What can go wrong?"

"You can faint for one thing."

"I'm hardly going to faint."

"No, you are not. Because I'll be with you. Finish that sandwich, and then we can go."

"You don't have to come."

"Of course I do. Someone has to look after you. Besides, Mom drove you to work, so you don't have your car, and I don't think you're up to the walk. I'll take you. We can borrow Fiona's car."

I took another bite of the sandwich. I have to admit, it was delicious, and I felt some strength coming back into my weary body. My phone rang, and I checked the display. Irene Talbot.

"Good afternoon, Irene." I wiggled my eyebrows at Jayne. "How are you on this fine day?"

"Better than you, I suspect. I've just heard the news. What the heck happened? Do you have a statement for the press?"

"Is Sherlock Holmes a Russian spy? Of course I don't have a statement for the press." She hadn't told me what she knew, and I wasn't about to fall into the trap of telling her.

"The police have said that a West London woman had been the victim of an assault last night. Passersby chased the perpetrator off. Is that about right?"

"If it was in a police statement, then it must be correct."

"Yeah, right. No mention was made of the victim's name, but Louise Estrada told me on the down low that it was you."

"She would." The office clock said five minutes before three. I was going to be late. "Sorry, I have to run. I'm going to the inn for drinks. Why don't you join us? You might learn something."

"I'd love to. See you soon." We both hung up.

"Why did you invite her?" Jayne said.

"The more the merrier."

Jayne plucked my hat off my desk and handed it to me. I put it on and we left.

"Won't be long," I called to Ashleigh. She rolled her eyes in response. Moriarty perched on top of the gaslight shelf. His eyes were narrow, and his tail flicked slowly back and forth.

"Sometimes," I said to Jayne, "I don't think that cat likes me very much."

"That's ridiculous. He loves everyone. Mrs. Morrison brings her kids into the shop just to play with him. They can't have a cat in the house because her husband's so allergic."

We drove the short distance to the Harbor Inn. As we pulled up, a familiar figure got out of a Ford Explorer: Grant.

"The gang's all here," I said.

Jayne dropped me at the front door, and I waited on the steps for her to park the car.

"Gemma," Grant said, "what brings you here?"

"A drink with Linda before she leaves. You?"

He peered closely at me. "You don't look too well. Are you okay?"

"Perfectly well, thank you."

"Don't believe a word she says." Jayne took my arm.

I shook her off. "You still haven't told me what brings you here, Grant."

We walked up the steps.

"I called Linda a short while ago," he said. "I asked her if she had some books signed by her mother she's willing to sell. A bit crass of me, I suppose, but business is business."

"What did she say to that?" I asked.

"She told me she was meeting some people for drinks at three and she suggested I join them."

As we crossed the lobby, Andrea called out, "Gemma, I heard what happened. Are you all right?"

"What happened?" Grant asked.

"I'll tell you later," I said. "I'm perfectly fine, Andrea. Thanks for asking."

The veranda of the Harbor Inn is one of the delights of West London. The footprint of the original garden remains visible: flagstone flooring and low stone walls, their cracks filled with moss and tiny flowers. Terracotta and ceramic pots full of blooms and greenery lined the walls, and the scent of lemons drifted from potted trees on either side of the door. On a sunny summer day, the views down the hill, over the harbor, and out to sea can't be beat. And today was a perfect sunny summer day.

I took a moment to admire the view. Irene ran into the lobby and caught up with us, and we went onto the veranda. Lunch service had finished and dinner had yet to begin, and only one table was occupied. A bottle of Prosecco resting in an ice bucket indicated that Linda and Kevin had been served already. Kevin gave us a smile and a wave, and

Linda watched me through wary eyes. She took a sip of her drink.

"Thanks for agreeing to see me," I said. "Everything settled for tomorrow?"

"Paperwork all done," she said.

They'd taken a large table with eight chairs. Linda sat at the head of the table, Kevin to her right. I dropped into a chair two over from Linda. I gestured to Jayne to take the seat between us. Grant pulled out the chair opposite me, and I said, "Why don't you come and sit beside me, Grant. I have some business to discuss with you, and we don't want to bore everyone else." I smiled at him. Irene took the chair opposite me, and Grant grinned as he sat down next to me.

"Sorry to be rude," I said. "I just remembered something very important." I pulled my phone out and sent a quick text.

Across the table, Irene's bag chirped, as I knew it would. A reporter can't chance missing an update. "Sorry," she said. She checked it, gave me a very startled look, and moved to the chair on her right, so she sat opposite Grant. She always carried a huge leather tote bag, full of the tools of her trade. She tossed the bag onto the chair at the foot of the table.

I made the introductions. "Now that we're all comfortably settled," I said, "how was the house viewing?" I wasn't trying to fill the time with idle conversation. I was hoping one more person would join us.

Linda shook her head. "It was far less impressive inside than the outside promised, and it's in need of an enormous amount of work. Hugely disappointing."

"You're moving to West London?" Jayne said. "That's great."

The waiter arrived and took our orders. Grant and Irene asked for pints of Nantucket Grey Lady, Jayne accepted the offer to share the Prosecco, and I ordered tea. Hot tea. They made a suitable cuppa here. They should: I'd taught them how.

"Prices can be jaw dropping around here," Kevin said. "Certainly for anything on the water."

"We're in no hurry," Linda said. "We have plenty of time. We're looking for the absolute perfect place." She smiled at Kevin. He smiled back. Jayne caught my eye and made a little circle with her lips.

The waiter arrived with the drinks. The beer glasses were thick with frost, and my tea was served in a white china pot emitting fragrant steam. "Kitchen's closed 'til five, but we can do a cheese plate or charcuterie."

Kevin politely asked if we wanted anything to eat, and we equally politely declined. I poured my tea and added a splash of milk. Jayne leaned across me and dumped in a spoonful of sugar. "You need the energy."

"Why is that?" Kevin asked.

"Coming down with a bit of a summer cold," I said. "Nothing to worry about. Isn't it a lovely day?" I hoped I wouldn't have to drag this out all afternoon. I am not an expert at small talk.

"Oh, good," Linda said, to my infinite relief. "Here he is now."

Robert McNamara was crossing the flagstone floor. He brushed Linda's cheek with his lips and dropped into the only empty chair: the one across from me. "Sorry I'm late. A beer, thanks. Whatever they're having will do," he said to the waiter.

Another round of introductions was made. Linda told us she would be in touch soon with details about her mother's funeral if we wanted to attend.

I took my phone out of my bag and sent a text, this time without making any apologizes. Jayne threw me a question; she knows how rude I consider using a phone in a restaurant to be.

"Isn't this pleasant." I put the phone away. "Nothing like a day in the sun with good friends."

Jayne clearly thought my brain really was addled. I adjusted my hat.

"Seems to me," I said, "that good friends shouldn't have secrets. Isn't that right, Linda?"

She looked at me for a long time. Only Kevin appeared to know what we were talking about. "I don't think this is a good time," he said.

"Gemma might be right. It's the perfect time," Linda said.

"Time for what?" Robert asked.

"The perfect time to tell you that my mother didn't write the books. I did."

Knowing what was coming, I watched his face. He showed no sign of shock or disbelief, only amusement. He chuckled. "I understand, Linda, I do. You want to continue her legacy. That's so admirable, but you have to understand it's not at all realistic. Ruth—Renalta—had such a distinctive writing style. We need to hire the absolute right person to finish the book so it's completely seamless. Isn't that so, Kev?"

"You're right about one thing," Kevin said, "no one can imitate that unique voice."

Robert coughed. "Let's leave this for another time. Y'all don't want to discuss our business in front of these nice people. That cheese plate does sound awful good. Anyone want to join me?"

"Don't patronize me, Robert," Linda said.

"I wouldn't dream of doing that, honey," he replied. "If you want to be a writer, why don't you start with a nice little short story? Maybe something from . . . what's the name of the character in Renalta's books?" He snapped his fingers rapidly as though the answer could be summoned out of thin air.

"Sherlock Holmes," Grant said.

"I mean the woman," Robert said. "An origin story, like they do in science fiction and fantasy. Something about her as a child that shows the woman she will grow up to be."

"Desdemona's past has been thoroughly discussed in the books," Linda said. "You'd know that if you'd read them."

"Not my job," Robert said. "That's why I have editors. Editors who've worked closely with Renalta and therefore are totally in tune with her voice and style. I'm thinking a short story by her daughter might be just the thing to keep fans interested until the new book comes out. Do you think you can do that? Almost anything will do. I can have it fixed up and made publishable."

Linda's eyes widened as he spoke, and her color was rising. I decided it was time for me to take control of the conversation before one of them stormed out of the room and my chance to confront Ruth's killer was lost, probably forever.

"You and your mother argued on your way to my shop on Saturday," I said. "Was that because you told her you didn't want to continue with the charade?"

"Yes," Linda said. "I've enjoyed writing those books, but I think they've come to a logical conclusion, and I want to try something new. She disagreed."

"To put it mildly," Kevin said.

"Ridiculous," Robert said. "The fans are eager for more. I can find a new writer. It'll be like Robert Ludlum. Renalta can keep writing even though she's . . . no longer with us. I'll let you have approval of the new ghostwriter. How's that sound?"

"What Linda is telling you," I said, "isn't that she wants to continue her mother's work herself. She's telling you she's the author and always has been."

"Don't be ridiculous." Robert's laugh was strained. "Her?"

Linda leapt to her feet, and Jayne grabbed her wine flute to keep it from tumbling over. "I am Renalta Van Markoff. I have always been Renalta Van Markoff. I wrote the books, every single word, and my mother acted the role of author in public."

"Wow!" Grant said.

"I'd love to interview you about that," Irene said.

I watched Robert. "You can't possibly be serious," he said.

"I'm serious, all right," Linda said. "Alert the press. Oh, look, the press is already here. Irene, I'll grant you an exclusive interview on the entire story."

"Cool," Irene said.

"Not only did I write all the books, I own the copyright to the published ones."

"Is this true?" Robert shouted at Kevin. "Did you know about this?"

"It's true," Kevin said. "I didn't know Linda intended to tell you now, here, but I respect her decision to do so."

"Furthermore," Linda said, "I'm leaving McNamara and Gibbons and taking the next book to a larger publishing house."

"What?" Kevin said.

"You can't do that!" Robert yelled. "We have a contract."

"No, we do not. That contract, as you are well aware, expired after the third book, and the new one hasn't been signed yet. I can take my books wherever I want. I've had an offer from one of the big five. It came in last week. They're offering a substantial amount more money than you ever have, Robert. I'm done with you and your cheap little publishing house. I'm only sorry my mother didn't live long enough to tell you herself. She always thought you were a nasty little weasel."

Robert perched on the edge of his chair, every muscle in his body tight with anger. Kevin, Jayne, Grant, and Irene stared at Linda. I sipped my tea and kept my eyes on the publisher. His color was not looking good. He opened his mouth and then closed it again.

"Except that Ruth did tell you, didn't she?" I said. "Ruth Smith told you she was accepting a better offer for the next book in the Hudson and Holmes series. She also told you it was almost finished, although she didn't inform you as to the true author. You killed her for nothing."

Everyone fell silent. Linda dropped into her chair, and Kevin rose out of his. Irene grabbed her big bag and surreptitiously slipped her notebook out of it. She placed her iPhone on the table and switched on the recorder.

"Now you're the one being ridiculous," Robert said with a forced laugh.

"When you and Linda argued over getting the unfinished manuscript, you mentioned that you had not yet paid an advance for it. I'm only a simple bookseller, but even I know that in traditional publishing, particularly at the Van Markoff level of sales, an advance on royalties is always part of the contact. No advance, therefore no signed contract. Meaning Renalta—either Ruth or Linda—is under no obligation to give you the next book."

"You're wrong, Gemma," Kevin said. "Paige Bookman killed Renalta . . . I mean, Ruth. She came here last night. While we were having dinner. She made another scene, demanding that McNamara and Gibbons hire her to continue writing the Hudson and Holmes series as well as some unfinished book she has."

"More like unstarted," Linda muttered.

"She also demanded that I act as her publicist," Kevin continued. "She's still claiming that Renalta ruined her writing career. She really has gone around the bend, and big time. The police were called, and Paige was arrested. The police are putting the case together to tie her to the murder."

"Except for the small matter that she didn't do it." I took off my hat. Linda sucked in a breath. Grant said, "Gemma, what happened?"

I rubbed at what curls remained on the top of my head. "I was attacked last night near the beach. West London's a low-crime town, but it still could have been a random act. I, however, don't believe in coincidences. I've been asking a lot of questions of a lot of people concerning the death of Ruth Smith." I studied Robert's face. A vein pulsed in his temple. "Believe it or not, I wasn't even close to discovering what had happened. I was getting nowhere and about to give up, to trust that Donald Morris's lawyer could get the charges dismissed before the case against him went much further. But your actions yesterday pushed me to the logical conclusion."

"I see you suffered a head injury," Robert said in what he no doubt thought a sarcastic drawl. "I can only sympathize and suggest your friends take you to your doctor."

"Linda told me you went home to Raleigh on Tuesday."

"Which I did." His voice was calm, but his eyes twitched.

"Maybe, maybe not. But you were back here yesterday. When I spoke to Detective Ashburton earlier, he told me Paige confronted Linda yesterday evening and that Kevin finally asked the police to charge her. Only later did I realize that Paige would never have asked Linda or Kevin to publish her. Linda is not a publisher. But you, Mr. McNamara, are."

"What of it?"

"You were here, in this restaurant, yesterday evening. I don't think even Detective Ashburton realized it. He assumed you and Kevin were dining alone, am I right, Linda?"

"I . . . I guess so. I don't think I mentioned that Robert was with us."

"He didn't ask me either," Kevin said. "We'd just arrived for dinner when Robert came in. He apologized for his harsh words the other day and said he hoped we understood that he only wants the very best for Renalta's last book. I told him that's what we want too and he was welcome to join us for dinner if he promised not to bring the subject up. I suggested it was a good time to toss around some ideas for a new marketing and promotion plan for *Hudson House* now that Renalta . . . uh . . . can't continue. We were enjoying our main courses when Paige arrived with all her demands and complaints. And yes, she did insist that Robert not only hire her to continue the series but publish her own book. Sight unseen, she wanted a contract.

"The police were called and she was taken away. It thoroughly spoiled the mood so we left the restaurant soon after without bothering with coffee or dessert. Robert, you told us you were going back to your B and B, and we said good night. I asked Linda if she felt like a nightcap, but she wanted to write, so we went to our respective rooms."

"That's right," Linda said.

"Very interesting," I said. "I have to wonder what you said, Linda, at this dinner that made Robert decide he had to come after me."

"What did I say?" Linda shook her head. "I said nothing. I haven't a clue what you're going on about. Kevin's right. Paige Bookman killed my mother. She's been living on her resentment of our success for years, and everything finally came to a boil."

"Ambition thwarted can be a dreadful thing," Robert said. "You're right, Linda. I'm sure you and I can settle our differences without the help of this interfering English busybody." He gave her a very strained smile. He hadn't met my eyes once since this conversation began even though I was seated directly opposite him. He picked up his beer mug in a shaking hand.

"Not Linda, but me," Kevin said. "Before Paige arrived, we were talking about Ruth's death. Linda said she was worried that no one would ever be brought to justice. She wondered if the West London police were up to the job. And I said maybe they're not, but Gemma Doyle is determined to see her friend exonerated, and that means finding the killer. You went rather quiet after that, as I recall, Robert."

Robert shoved his chair back. "I don't have to listen to this. So I was in West London yesterday. A lot of people were. As long as we're being brutally honest here, I'll confess that I was worried about Renalta's manuscript and I came back to try to talk you into handing it over, once again. But we were interrupted by that stupid, delusional woman, and it wasn't the best time. I did not then go out and attack anyone."

"Should be easy enough to check what time you arrived at your B and B," I said.

His eyes moved toward me, and I saw something very dark in their depths. He got to his feet. "I've had enough of this. Enough of her and her preposterous ideas and enough of arguing with you about the new book. My lawyers will be in touch, Miss Marke. I had a verbal contract with Renalta, and I expect you to honor it. I want that manuscript by the end of the week." He headed for the door.

I also stood. I stepped away from the table and called after him. "Your wife's photographs are wonderful. I'd like to place an order for the book you made of them. She's been taking pictures for a long time, I understand. Since the days of film."

Robert hesitated for a moment, and his shoulders stiffened. Then he continued walking. I followed him.

Ryan Ashburton stepped onto the veranda. "Why don't we continue this conversation down at the station? I'm also interested in your whereabouts after dinner last night, Mr. McNamara."

Robert whirled around. He stared at me. "I should have finished you off when I had the chance."

The tables in the restaurant would soon be set for dinner. China, cutlery, and crisp linen napkins were stacked on a small table next to the doors, along with an arrangement of wineglasses. In one swift move, Robert McNamara snatched up a crystal glass and smashed it against the edge of the table. He clutched the stem to which shards of crystal remained fastened.

Ryan yelled a warning and reached for his gun.

Before I could move, Robert grabbed me, whirled me around so my back was pressed against him, and held the broken glass against my exposed throat.

Chairs overturned as everyone leapt to their feet. Jayne yelled, "Gemma!" and Linda screamed.

"Careful there, buddy," Grant said.

"Put that gun away," Robert yelled to Ryan. "Now!"

"No need to get excited." Ryan slipped the weapon into the holster. "I just want a little chat, that's all. Accusations have been made against you. I'd like to hear your side of the story."

Ryan was the picture of calm authority. He held his arms loosely to his sides, kept his face relaxed, and allowed the visible tension to drain out of his body. But his fingers were clenched into fists, and his eyes didn't stop moving. He glanced at me, gave me an almost imperceptible nod, and then moved on, checking out whatever was behind us.

Robert backed up slowly, dragging me with him. His left arm was tight around my neck, and his right hand kept the broken glass pressed against my throat.

Grant took a step forward, his hands held out of front of him. "Don't do anything you might regret, buddy."

"I regret nothing. Nothing except not killing this one when I had the chance." Robert continued walking backward. I staggered, trying to keep myself upright.

"You won't get very far, Robert," Ryan said calmly. "This is the Cape, remember? Only two bridges out."

"We'll see about that," Robert said.

Andrea, her husband Brian, and several of the staff had come to see what was going on. They clustered behind Ryan, faces white. Andrea held up a phone. "I've called nine-one-one."

"Thank you, Andrea," Ryan said. "Please meet my colleagues at the door and ask them to wait in the lobby. The rest of you, stay inside, please."

I took a quick glance to my left. Recognizing that control had to be left to Ryan, Grant retreated. He held Jayne tightly. Kevin and Linda stood close together. Her eyes were round and her face white with anger. Irene had her phone in hand and snapped pictures. She was smart enough to keep the phone down, not hold it up to aim for a proper shot, which might serve to push Robert over the edge.

He stopped abruptly. His knees buckled, but he quickly recovered. He'd bumped against one of the low stone walls.

"You might be able to get off the death of Renalta," I said in a low voice. "But you certainly won't if you kill me in front of a restaurant full of people, some of whom are taking pictures."

"Shut up!" He tightened his grip on my neck. He was surprisingly strong. Madness does that to a person, or so I've been told.

He bent his right knee and reached behind him with one leg to test out the height of the wall. "I'm going to pull you over. Don't make any sudden moves."

His grip on me loosened as his body rose, but the broken glass remained pressed against my throat. There was no possible chance he would be able to get away. I could hear sirens rapidly approaching. The inn would be surrounded in minutes. I didn't want to find out what he was going do when he realized that.

I took a deep breath and forced my body to relax. I dropped my shoulders, loosened my hips, and flexed my knees. When the time came, I had to be ready to move. The wall was only about one foot high, and he was scrambling across it. "Up you come," he said.

We were approximately the same height, so he'd be vulnerable if I could stand on the wall above him. Half-dragged, sore knee protesting, I scaled the wall. Ryan had taken a couple of small steps toward us. He stared into my eyes.

Robert moved before I was ready, and he pulled me down after him. I fell against him; he grunted, and the tip of broken glass came away from my throat. I let out a huge scream and threw myself forward, intending to leap over the wall and make a dash for safety.

Instead my right knee collapsed in a blaze of pain, and I stumbled.

Robert grabbed me before I hit the ground and hauled me tight against him. "Don't try that again." No trace of Southern charm now; his voice was hard and full of menace.

Ryan stood next to the wall. "Are you all right, Gemma?"

"She is for now," Robert answered. "Up to you how long that lasts."

At this point the ground sloped gradually away to the street below. This wasn't part of the gardens, so the area was covered in small rocks, low scruffy bushes, and wild plants. All was quiet. Too quiet. No cars moved on what was normally a busy road.

We started down the slope. Robert's arm didn't ease away from my upper chest, and the glass didn't move from my throat. He walked backward, dragging me with him, his attention fixed on Ryan. If Robert tripped on a stone or slid in a patch of loose earth and the broken glass slipped, I'd be done for.

I heard a branch snap and then a thud, loud and very close. Robert let out a soft grunt, and his grip on me broke as he toppled to one side. I leapt forward and spun around.

Robert McNamara lay on his side in a patch of weeds. He groaned.

Louise Estrada stood over him, a Maglite in her hand. "I thought," she said to me, "I told you not to get involved." She pulled handcuffs off her belt.

My sore knee gave way, and I dropped to the ground.

Chapter 17

I spent a substantial part of the evening at the police station. This time, they treated me with great courtesy, showing me to the nice interview room—the one with a picture on the wall, a box of tissues at hand, and a comfy chair that was not bolted to the floor. Officer Johnson even brought in an office chair so I could put my foot up to rest my aching knee.

The chief of police himself sat in on the interview. I explained my reasoning calmly and laid out my points one by one.

"What does Mr. McNamara have to say for himself?" I asked when I'd finished.

"That he didn't kill Ruth Smith, and if he did, he didn't mean to," Estrada said. "He's called his lawyer and is now resting comfortably in a cell. We'll talk to him again tomorrow."

"He might have been able to bluster his way out of your accusations," Ryan said, "but to attack you in a public place in a room full of witnesses, not to mention a police officer, was not very smart. Not to mention tantamount to a confession."

"Which was, of course, what I was counting on. 'The emotional qualities are antagonistic to clear reasoning.'"

"Say again?" the chief said.

Estrada groaned. "Not Sherlock Holmes, I hope."

"*The Sign of the Four*," I said.

The chief lumbered to his feet. He held out his hand. I accepted it with some surprise, and we shook. "Thank you, Ms. Doyle. You've been very helpful. I'll call a car to take you home now."

"I can take her," Ryan said.

"We would have gotten him anyway, you know," Estrada said, somewhat ungraciously. "Without putting lives in danger."

"As it was only my life, I'm sure you don't consider that to be too steep a price to pay, Detective," I replied.

"Whatever," she said. "I'll be watching you, Gemma. Try to stay out of trouble."

"Trouble," I said, "finds me."

* * *

"I'm having a party?" I asked Ryan when we turned into Blue Water Place and I could see cars filling my driveway.

"You don't think Jayne and the rest would have gone quietly home to bed after all that, do you? Let them give you a hug and ask a question or two, and then I'll tell them you need your rest."

"I'm feeling quite invigorated, truth be told," I said. "Something about successfully escaping a brush with death can do that."

"You might be fine now, but you're going to crash sooner or later. And crash hard."

"Probably."

Violet was first to greet us at the door, but Jayne, Robbie, Grant, Irene, and Donald followed closely.

Donald swept me into his arms and hugged me with gusto. Then everyone else had a turn, and hugs were exchanged all around, although the men merely shook hands. Donald might have intended to give Ryan an enthusiastic embrace, but Ryan stepped nimbly out of the way. Greetings taken care of, I was bustled into the living room and settled onto a sofa. Jayne tucked a cushion behind me and a woolen throw around me, pressed a cup of tea into my hands, and asked if I wanted anything to eat. I said no, but she ran off anyway, calling, "Don't say a word until I get back."

She reappeared with a platter of crackers and cheese.

"Got any beer, Gemma?" Robbie asked.

"I'll have one too," Irene said, and Jayne returned to the kitchen.

I sipped my tea, enjoying the delicious warmth. Now that I was sitting down, I was suddenly totally exhausted. I closed my eyes.

Irene asked Ryan if Robert had been formally charged with the murder of Ruth Smith, and Jayne hissed, "Shush, don't wake her."

"I'm not asleep." I struggled to open my eyes. "Just resting." I lifted my teacup. "Cheers."

"I have to know one thing before we leave you in peace," Jayne said. "What did that comment about Robert's wife mean? It obviously meant something to him. Was she in on it?"

"Not at all," I said. "Far as I know, anyway."

Ryan said, "Irene, anything Gemma says about the evidence against Robert McNamara is off the record. You can't be reporting it."

"Understood," she said. "But I want an exclusive later."

"I'm not going to tell you how it felt to have a piece of broken glass pressed against my carotid artery," I said. "Now or at any other time."

"Just the facts, ma'am," she said.

"I'm thinking I can use that image in my new art project." Robbie held his hands in front of him as though attempting to imagine how it would look.

"That sounds appealing. Not," Irene said.

"Mrs. McNamara?" Jayne prompted me.

"The McNamara and Gibbons Press website contains brief biographies of the staff, including Robert. His bio mentions that his wife is a professional photographer. Simply out of curiosity, I followed the link to her website and found it very impressive. She has a long list of credits with highly respectable magazines going back twenty or more years. All the way back to the days of film."

Donald let out a bark of laughter. "Of course."

"I don't get it," Grant said. "No one photographed Renalta's death, or did they?"

"Other than a handful of pictures that were given to us, no," Ryan said.

"Photographers today, professional and amateur, use digital cameras," I said. "Film is almost dead, but not entirely. Many serious photographers still like to use it on occasion. I'm not an expert in photography . . ."

"Imagine that," Irene muttered.

I ignored her. ". . . but some say film has distinct advantages. In an interview with a photo magazine that was posted on her website, Mrs. McNamara said she prefers to use film in some situations, particularly for shots that need a long exposure."

"I've been thinking of maybe using photographs in my art," Robbie said. "That's called mixed media."

"Get to the point, Gemma," Jayne said.

"The point," I said, "is that as an important photographer of long standing, Mrs. McNamara would have learned to work in film. She would almost certainly have done most of her own developing, and it is entirely likely she still has a darkroom in her house."

"Elementary!" Donald said.

"I still don't get it," Grant said.

"Give her time," Jayne said. "She needs a long introduction. Sometimes I wonder if I'll live so long as to hear it all."

Ryan grinned. I'd told the police my theory at the station.

"Potassium cyanide is used in the developing process. I believe it's somewhat out of date these days, but some photographers still like to use it."

"How do you know these things, Gemma?" Irene asked.

I considered giving them a casual wave of my hand and saying, "Doesn't everyone?" Instead I confessed. "My father was an enthusiastic amateur. He was extremely strict about forbidding us entry to his darkroom unless he was there to supervise. The place had about as many locks as the jewelry room at the Tower of London. The first time I met Robert, he mentioned that his wife was traveling and thus not able to attend his mother's birthday party. When I began to put the pieces together, I concluded that only in her absence would he be able to search her darkroom and remove what he needed. It's likely that over the years, he picked up some knowledge from her."

"Amazing," Irene said.

"Diabolical," Donald said.

"We can get him on premeditated," Ryan said. "This took some considerable degree of foresight and planning."

"Renalta Van Markoff is the only bestselling author McNamara and Gibbons has. Without her, they'd be in danger of going under. Robert was furious when Renalta—Ruth—abruptly canceled several of her promotional appearances on the book's opening week. He called her to try to convince her to get back on schedule, and they argued. She told him about the contract offer from another publisher for the next book, which she said she'd almost finished. I suspect she threw that detail into his face, twisting the knife a bit deeper, not realizing she was sealing her fate. He decided he had to kill her to get the unfinished manuscript. Not knowing Linda was the real author, he thought she'd simply hand it over and he could get a ghostwriter to finish it and then publish it quickly to take advantage of the publicity that would be generated by the author's death."

"She wasn't suspicious when he came here and joined her for the book signing at your store?" Irene said. "I would have been."

"She was, sorry to say, a vain and self-absorbed woman. He put on a friendly front and probably said something along the lines that he recognized she'd made a practical business decision and they could remain friends."

Irene snorted.

"He made a serious mistake underestimating Linda's role," Grant said. "Aside from being the true author, she's the one who made all their business decisions."

"It was easy to underestimate Linda," I said. "Everyone did. Ruth completely intimidated Linda, and Linda made no effort to stand up for herself."

"Sad, isn't it?" Jayne said. "Without that bullying, Ruth might still be alive."

I yawned.

"Bed time," Jayne said. "I haven't forgotten, although everyone else seems to, that you had a blow to the head recently."

I yawned again. "I think you might be right."

*   *   *

When I arrived at work the following morning, I went to Mrs. Hudson's for a cup of tea. Standing in line reminded me that I had one last task to do, and I placed a phone call while I waited.

Jayne heard my voice and hurried out of the kitchen. "Why are you not at home in bed?"

"Because I'm not sick."

She studied my face. "I'll admit that you look okay, as long as you keep that hat on. How's the knee?"

"Perfectly fine," I lied. It hurt like the blazes. "If anyone should be home in bed, it's you. It was after midnight when you left my house last night, and you got almost no sleep the night before because you were looking after me. What time did you get up this morning?"

"The usual," she said. Meaning four o'clock.

Jayne had hustled everyone out the door and, over Robbie's protests, stayed with me until I was ready to crawl into bed. She offered to spend the night, but I told her that wouldn't be necessary. I fell asleep almost immediately and slept what remained of the night through.

"I have special guests coming for tea at two," I said. "Can you do a table for eight, Fiona?"

"Yup," she said.

"I'll be here to greet them." I took my tea and opened the bookshop.

I wanted to tell Moriarty about yesterday's excitement, but he didn't appear at all interested.

At two o'clock, I left Ashleigh helping customers and went to Mrs. Hudson's. A few minutes later, a large group came through the doors. Jason and Jolene introduced me to their pastor and his wife and the leaders of their youth group. Everyone complimented me on the decorating of the tea room, and Fiona showed them to the largest table.

"It's so kind of you to treat us, Ms. Doyle," Pastor Grayson said, "but unnecessary. Doing good should be its own reward."

"Quite right, but it's my pleasure. You're so fortunate to have such lovely young people in your group." Jason bowed his head, and Jolene flushed. The pastor's wife beamed. The group took their seats in a burst of excited chatter. Jason politely pulled out a chair for Jolene, but when he went to take the one next to her, a broad-chested, no-nonsense woman dropped into it. Jason slunk into the last empty chair, across the table from Jolene. He saw me watching him, gave me a big grin, and mouthed, "Thank you."

"Thank you," I said. I left the group consulting with Fiona on what teas to order.

Back in the bookshop, I found Donald Morris browsing the pastiche shelf while Moriarty supervised. "Can I help you with anything, Donald?"

"No! I mean, maybe. Well, yes, I suppose you can. That book that caused me so much trouble was nothing but nonsense. And badly written nonsense, at that. But it did get me thinking—these Holmes-related stories are so popular, surely some of them must have *some* merit." He peered at me. "Or am I being overly optimistic?"

"Not at all. Many of them are very loyal to the spirit of the canon."

"What about that one?" He pointed to *A Study in Scarlet Women* by Sherry Thomas. "The title is intriguing."

"Perhaps not the right place to begin," I said, thinking that Thomas's interpretation of Sherlock as a woman might not be the best way to introduce Donald to the complex world of the pastiche. I plucked *The Sherlock Holmes Stories of Edward D. Hoch* off the shelf. "Read this by a master of the short story form. His stories are respectful to the original but not tied to an attempt to imitate."

He carefully took the book from me.

The bells over the door tinkled, and Linda and Kevin came in holding hands. She had a yellow scarf loosely tied around her neck, giving a pop of color to her otherwise drab brown ensemble. She enveloped me in a hug, and I caught the scent of citrus shampoo and vanilla hand lotion. "I can't thank you enough for what you did yesterday."

"What happened yesterday?" Ashleigh said.

"We're on our way to the airport," Kevin said. "We wanted to come and say good-bye."

"Not good-bye," Linda said. "I'll be back. Back to West London and back to this store. *Baker Street Showdown* will be coming out soon. It's being rushed into production by my new publishers, and I'd like to do a signing here for it."

"You're very welcome," I said.

"What happened yesterday?" Ashleigh said again.

Donald's face might have showed a moue of disapproval at the title of the newest Hudson and Holmes book, but he wisely said nothing.

"Your store will be the only signing I plan to do for it. In honor of my mother. That's the last Hudson and Holmes book."

"Isn't that too bad," Donald said.

"I had a lot of fun writing that series, and it was great trying to re-create Sherlock Holmes's mind in Desdemona."

Donald tut-tutted in disapproval. "As if anyone could have a mind like his."

"But I've had enough of it. I want to write something more serious, and my new publisher is excited about that. We're thinking maybe something on the periphery of Holmes. Characters who live in the world he lives in and who are aware of him, but he doesn't have much of a role to play in the books."

"That might be interesting," Donald admitted.

"I'm glad you think so, Mr. Morris. I'll keep him faithful to the Conan Doyle representation."

"Glad to hear it." Donald dug in his pocket. "Let me give you my card. I'd be happy to help with any research you need. As well as being a noted Sherlockian, I am somewhat of an

Vicki Delany

expert in the life of Sir Arthur Conan Doyle. Did you know he was heavily involved in spiritualism? That would make an interesting storyline in your book. Perhaps rather than being in Holmes's world, your book could be in Sir Arthur's world."

"That's a marvelous suggestion. I'd love your help." Linda slipped Donald's card into her purse. She gave me another enthusiastic hug, Kevin thanked me again, and they left.

My phone buzzed with an incoming text.

It was Great Uncle Arthur: *What's going on at the house? When will we be able to move back in? Are you sure Violet is OK at Jayne's?*

I'd forgotten to tell Great Uncle Arthur he could come home.

Donald placed his new book on the sales counter.

"What happened yesterday?" Ashleigh asked him.

Moriarty yawned and began to wash his whiskers.

Acknowledgments

I'd like to thank Luci Zahray, a.k.a. the Poison Lady, for helping me consider various poisoning methods. And what fun was that! I've had the pleasure of listening to Luci speak at mystery conventions, and it's always great fun, and informative too. Thanks also to my good friend Cheryl Freedman for reading my manuscript with her keen editor's eye and sense of fun.

And to my agent, Kim Lionetti, and the good people of Crooked Lane for believing in me and Gemma.